THE GHOST

AND THE MEDIUM

HAUNTING DANIELLE

THE GHOST
AND THE MEDIUM

USA *TODAY* BESTSELLING AUTHOR
BOBBI HOLMES

The Ghost and the Medium
(Haunting Danielle, Book 30)
A Novel
By Bobbi Holmes
Cover Design: Elizabeth Mackey

ISBN: 978-1-949977-70-7

To the mediums who give us a glimpse into the other side.

ONE

E den Langdon sat alone, waiting for her date to return from the restroom. They had given them a booth by the window, and while Pearl Cove offered an ocean view, the sun had set hours earlier. Yet, even at noon, there still would be nothing to see, because the foggy and dismal gray November weather of Frederickport would have obstructed the ocean view. She found it drafty by the window. Shivering, she pulled her sweater tighter around her shoulders and cursed the cold, damp climate. If she had her way, she would have already moved somewhere sunny, like Arizona or Palm Desert. Shannon made it almost impossible to leave—an albatross Eden never wanted. Yet all of that was going to change, Eden vowed.

She glanced from the window to the dining room, wondering what was taking her date so long. Not that she particularly cared if he hurried back. The only reason she accepted the date, Pearl Cove served excellent food, and she was always up for a free meal. Her date was a nice enough guy, but she didn't imagine she would see him after this evening. If things worked out, Eden planned to be packing up and moving after Thanksgiving.

Taking a sip from her cocktail, she lazily looked around the restaurant, observing the other diners. Her gaze set on a nearby table—a party of eight. Or was it nine, she asked herself before taking a quick head count. She wondered who was the odd one out.

Eden leaned back in the chair, cocktail still in hand, and studied the group. She knew who they were, yet she only knew one personally. An odd, mismatched collection of people, she thought before taking another sip of her drink.

She had immediately recognized the couple at the end of the table, Walt and Danielle Marlow. They lived in that big old Victorian house on Beach Drive. Well, it wasn't a Victorian, exactly. From what she once read in a brochure, back when Marlow House first opened as a bed-and-breakfast, the house's architecture was a Second Empire mansard house. The brochure discussed the house's history and how the town's founder, Frederick Marlow, built it in 1871. Frederick passed Marlow House down to his grandson, Walt Marlow, who then left his estate to his housekeeper, which was how Danielle Marlow inherited it—through some shirttail relative.

The Walt Marlow now sitting across the restaurant, a distant cousin of the original Walt Marlow, first visited Frederickport a few years back and stayed after hooking up with Danielle. Eden wondered about their story. She could understand Danielle's attraction to Walt Marlow. Younger than Eden, in his mid-thirties, an attractive man with wavy dark hair and mesmerizing blue eyes, he carried himself with style. Walt always dressed like some character out of *The Great Gatsby*.

Of course, he was a successful author, so Eden assumed it might all be part of some persona he created for marketing purposes. As for the wife, Eden found her a reasonably attractive brunette. Danielle often wore her long hair in a fishtail braid. Of average height, she wasn't slim, nor would Eden call her overweight. Danielle dressed alright—nothing particularly out of the ordinary, not like her husband. The local rumor mill claimed Danielle was expecting, but when Eden had watched her walk into the restaurant thirty minutes earlier, she didn't look pregnant.

When Danielle Marlow—then Danielle Boatman—first moved to Frederickport, she'd turned Marlow House into a bed-and-breakfast but closed it down after she married Walt Marlow. Yet, from what Eden heard around town, the bed-and-breakfast recently reopened.

The attractive couple to Danielle's right, Eden knew as Lily and

Ian Bartley. Ian Bartley was also an author, even more famous than Walt Marlow. But he didn't dress like Walt, more preppy. His wife, a petite redhead, had been a local schoolteacher before becoming a stay-at-home mom. From what Eden understood, Lily had moved to Frederickport with Danielle, where she had met her husband and stayed. There was also a story about Lily being involved with some scandal with the Gusarovs, but she hadn't really followed that story, as it had been one of the rare times Eden managed to get away from Frederickport for a few weeks.

She turned her attention to Adam Nichols and Melony Carmichael. They had gone to the same high school as her cousin, Shannon, but were a few years younger. Adam owned a local property management company and sold real estate, and Melony had become some hotshot attorney, but she looked more like a high-priced call girl to Eden. Melony had left town years earlier and ended up in New York. But after her mother died, Melony had moved back to Frederickport, and she had recently become engaged to Adam. That's if Eden's hairdresser was to be believed.

Eden's cousin once told her the two had dated in high school. The then young teenagers had run away, and after their parents found them and dragged them back to town—after causing a major scandal—Melony's parents had shipped her off to a boarding school in Europe.

Eden's gaze turned to the last couple at the table. They seemed totally out of place with the rest of the group and with each other. He was the only person at the table she knew personally. A local cop, Brian Henderson was a nice-looking man for his age, with gray hair and a husky physique. But he was a major jerk. Yet it was his date—and she assumed the woman was his date considering the way she sat close to him—Eden found so out of place. Young enough to be Brian's daughter, the woman, an Elvira wannabe with braids, looked ready for a Halloween party. And Halloween was last month.

"Is it possible Brian has a daughter, and that's her?" Eden muttered aloud.

The ninth person at the table was Chris Johnson. He worked for the Glandon Foundation—a philanthropic organization that had set up office in the old Gusarov estate. Chris was the only one at the table who didn't have someone with him. Eden would love to ditch her date and volunteer to keep Chris company. Chris Johnson was gorgeous. He was probably one of the best-looking men she had ever seen. Sure, he was younger than her, but maybe he liked older women.

"Sorry I took so long." A voice interrupted Eden's mental rambling. She looked up to see her date taking his seat at the table. "I ran into someone on the way back, and I just couldn't get away from them."

"That's okay." Eden glanced briefly at Chris, gave a wistful sigh, and then reluctantly looked back to her date.

HAD IT BEEN SUMMER, they might have each parked their cars at their respective homes and then walked to Chris's, except for Melony and Adam, who didn't live on Beach Drive. But it was raining, so they drove to Chris's house after leaving Pearl Cove.

The plan was to have dessert at Chris's. Thirty minutes after arriving at his house, they had already finished their dessert and now sat comfortably in his living room. Had it not been dark out, they could have enjoyed a spectacular ocean view from his west-facing sliding glass doors.

"Are you sure you're up to having us over for Thanksgiving dinner?" Chris asked Danielle. He sat on a recliner in his living room, a glass of brandy in hand.

"Do you mean because I'm pregnant?" Danielle gave her stomach a pat. She could still wear her slacks, providing she left the top button unfastened and wore a long sweater to cover the zipper. Next to her on the oversized recliner sat Walt, who, like Chris, sipped on brandy.

"That and the fact you'll be reopening the B and B. I'm surprised you're willing to have all of us over that weekend," Chris said.

"I think Danielle wants us as a buffer," Lily teased. "She doesn't want to be alone with the ex-mother-in-law for Thanksgiving."

"Is she really an ex since you didn't divorce her son?" Adam asked. Instead of brandy, he sipped a beer.

Melony turned to Adam. "She's considered Danielle's former mother-in-law."

"Because Danielle remarried Walt?" Heather asked.

Melony shook her head. "No. When your spouse dies, their parents become your former in-laws."

"Spending Thanksgiving weekend with a former mother-in-law sounds awkward. I certainly wouldn't want to spend one with either of mine." Brian cringed at the thought. He, Heather, Ian, Lily, Adam, and Melony sat on Chris's large living room sectional sofa.

Danielle snuggled closer to Walt, who wrapped one arm around her.

Melony looked at Danielle. "Are we buffers?"

Danielle shrugged. "Sorta. But not entirely. You know I love to entertain, and I'm excited to reopen the B and B. But I understand in a few months I'll be curtailing my entertaining for a while, and when it gets closer to the arrival of our new family member, we'll be closing the B and B again—but just until we're ready to reopen."

Brian set his drink on the coffee table and looked at Walt and Danielle. "Joe thinks you're crazy to reopen."

Danielle chuckled. "No surprise there. Joe never understood the B and B."

"I have to agree with Joe. We are crazy." Walt laughed.

Danielle frowned at her husband. "Walt?"

Walt laughed again, kissed Danielle's forehead, and said, "I didn't say I don't want to reopen the B and B. But I do question our sanity." Walt refrained from saying more, as Adam and Melony, unlike the rest of their friends in the room, did not know of Walt's past life—or death. The ghost Walt Marlow, whom Danielle had first met when moving into Marlow House, had been against turning his home into what he termed an inn.

"Back to Thanksgiving. How many are going to be there?" Chris asked.

Danielle took a mental count. "I think fifteen. All of us here, plus Ian's parents and Kelly and Joe."

"Your parents are coming?" Heather felt Ian's parents disliked her.

"They are," Lily answered for her husband.

"What about Joe's family?" Heather asked. "Joe and Kelly aren't spending it with them?"

"Joe's family is going to Portland to spend Thanksgiving with some cousins," Lily explained. "Joe can't go because he's working that morning. So he and Kelly will be there."

Melony looked at Danielle. "What about your former mother-in-law and her gentleman friend? They'll be joining us, right?"

"Yes… her gentleman friend," Danielle murmured.

"They'll be the only guests at Marlow House for the weekend," Heather told Melony.

"Your former mother-in-law's boyfriend is really Finn Walsh?" Adam asked

"We don't know their relationship," Walt answered for Danielle. "We know they're coming together, because Danielle's former mother-in-law booked the reservation, but they have separate rooms."

"Are you sure it's *the* Finn Walsh?" Brian asked.

"It's him," Danielle said. "I didn't recognize the name at first. Lily did. And then I figured it was probably just someone with the same name."

"Dani is such an excellent spy," Lily said. "She did a Google search on the email they left with his reservation. It took her to his website."

"I'm excited to meet him," Melony said. "I almost went to one of his shows."

"He's just a con man," Danielle scoffed.

Melony frowned at Danielle. "How can you say that? Come on, I know you believe in the possibility of mediums."

"You mean ghosts," Adam grumbled.

"It doesn't mean I believe in every charlatan who claims he can talk to spirits—while emptying his sucker's pockets."

"Wow, that's pretty harsh." Adam laughed. "I'm surprised you feel that way. After we found out he was going to be one of your first guests, Mel and I watched some of his YouTube videos. I admit, I usually think those guys are fakes, but he seemed pretty spot on in those readings. Almost got me to believe all that stuff."

"Because he's good at his job. Not because he's a medium," Danielle insisted.

TWO

It's almost my birthday. Just five days, Shannon Langdon thought. Had someone not murdered Rusty, they would celebrate their birthdays together. Headlights briefly illuminated the living room, bringing Shannon to her feet and interrupting her thoughts of birthdays and tragedies. Wearing a worn, floor-length, powder blue fleece robe, Shannon scurried from the sofa to the front window. She pulled the curtains to one side, looked outside, and spied the vehicle attached to the headlights. It parked in front of the house next door—Eden's house. Shannon watched as Eden got out of the passenger side of the car into the rainy night. The driver didn't turn off his engine and get out of the vehicle to walk Eden up to the front door.

"A real gentleman," Shannon muttered to herself as she watched her cousin pull up the hood of her rain jacket while giving a quick wave to the driver before hurrying up to her front door, its porch light already on. The driver waited for Eden to go inside the house before pulling back into the street.

After the car's back lights disappeared into the night and Eden turned off her front porch light, Shannon moved from the window and allowed the curtain to fall back in place. The next minute, her landline rang.

Shannon returned to her place on the sofa and picked up the

phone's receiver. She expected to find Eden on the other side of the line to tell her she had gotten home and ask if Shannon needed anything. No one else ever called.

Shannon held the phone's handset's earpiece to her ear. "Hello?"

"May I speak to Shannon Langdon?" a male voice asked.

Momentarily moving the phone's handset from her ear, she stared at it.

"Who is this?" Shannon demanded after placing the handset back next to her ear.

"Do I have the wrong number?"

Shannon thought the voice sounded familiar, but she couldn't place it. "Who's calling?"

The man on the other end of the phone did not answer immediately. Finally, he said, "My name is Finn Walsh, and this is the number Shannon Langdon gave us. Is she there? Do I have the wrong number?"

"Finn Walsh?" Shannon whispered in disbelief.

"Is this Shannon Langdon?" he asked.

Instead of answering, Shannon closed her eyes and took a deep breath. The last time she had heard Finn's voice—aside from on some video—was the day before her brother's death. The day her world changed.

"Hello? Are you still there?" he asked.

"Yes. This is Shannon. I… I can't believe you're really calling."

"I'm coming to Frederickport in a few days. Cameron Lowe suggested I meet with you. Would that be possible?"

"You are? I read nothing about it in the newspaper."

"I'm spending Thanksgiving weekend in Frederickport with a friend. If you still want to meet—"

"Oh yes! Yes, please. Of course I want to. When can I see you?"

"I'll be arriving on Wednesday. Perhaps we can meet on Friday?" he suggested.

"If you're coming Wednesday, why do we have to wait until Friday? I'm sure Cameron told you how anxious I am and how long I've waited."

"I assumed with it being Thanksgiving, you'd want to wait until Friday."

"No. I don't want to wait. I've waited long enough," she said.

"At the moment, I can only promise to see you on Friday. And if I find it's possible to see you Wednesday or Thursday morning, I'll call you to change plans. Where would you like to meet?"

Wednesday is my birthday. He has to come on Wednesday, Shannon told herself.

"Where would you like to meet?" he asked again.

"At my house. We need to do this alone."

They talked for a few minutes longer. After the call ended, Shannon hung up the receiver and sat quietly on the sofa, staring ahead while processing what had just happened. Finally, she let out a sigh and said, "There will be justice for Rusty."

LATER FRIDAY EVENING, Brian Henderson pulled his car up in front of Heather Donovan's house and parked. It had been a short drive from Chris's house.

"Are you sure you don't want to stay over?" Heather asked, still sitting in the passenger seat and making no attempt to take off her seatbelt and open the car door.

Brian turned off the ignition. "I'd better not. I go to work early in the morning."

"No fun when you have to work weekends." Heather removed her seatbelt and turned to face Brian.

"Tell me about it!" Brian unfastened his seatbelt.

"You changed your mind?" Heather asked hopefully.

"No. But I'm walking you to the door."

"Don't be silly; it's raining. No reason for us both to get wet."

"I already did, walking from Chris's to the car," Brian reminded her.

Heather brushed her fingers through Brian's damp hair. "You don't need to get wet again."

Brian reached out and took hold of Heather's hand, gently moving it from his hair while continuing to hold it. "Can I ask you a question?"

"Sure. What?"

"I couldn't ask back at Chris's. Not with Adam and Mel there. But why is Danielle so convinced Finn Walsh is a con man? Perhaps he's like her... like you... and can see ghosts."

"It's because he's not like Danielle or me."

Brian frowned. "What do you mean?"

"Have you ever watched one of his readings?"

"Yes. After you told me he was coming to Marlow House, I was curious. I watched a few of his videos on YouTube. I was impressed. He had me convinced he's the real deal."

"In the readings, remember how he'll tell someone their grandmother or husband or whoever is standing behind them?"

"Sure. Reminds me of when Marie is standing near Adam, and he has no clue."

"And then he talks about how the spirit is in heaven? He even explains what heaven's like?"

Brian nodded. "Yes."

"Once a spirit moves over to the other side—be it heaven or whatever you want to call it—we no longer communicate with them. Only in a dream hop. And Finn Walsh is wide awake when he claims to connect with the spirit—the spirit who obviously has moved over, since they discuss heaven."

"Perhaps he can see spirits who have moved over," Brian suggested.

Heather rolled her eyes and let out a snort. "No. I agree with Danielle. He's an entertainer. Not a medium. And if you noticed tonight, Chris and Walt didn't disagree with Danielle. We've all discussed this and concluded that the man is a fake."

"You'll know for sure if he's a fake or the real deal when he gets here on Wednesday." Brian chuckled.

"Why? Will he convince us otherwise?"

"I was thinking of Marie and Eva."

"Oh... yeah. That will be the ultimate test. If Finn Walsh doesn't see Marie or Eva, we have our proof. The man is a fake."

MADELINE SAUNDERS and Finn Walsh sat together on the balcony of their Honolulu hotel room, enjoying the evening view. Neither one had changed out of the clothes they had worn to dinner earlier that evening.

"I doubt the beaches of Oregon will be this warm." Finn took a sip of his wine. He glanced over at Madeline, noting what an attractive woman she was for her age. He didn't imagine Madeline would appreciate him using the term "her age," considering he was a few years older than her. Of course, the women he had dated the last few years were typically closer to the age of Madeline's dead son.

"I'm getting nervous," Madeline confessed, looking over at Finn. "I haven't seen Danielle for almost five years. Maybe we shouldn't go."

Finn leaned over to Madeline and briefly patted her hand. "Lucas wants you to go."

Madeline smiled weakly. "But I'm afraid. She's going to think I'm crazy."

"No, she won't. Trust me."

They sat in silence for a few minutes while Madeline stared out into the night, lost in her private thoughts, and Finn sipped his drink and studied Madeline's profile. Finally, Madeline said, "I considered Danielle a daughter. It broke my heart when she sold the marketing company and returned the engagement ring. I didn't want the ring back. It was her ring. And then she gave me the portrait. It was like she just wanted to erase everything about her marriage. Including me." She looked back at Finn and added, "Lucas could be wrong."

"I don't think he is. Not considering how adamant he is about this," Finn said.

Madeline grinned. "I'm sorry, but when you say things like that, it... well... it just sounds so funny."

"You believe, don't you? That Lucas came through?"

Madeline smiled again. "Yes. I do. But it still sounds strange when you say it—when I say it." Madeline laughed and then asked, "Tell me, is he here now?" She glanced around.

Finn shook his head. "No. Lucas felt you and I should have some time alone without him hanging around. He'll meet us in Frederickport."

"I'll admit, I'm rather glad to hear that. As much as I'm thrilled about all this, well, sometimes it is unnerving to know Lucas is always there—listening in. I feel as if I need to always be on my best behavior." Madeline laughed.

Finn flashed Madeline a grin while reaching over and taking hold of her right hand, giving it a gentle squeeze. "You don't want your son to see his mother being naughty?" He glanced over at the sliding glass door leading to the motel room.

"Finn!" Madeline said with a blush, pulling her hand from his. "You are incorrigible!"

"I try." He laughed and settled back in his chair.

"I should just be grateful someone other than Danielle answered the phone and took my reservation. I'm not sure what I would've said if she answered the phone that day. And it's always possible that if she had been the one to take the call, she might have made some excuse—like they didn't have any vacancies."

"I told you, this was meant to be. That's why I asked you to call Marlow House on that day to make the reservations. I knew your daughter-in-law would not be there to answer the phone."

"You were right. You are always right."

Finn grinned.

"You know, I'm not surprised Danielle remarried. I expected it. She is a young, attractive woman. But the other thing…" Madeline didn't finish her sentence.

"You mean the money?"

Madeline nodded. "Yes. She's a very wealthy woman now. Which, honestly, makes me wonder why she reopened the bed-and-breakfast. I understand why she opened it initially; she had to make a living. But why, why now? Why reopen it? She doesn't need the money."

Finn laughed. "Madeline, you continually ask questions with obvious answers. She had to reopen the bed-and-breakfast, because that way, you could make a reservation and see her and do what Lucas wants you to do. It's all part of the plan. The universe's master plan. No reason to question it or be afraid. And remember, I'll be there for you every step of the way."

THREE

Kelly Bartley leaned against Joe's car and stared at her engagement ring—her ugly engagement ring. She didn't understand how Joe couldn't see how his grandmother's ring— albeit with a generous diamond—had the most hideous setting. *Perhaps I could just lose it?* she thought. Extending the fingers on her left hand, she held it downward and gave a little shake. The ring didn't budge.

She looked up toward the house and felt a smidge of guilt. Joe didn't need to catch her trying to shake off his grandmother's ring. *Where is Joe?* Kelly wondered. *What is taking him so long?* The next minute, the front door opened, and Joe stepped outside. Kelly watched as he turned back to the door, locked it, and then turned again and headed down the steps and then the walkway to his car and her, his waiting fiancée.

"I thought I'd have to go to lunch alone. What took you so long?" Kelly asked when Joe got within earshot.

"Sorry, my mom called right as I was about to head out the door." He walked over to the driver's side of the car and unlocked it.

"Any problem?" Kelly walked to the passenger side of the car.

"No. She just wanted to double-check to make sure we weren't going with them to Portland for Thanksgiving."

13

"You told her you had to work, right?" Kelly watched Joe unlock the driver's door and then hers. She got into the car.

"Yes. But she wondered if my work schedule changed."

Now sitting in the car, Kelly slammed the passenger door shut and pulled out her seatbelt. "I suppose you didn't tell her you volunteered to work that day?"

"No." Joe chuckled, closed the driver's door, and buckled his seatbelt. "I really don't want to spend Thanksgiving with my cousin. I couldn't stand him when we were kids, and he hasn't improved as an adult."

Joe shoved the key into the ignition, and Kelly said, "Joe, can we stop somewhere before we go to lunch?"

Instead of turning the ignition on, Joe looked at Kelly. "Where?"

"Frederickport Vacation Properties."

Joe groaned and slumped back in the car seat, making no attempt to turn on the engine.

"I spoke to my brother this morning," Kelly said hurriedly. "And he said Adam and Mel had dinner with them last night, and Adam mentioned he was working today."

"Kelly, I told you, until Adam actually lists Pearl's house, we can't even think about making an offer on it."

"Ian also told me Melony wants the house."

Joe stared at Kelly for a moment before asking, "Then what is the point? If Melony wants to buy Pearl's house, and Adam is the listing agent, then she's going to get it."

Kelly shook her head. "It doesn't work that way."

"What do you mean it doesn't work that way? It certainly does."

"No," Kelly said primly. "Adam's fiduciary duty is to his seller. He is obligated to bring them the best offer. He can't just show them the offer he wants them to take."

"Real estate agents do that all the time," Joe said with a snort.

"Sure, disreputable agents. But I figure if we go to Adam, tell him we want to present an offer to the buyers as soon as he lists the property, he's obligated to give it to them."

"You're suggesting Adam is a reputable agent?" Joe scoffed. "You don't think Adam won't tell Mel how much we're offering so she offers more?"

"I suppose. But we need to try. If we do nothing, we will for sure lose out."

"And what do you want to offer?" Joe asked.

After Kelly told him, Joe let out a low whistle. "Kelly, that's a lot of money. We aren't even sure about the condition of the property."

"True, but if they accept our offer, we still get an inspection period. And if we find something we don't like, we can cancel the deal or negotiate for better terms."

Joe silently considered Kelly's idea. Finally, he said, "I think this is going to be a waste of time."

"Can we at least try? If Mel knows we want it, maybe she'll look for something else. After all, they can afford a lot more than we can."

"Which is why I say this is going to be a waste of time. They can easily outbid us." Joe turned on the ignition.

WHEN JOE and Kelly walked into the outer offices of Frederickport Vacation Properties on Saturday afternoon, they found Adam's assistant, Leslie, alone in the office.

"Hello, Joe, Kelly," Leslie greeted them when she looked up from her desk.

"Is Adam in?" Joe asked.

"You aren't planning to arrest him, are you?" Leslie teased.

"Not today." Joe flashed Leslie a grin. "At least, not while Kelly's with me."

Leslie glanced at the doorway leading to Adam's private office. She looked back at Joe and Kelly. "He's with someone right now. Is there anything I can help you with?"

"Has Adam listed Pearl Huckabee's house yet?" Kelly asked impatiently.

Leslie shook her head. "No, not yet. They had repairs the sellers wanted to complete before listing."

"But Adam is getting the listing? Right?" Kelly asked.

"Oh yes. I doubt the sellers will change their minds. Chris is the one who recommended Adam, and from what I understand, the seller has done a lot with the Glandon Foundation."

The next moment, their conversation stopped when Adam walked out from his office with another man.

"Morelli?" the man with Adam blurted when he saw Joe.

Joe turned to the voice. The moment he saw the man with Adam, his eyes widened. "Charlie Cramer? Is that really you?"

The man laughed in response, hurried to Joe, and the two men exchanged a bear hug. When the hugging and patting each other's backs ended, the two men stepped back from each other and looked the other up and down.

"When did you get into town?" Joe asked. "You were going to call me?"

"Of course. I just pulled into town an hour ago. This was my first stop."

Kelly, along with Leslie and Adam, silently observed the exchange. Kelly recognized the name Charlie Cramer. While she had never met him, Joe often talked about his old friend Charlie Cramer.

"You wanted to see Adam before me?" Joe teased.

"I'm thinking of listing Mom's house," Charlie explained. Joe knew Charlie's mother had passed away years earlier, leaving her house to Charlie, which he had put in a rental program.

"You decided to sell?" Joe asked.

Charlie gave a shrug in reply, and Kelly cleared her throat.

Joe glanced to Kelly, looking chagrined, and then looked back to Charlie. "You haven't met Kelly yet." Joe reached for Kelly and pulled her to his side.

"Ahh, so this is the lovely lady who finally got our boy Joe to settle down." Charlie flashed Kelly a flirtatious grin.

"I take it you're Charlie Cramer; Joe's spoken about you." Kelly offered Charlie her hand. "Nice to finally meet you."

Charlie shook her hand and grinned. "Nice to meet you, too."

"Who told you about the engagement?" Joe asked.

"Eden," Charlie said.

Joe wrapped an arm around Kelly's shoulders and told her, "We had some good times, Rusty, Charlie and me."

"Rusty Langdon?" Adam asked, sitting down in an empty desk chair next to Leslie.

"You knew Rusty?" Joe asked.

Adam shrugged. "No, but I remember all his track trophies back in high school. I imagine they're still in that case."

"You guys all went to high school together?" Leslie asked.

"Yes, but I am much younger than Joe." Adam grinned.

Joe laughed. "Not that much younger." Joe turned to Leslie. "But we graduated before Adam started high school."

"Joe has mentioned Rusty. He was the one who was murdered, right?" Kelly asked.

"Yeah. What has it been, ten years now?" Joe asked.

"Next week it will be ten years," Charlie said.

"Murdered? What happened?" Leslie asked.

"He was killed at work, a robbery. It was in Portland, not in Frederickport," Joe explained. "They never found out who did it."

"That's horrible," Leslie muttered.

"Yes. It was." Joe turned to Charlie. "Kelly and I need to talk to Adam about something. But afterwards, we're going to Lucy's Diner for lunch. You want to join us, and we can catch up? We won't be with Adam long."

"I'd love to."

"SO YOU AND Charlie Cramer were high school buddies?" Adam asked after escorting Joe and Kelly back to his office. He closed the door and walked to his desk to sit down while motioning to two empty chairs.

"Yeah. We were tight back in high school, the three of us," Joe said as he and Kelly sat down and faced Adam's desk.

"I never met Rusty, but I'm familiar with his sister, Shannon," Adam said. "Or at least, who she is. I know her cousin, Eden."

"Shannon used to be a friend back in high school. But that was a long time ago," Joe said.

"She's a recluse now. Her cousin says she's agoraphobic," Adam said.

"You mean, like, she can't leave her house?" Kelly asked.

"Pretty much," Adam said. "I don't think she's stepped out of that house in years."

Joe nodded. "That's what I understand."

Kelly looked at Joe. "Was she always like that?"

Joe shrugged. "She was always shy, unlike her brother. She and Rusty were twins."

"From what Eden told me, Rusty's death hit Shannon hard, and she never got over it," Adam said.

"That's true," Joe said with a nod.

"But I don't imagine you stopped in to rehash old friends from high school," Adam said. "What did you want to talk to me about?"

"Joe and I have been thinking of selling his house and buying something together."

Adam perked up. "Really? You want to find out how much Joe's house is worth? Find you something to buy? Do you have an agent yet?"

"We were hoping to work with you," Kelly said.

Adam's smile broadened. "I'd love to help you."

"In fact, we're already interested in one of your listings," Kelly said.

"Terrific. Which one?"

"Pearl Huckabee's," Kelly said.

Adam's smile fizzled. After a moment of silence, he said, "I'm afraid it's not listed yet."

"We understand that," Kelly said. "But we were hoping we could write up an offer now, and as soon as you list the property, you can present our offer to the seller."

Adam let out a sigh and leaned back in the office chair. "I'd love to help you guys. But until I list the property, I can't present an offer. I'm sorry."

"That's what I thought," Joe said.

"But as soon as it's listed, I'll call you. I could show you some other listings now. Perhaps I can find you something you'll like better," Adam suggested.

"I ALMOST ASKED Adam if Mel wanted the house," Kelly told Joe after they stepped out of the office building. They left Joe's car in the parking lot while they walked down to Lucy's Diner to meet Charlie for lunch.

"I'm glad you didn't," Joe said.

"I really want that house."

Looking at Kelly, Joe arched his brows. "Even with the dead bodies in the backyard?"

"They aren't in the backyard anymore," Kelly reminded him.

FOUR

The moment Kelly stepped into Lucy's Diner with Joe, she spied Charlie Cramer alone in a booth on the other side of the restaurant, menu in hand. Long ago, Joe had told her all about Charlie and how he, Charlie, and Rusty had been best friends through high school.

Rusty's impressive track career in high school earned him a college scholarship. To his parents' disappointment, he turned it down. Joe said Rusty wasn't interested in college; he wanted to open a motorcycle shop in Portland. Rusty didn't just run fast, he liked to drive motorcycles fast.

Charlie shared Rusty's dream and passion, and while Joe rode motorcycles back in high school, he didn't want to go into business with his two best friends, although they had tried talking him into it. With a loan from Charlie's mother and a small inheritance Rusty had from a great-uncle, his dream became a reality. That dream ended when the police found Rusty's body on the floor of the motorcycle shop ten years earlier. Someone had bashed him in the head during closing and cleaned out the cash box.

According to Joe, Rusty's murder didn't just end his life, it forever changed the lives of those closest to him. Unable to keep working at the murder scene of his best friend, Charlie had sold the business and took a sales job with a motorcycle company, which kept him perpetually traveling around the country.

Rusty's sister, Shannon, had fared even worse. At the time of her brother's death, she had been sharing an apartment with him. But after he died, she left Portland and moved back into her parents' home in Frederickport. Heartbroken over his son's death, Shannon's father died a year later, and two years after that, her mother passed away, leaving Shannon living alone in her childhood home.

As Kelly and Joe approached Charlie's booth, a thought occurred to her. If someone hadn't murdered Rusty, Joe probably would have asked either Rusty or Charlie to be his best man.

Charlie glanced up at Kelly and Joe and smiled as they neared the table. Kelly found Charlie an incredibly handsome man—clean shaven, husky physique with black, horn-rimmed glasses. She thought he would look great in a tux. A best man's tuxedo.

"SO EDEN TOLD you I was engaged? You guys keep in touch?" Joe asked. He and Kelly sat in the booth across from Charlie. The server had already taken their order and left the table.

"Not really. I knew I was coming to town, so I called her to see how Shannon was doing. The last time I was in Frederickport was when you saw me five years ago. I haven't been terrific at keeping in touch with you, but Shannon and I exchange emails from time to time."

Joe nodded. "I understand."

"I considered stopping in to see her, but I wanted to find out what I might walk into. You can't tell much from emails."

About to take a sip of his water, Joe paused and looked across the table at Charlie. "How did Eden say she was?"

Charlie gave a shrug. "About the same."

"Why aren't you guys Facebook friends?" Kelly asked. "Joe told me you were a sales rep and traveled all over the world. These days everyone keeps in touch online. Even if you don't email each other, you can touch base on Facebook."

"I don't do any of that social media stuff," Charlie said.

Kelly wrinkled her nose. "I thought that was part of sales these days."

Charlie grinned sheepishly. "Well, I'm not doing sales anymore. The only communicating I do on the computer is email."

"What are you doing now?" Joe asked.

"I'm in between jobs. So I figured I should probably take the opportunity to come to Frederickport and check on Mom's house. I might sell it since the renters just moved out. I figured this would be a good time to sort through all the boxes I shoved in the attic when I put the place in the rental program."

Kelly already knew—because Joe once told her—Charlie had been raised by a single mom, who died not long after Charlie and Rusty opened their business in Portland. After her death, instead of selling his mother's house, he put it in a rental program.

"Does this mean you'll be in town for a while?" Kelly asked brightly.

Charlie flashed Kelly a grin. "It depends how fast I go through all those boxes."

"I think you should stick around for our wedding," Kelly said. "I bet Joe would love to have you there."

Joe broke into a smile. "Yes, I would."

Charlie returned the smile and said, "I would like that too. See my old buddy walk down the aisle… oh, wait a minute… he doesn't do the walking, right?"

Kelly chuckled. "Haven't been to many weddings?"

Charlie shrugged. "Not really."

"No one special in your life?" Joe asked.

Charlie shook his head. "With my job, I moved around too much. Hard to establish any serious relationship with that lifestyle."

"It would be nice if you stuck around for a while," Joe said.

"Perhaps I will."

The next moment, the server arrived with their beverages. When she left the table, Charlie asked, "Do you ever talk to Shannon?"

Joe shook his head. "No. Like I told you, the last time you were here, I tried to at first. I would stop by her house, check on her, but it was obvious she didn't welcome my company. But I was never close to Shannon, even before Rusty's death. She wasn't really my friend. Not like she was yours. Of course, you're the one she had the crush on."

Charlie chuckled at the comment and shook his head. "Well,

that was not happening. I considered Shannon a good friend, but the fact was, I just couldn't get over the fact she looked so much like her brother."

"They were twins," Kelly reminded him.

Charlie looked at Kelly and grinned. "Hey, I have nothing against someone if they're gay. But I happen to be straight, and the thought of kissing someone who looks so much like Rusty, well, it was kind of a turnoff."

Joe laughed. "Yeah, those two looked a lot alike."

"She had a crush on you?" Kelly asked Charlie. Joe had never mentioned that when discussing his friends. In fact, he had barely mentioned Rusty's sister aside from the fact she was Rusty's twin.

Charlie gave a nod. "Yeah. But like I said, nothing ever came of it."

"So you're planning to see her?" Joe asked.

Charlie shrugged. "To be honest, I'm not sure. She doesn't know I'm coming. I asked Eden not to say anything to her."

"Who exactly is Eden?" Kelly asked.

"She's Shannon's cousin," Charlie explained. "Rusty and Shannon lived next door to their grandparents. Eden's the same age as we are. She used to spend summers with her grandparents. The grandfather died years ago, and the grandmother passed away a couple of years after Rusty. She left her house to Eden and Shannon, and Eden lives in it."

"She looks after Shannon," Joe told Kelly.

"Does she really need looking after?" Kelly asked.

Charlie shrugged. "It's Shannon's agoraphobia that we mentioned. While she has always been shy, she wasn't a recluse like she is now. I think Eden regrets moving into her grandmother's house, because it makes it easier for Shannon to survive without ever stepping foot outside."

"She has to leave sometime," Kelly said.

"Nope." Charlie shook his head. "Eden told me Shannon does all her shopping and banking online. If she needs something picked up at the grocery store, she has Eden get it for her."

"What about trips to the doctor or dentist?" Kelly asked.

"Eden says she doesn't go," Charlie said.

"That's pretty much what I heard," Joe said.

"How does she support herself?" Kelly asked.

Charlie leaned back in the booth and absently ran his right index finger around the rim of his water glass as he looked across the table at Kelly. "Her parents left her the house and some money. Which I imagine she's living on. Plus, whatever her grandmother left her and Eden, aside from the house. I don't know how much it was."

Joe picked up his water glass. Before taking a drink, he looked at Charlie. "I suppose I can understand why you're reluctant to see her."

Charlie let out a sigh. "I just don't know what the point would be. After Rusty died, she got a little…"

"Dependent on you," Joe finished for him.

Charlie cringed and nodded. "Yeah. It was awkward, but back then her parents were both alive, so when I could sell the shop and leave, I figured she had them to lean on. And honestly, I was having a hard time dealing with everything myself. Rusty was like a brother to me, and the shop had been our dream. I just needed to get away."

"IF YOU THINK ABOUT IT, Shannon and Charlie have more in common than he realizes," Kelly told Joe after Charlie left the diner an hour later. They had stayed behind to have dessert, while Charlie said he needed to get back to his mother's house to meet a repairman.

"What do you mean?" Joe asked.

"After Rusty's murder, they both checked out. Shannon locked herself in her parents' house, while Charlie took a job that kept him on the road, making it impossible to establish close relationships, while abandoning old friends, like you."

Joe let out a sigh. "You know, you have a point."

The server brought their dessert. After she left the table, Kelly said, "I like him. He reminds me of Clark Kent."

Joe, who had just picked up a clean fork to take a bite of his apple pie, paused and looked at Kelly. "Clark Kent? You mean like in Superman?"

"Yeah. With those glasses, his all-American good looks." Kelly grinned. She picked up a fork and took a bite of her chocolate cake.

Joe laughed. "I have to be honest; I never saw Charlie as a Clark Kent."

"He would make a great best man." Kelly took another bite of cake.

Joe paused and looked at Kelly. "I assume you're talking about a best man for our wedding?"

"Well, I'm not talking about one for Adam and Melony's wedding."

"I already have a best man."

Kelly set her fork on the table next to her plate of cake and looked at Joe. "You know, if Rusty hadn't been murdered, I bet you would have asked either him or Charlie to be your best man."

"Maybe. But that was a long time ago. I've only seen Charlie a couple of times in the last ten years."

"Do you feel like he's a stranger?" Kelly asked.

Joe considered her question. After a moment, he smiled. "No. Actually, it kinda felt like I had just seen him last week. He seemed like the same ol' Charlie to me. It was nice."

Kelly picked up her fork again and smiled at Joe. "Then you should seriously consider asking him. I think Brian would understand."

FIVE

L ily stood silently by the open doorway of her son's bedroom and watched as toy blocks floated from a red storage bin to her son, Connor, who sat in the middle of the room on the braided rug. Before each block hit the floor, Connor snatched it and placed it on the tower of blocks he had assembled. If he added many more blocks, Lily figured the tower would tumble down. But that was okay with Connor. He would just build it again, with Marie's help.

Leaning against the doorjamb, her arms folded across her chest, Lily tried visualizing the scene through Connor's eyes. Unlike her, he didn't see floating blocks. He saw an elderly grandmother bringing him blocks to add to his tower. Marie made the ideal babysitter and playmate. Yet, unlike Connor, Lily couldn't see her. Only the mediums saw Marie—and some small children, like Connor. *Could he really be considered a medium?* Lily wondered. She imagined she would have an answer to that question when Connor was much older.

Lily stood up straight and dropped her hands to her sides. "Marie, I'm going over to Dani's house. I'm meeting Heather over there; we're going to discuss what we need to bring for Thanksgiving dinner. Ian's in his study, working. He knows you're here."

The next moment, Connor's Winnie the Pooh stuffed animal lifted from the rocker. Its right paw rose, making a waving motion.

Lily laughed at the gesture, knowing it was Marie's way of saying, "Okay, goodbye!"

Before leaving the room, Lily walked to Connor, dropped a kiss on his forehead, and told him to behave for Grandma Marie. While she couldn't hear Marie, Lily imagined Marie had probably just said, "Connor always behaves for me."

HEATHER SAT on the edge of her sofa and slipped on a pair of black, water-resistant ankle boots over her wool socks. That morning, she had dressed in black denims and a long gray pullover fleece sweater. She wore her black hair in two straight braids, with her bangs half-covering her dark eyebrows. She stood up and headed for the door. Before going outside, she grabbed her black puffer vest from the coat rack and slipped it on.

The rain had stopped, but even if it had been raining, Heather wouldn't be carrying an umbrella. She headed up the sidewalk, en route to Marlow House. Just as she started to pass the house between hers and Marlow House, Heather paused. She looked up at the empty building. A wave of sadness washed over her.

"Do I actually miss Pearl?" Heather asked aloud, studying what had been Pearl's home.

"Hey, Heather!" A shout broke Heather's concentration. She looked from Pearl's house to Marlow House and saw Lily had just crossed the street and was stepping onto the sidewalk in front of Marlow House's side gate. It had been Lily who had called out.

"Wait up, Lily!" Heather called before jogging to meet her. When she reached her a moment later, Lily stood at Marlow House's side gate, looking her way.

"I saw you staring at Pearl's house." Lily smiled at Heather with a hint of sadness.

"It's weird, her not being there anymore. I wonder who our new neighbor is going to be. You think Mel will talk Adam into buying it?"

Still standing by the gate, Lily glanced briefly at Pearl's house and then looked back at Heather. She shrugged. "I don't know. Guess who else wants the house?"

Curious, Heather studied Lily. "Who?"

"Kelly." Lily grinned.

"Oh no!" Heather cringed.

Lily laughed.

"I'm sorry. She's your sister-in-law, and Ian loves his sister and all that, but she doesn't like me. And I can't imagine living next door to her and Joe. Especially when Brian stays over."

"Well, if you weren't such a ho," Lily teased.

"Oh, shut up!" Heather laughed and reached for the gate. Before her hand touched the latch, Lily grabbed it and pulled Heather's hand to her so she could inspect her manicure.

"Oh, I love that color! It's sort of orange, but not an orange. I couldn't get away with it. Not with my red hair. It would clash. But I love it!"

Heather took back her hand and glanced briefly at her long, painted nails. "Thanks. It's my Thanksgiving color."

HEATHER AND LILY found Danielle in the kitchen at Marlow House. They didn't bother knocking, but just walked in.

"I made coffee," Danielle said in greeting. "Which I believe was a noble gesture, as I can't drink the stuff."

"I read somewhere that you can have a little coffee if you're pregnant," Heather said as she closed the door behind her and Lily.

"They also say you're supposed to limit caffeine intake if pregnant. Since I'm not giving up chocolate—which has caffeine—it'll have to be the coffee," Danielle said.

"Thanks for making it, but I'm kinda in a tea mood." Heather walked to the pantry and helped herself to a tea bag.

"I appreciate the coffee." Lily walked over to Danielle, who poured her a cup. "But where's Walt? Doesn't he normally make the coffee?"

"Walt's not here," Danielle said. "He's at the Glandon Foundation office, helping Chris."

"On a Sunday?" Lily took her coffee to the kitchen table.

"Ah, that's right. Chris mentioned it," Heather said as she filled a mug with water to put in the microwave. "Chris wants to move some furniture, so they need to do it today when no one is there."

"You mean Walt needs to move furniture," Lily snarked as she sat down at the table. With Walt's telekinetic powers, he could easily move furniture without lifting a finger, in much the same way as Marie could move toy blocks and stuffed animals without having physical hands.

Ten minutes later, the three friends sat around Marlow House's kitchen table—Lily drinking coffee, Heather hot tea, and Danielle a glass of chocolate milk.

"Lily told me Kelly wants to buy Pearl's house." Heather wrapped her hands around her mug, warming them while waiting for her tea to steep.

"Yeah, Lily told me." Danielle sighed. "Not sure how I would feel about living next door to Joe."

"I can't believe Joe wants to live on our street." Lily shook her head at the thought. "I think this is just something Kelly wants."

"Can they afford it? I couldn't have without my inheritance after Mom died, and prices have gone up since I moved here," Heather said. "I know from Brian, the local police don't make all that much, and can Kelly really make enough from her blogging?"

"Kelly has her inheritance. She got some money from her grandmother. Ian figures that's what she's intending to use if they make an offer." Lily picked up her mug and took a sip of coffee.

"Of course, Mel wants the house too," Danielle reminded them.

"I'm on Team Mel," Heather announced before taking a sip of tea.

"So Joe hasn't said anything about Pearl's house?" Danielle asked Lily.

"Not much. They stopped by last night. But we didn't discuss the house. Kelly was more talkative about some old friend of Joe's who's in town. I guess he was one of Joe's best friends from high school. Joe hasn't seen him in years. Kelly hopes he'll stick around for the wedding, but that's months away, and Joe figures he won't be here that long. He's just in town to list his mother's house. In fact, they ran into him at Adam's office. It was a total surprise seeing him."

"Don't tell me, she wants him to replace Brian as best man, right?" Heather asked.

Lily frowned at Heather. "A medium and clairvoyant?"

The next moment, Marie appeared. "Morning, ladies!"

"Morning, Marie," Heather and Danielle chimed.

It wasn't just Heather and Danielle's greeting that alerted Lily to Marie's presence. It was the fact the empty chair at the table pulled out, as if someone was sitting down.

"Tell Lily Ian took Connor to meet Walt and Chris at Pier Café. The boys are all having breakfast together."

Danielle repeated Marie's message, and Lily resumed her conversation, telling the others what Kelly had told her about Joe's long-lost friend. When she finished the telling, Marie said, "Oh, I knew Mrs. Cramer and the Langdons. I remember when the Langdon boy was murdered. Those poor people, they were devastated."

Danielle repeated Marie's words for Lily, and Heather asked, "And they never caught the killer?"

Marie shook her head. "Not that I'm aware of. From what I was told back then, there had been a series of break-ins along the businesses near their motorcycle shop. No one had been hurt, not until Rusty Langdon's death. It was after closing, and they felt Rusty must have returned to the shop for some reason and walked in on the robber. The robber panicked and then killed him. After that, the robberies stopped. The police figured the killer must have left the area."

"How was he killed?" Heather asked.

"Someone bashed the poor boy over the head with a tool from the shop. They wiped their prints off, took the cash, and got the heck out of there," Marie said.

Again, Danielle repeated Marie's words for Lily.

"Sounds to me like the burglar panicked. And then, after realizing his life of crime had escalated to murder, probably figured it was time to take his act elsewhere," Lily suggested.

"Exactly what the police thought," Marie said.

"Joe never mentioned this Rusty or Charlie to me," Danielle murmured.

"Well, I guess you guys didn't date for that long," Lily said.

Danielle shrugged. "True."

"Okay, guys, we're here to talk about Thanksgiving," Heather reminded them. She turned to Danielle. "What do you want us to bring?"

"I told you, I'm handling it," Danielle said.

"No, Heather is right. We want to help. Don't be silly. You will have guests to worry about. At least we can help with Thanksgiving dinner," Lily said.

"Speaking of guests, when does your mother-in-law arrive?" Marie asked.

"Former mother-in-law, Marie," Danielle said primly. "At least, that's what Mel said she's considered. They're arriving Wednesday morning."

"What is this former mother-in-law like? The stereotypical shrew?" Heather asked.

Danielle shook her head. "No. Actually, she is a very sweet lady. She was always nice to me. And even though she doted on Lucas—she adored her son—she never made me feel like I wasn't good enough for him, like some mothers-in-law do. She was a good mother-in-law."

"I remember Madeline. I liked her." Lily smiled.

"But you haven't seen her since you moved here?" Heather asked.

"No." Danielle let out a sigh. "The entire thing was so awkward. After Lucas died, I was totally blindsided when I learned the woman in the car with him had been his lover. It was like our life had been a lie. I never felt it was something I could discuss with his mom. I was angry with him. But I also understood Madeline was hurting. She had lost her only son. He had been the world to her. She didn't need to hear how her only child cheated on me."

"She didn't know?" Heather asked.

"I never told her, but there were some articles in the newspaper. I assume she saw them. But I suppose it's possible she didn't read them, and unless someone she knew told her, maybe she didn't know. Yet I find that hard to believe."

"She never discussed it with you?" Heather asked.

Danielle shook her head. "No. I figured she probably knew yet didn't believe it. That seemed the most likely scenario."

"What I want to hear about is this medium she's bringing with her, and why," Marie said.

"He is not a medium," Danielle insisted.

"I intend to be here when they arrive. And that way you'll know for certain, one way or another," Marie said.

SIX

W alt and Danielle sat at the table in Marlow House's kitchen on Sunday evening. Danielle had prepared a simple dinner of roasted chicken, a tossed green salad, and several slices of home-made sourdough bread fresh from a loaf Heather had given them.

After Danielle mentioned something to Walt about Lily and Ian having Sunday dinner with Ian's parents, Walt looked up from his salad plate to Danielle. "I'm surprised Ian's parents accepted our invitation for Thanksgiving dinner." Walt looked back to his plate and added dressing to his salad.

"Lily told me June's not thrilled with the oven in the rental. I guess it's okay for their weekly family dinner, but not for a turkey." Danielle picked up a slice of bread from her plate and tore it in half before continuing. "Plus, Lily told June that Finn Walsh is one of our guests for Thanksgiving. She's dying to meet him."

About to take a bite of his salad, Walt looked across the table at Danielle and arched a brow. "I got the impression Ian's mother doesn't believe in ghosts and things that go bump in the night?"

"Oh, you don't have to actually believe in the supernatural to be a fan of someone like Finn Walsh. It's like you don't have to believe in magic to enjoy a good magic show."

"You are suggesting June enjoys parlor tricks?"

Danielle shrugged. "Something like that."

ON MONDAY MORNING, Danielle wrote out her menu and grocery list for the week while Joanne Johnson cleaned the guest rooms. Walt and Danielle shopped in the afternoon, stopping at the grocery store, meat market, and Old Salts Bakery. When they returned to Marlow House, Joanne helped them unpack and put away the groceries.

Joanne returned to Marlow House on Tuesday to finish up her housekeeping chores and to put clean linens in the guest bedrooms and baths. Danielle spent her day baking for the week, which included a double fudge chocolate cake, brownies, and chocolate chip cookies.

Late Tuesday afternoon, when Walt wandered into the kitchen as Danielle plated up her baked goods, Walt asked, "Do you have enough chocolate?"

To which she responded, "We can never have enough chocolate."

After Joanne headed home on Tuesday evening, Walt insisted they go out to dinner at Pier Café. He figured Danielle had been on her feet enough while baking, and she would be doing her share of cooking once their guests arrived. They didn't have dinner alone; Chris and Heather joined them.

Danielle sat next to Walt in a booth, while Chris and Heather sat across from them. After picking up a menu, Danielle looked at Heather. "Where's Brian tonight?"

Heather peeked over her menu. "He's been putting in crazy hours. "They're kind of shorthanded. I figured Lily and Ian would join us tonight." Heather closed her menu and set it on the table.

"We asked them. But Lily didn't feel like taking Connor out in the rain, and she had already put something in the Crock-Pot this morning." Danielle closed her menu and tossed it back on the table.

"You ready for your guests?" Chris asked. Before they could answer, Carla came and took their order. After Carla left the table, Chris repeated the question.

"Joanne cleaned Marlow House from top to bottom." Danielle grinned. "I love a clean house."

"Yeah, especially when you don't have to do the cleaning," Heather said with a snort.

"Danielle *did* spend all day baking. Not sure if it's for the guests or herself." Walt chuckled.

Danielle looked at Walt and scoffed. "Look who's talking. You tried to talk me into cutting into the chocolate cake."

Chris leaned closer to the table. "Is it your double fudge?"

Danielle reached for her water glass, paused, and looked at Chris. "Yeah."

"Then who can blame him? I say we go to your house after dinner for dessert." Chris grinned.

"Sounds like a good idea." Walt raised his water glass to Chris in a mock toast.

"Sorry, you guys have to settle for Pier Café pie tonight." Danielle chuckled.

A few minutes later, the conversation shifted from dessert choices to Marlow House's next guests.

"You still have no idea what the relationship is between your former mother-in-law and Walsh?" Chris asked.

Danielle shook her head. "No. I did a little research on Walsh's personal life. He's been married once, divorced. But that was, like, twenty years ago. He's about the same age as Madeline, but from what I found on him, he typically dates younger women. At least, according to the photos I found of him online. Pretty young women on his arm at various events. Never saw the same woman twice."

"You said they're staying in separate rooms; it's possible they're just friends," Chris suggested.

"Joanne told me, when she took the reservation, it was my mother-in-law, Madeline, she talked to."

"Former mother-in-law," Heather corrected.

Danielle shrugged. "Madeline never told Joanne who she was. She gave her name and other information we require when taking a reservation, but she said nothing about knowing me. When making the second reservation, she said it was for her traveling companion. Joanne later mentioned his name sounded familiar, but she figured it was probably someone with the same name. I didn't recognize the name when I first read it. It wasn't until I was talking to Lily about Madeline coming with some man. Lily recognized his name."

"And then you did a Google search on his email," Heather finished for her.

"Yeah." Danielle flashed Heather a smile before continuing, "I didn't read about any of his events in the area. It might just be a vacation for him. I imagine he doesn't want us to broadcast his visit if it is just a vacation."

"You haven't actually kept it a secret," Chris reminded her. "We know."

"It's not public knowledge. I didn't tell Carla." Danielle glanced briefly at the server, who stood on the other side of the dining room, talking to a customer. "I wish I could figure out why Madeline is coming here. We haven't talked to each other in over four years. Why would she make a reservation at our bed-and-breakfast?"

"Maybe she doesn't know. Maybe this is just a bizarre coincidence. Maybe she will be shocked to find you at Marlow House," Heather suggested.

Danielle arched her brows at Heather. "I seriously doubt that. While I didn't keep in contact with her after moving here, we spoke one final time before I left California. I told her about the property I inherited in Frederickport from my aunt Brianna. After I sold our business, she asked me what I planned to do in Oregon. I told her, depending on what I found here, I hoped to open a bed-and-breakfast."

"Perhaps this is nothing more than a simple visit from someone from your past," Chris suggested.

———

"I CAN'T BELIEVE this is our last night in Hawaii," Madeline said with a sigh. "It went so fast." She and Finn sat alone at a small table at a seaside restaurant, enjoying a lobster dinner, while the faint sound of live Hawaiian music drifted out from the lounge.

Finn reached across the table and patted her hand. "What is that old saying? Time flies when you're having fun?"

Madeline grinned. "True words. But I admit, I'm nervous. I don't imagine the rest of our trip will be as relaxing."

"There is nothing to be nervous about."

"Tell my nerves that."

"Remember, it won't just be me with you. Lucas will be there, too. In fact, he's here now."

Madeline glanced around, not really expecting to see anyone.

She looked back at Finn and frowned. "He is? You said he'd be joining us in Frederickport?"

Finn shrugged. "I guess he changed his mind. He's standing right behind you. I imagine he sensed your anxiousness. But he wants me to tell you, don't be nervous. He will be with you."

"Can you tell him—"

Before Madeline finished her sentence, Finn said, "You keep forgetting. You don't need me to tell him anything. Tell him yourself. He can hear you. Even if I'm not here."

"Lucas…" Madeline began hesitantly, "do you promise Danielle will understand? She won't think I am crazy?"

"Lucas says she'll understand. Now, stop fretting, and let's enjoy our last night in Honolulu, shall we?"

SHANNON STOOD ALONE at her living room window, gazing out into the darkness. Tomorrow was her birthday. Until Rusty's death ten years earlier, she and Rusty had always spent their birthdays together.

Last year Eden had brought her a birthday dinner. Of course, that was after Eden offered to take her to Pearl Cove, something she offered every year except for this one. This year, Shannon would spend her birthday alone. Eden planned to visit friends in Palm Springs for Thanksgiving, and she intended to leave early Wednesday morning. Turning from the window, Shannon walked from the living room into the den. Once there, she went to the desk, sat down, and turned on the computer. A few moments later, she opened her email.

Beginning a new message, Shannon sat there for a moment and wondered how best to express what she wanted to say. Finally, she began to type.

Hi. It's me. Tomorrow is my birthday. Of course, that means it's Rusty's birthday too. Can you believe it has been ten years since his death? Ten long years, not knowing who was responsible. That is finally going to change. I thought you would want to know.

I will be meeting someone on Friday. He'll be able to give me the answers. I can't say who he is, and why he hasn't come forward until now, but you might say he was there the day Rusty was killed. He holds the key to what really happened. The reason he hasn't come forward before, he didn't realize what he knew. I've been trying to contact him for a long time now, and he's finally gotten back to me and agreed to meet me. He doesn't know why I need to see him, and I hope when I tell him, it doesn't scare him away. But I have faith this will all work out. Rusty will finally get justice. As soon as I see him, I'll let you know what he says. Shannon.

Shannon reread her words and then hit the send button. After she heard the little whooshing sound, she started another email message to another person.

———

SHANNON WAS ABOUT to go take a shower when her phone rang. A moment later, she answered it.

"Hello?"

"Hey, are you still up?" came Eden's voice.

"I'm talking to you, aren't I?"

Eden laughed. "I mean, are you in bed?"

"No, I was just about to take a shower."

"I… I got your email," Eden said. "You can always just call me if you need to talk."

"I know."

"I was wondering, I was hoping I could stop over before you go to bed."

"I'm really tired—" Shannon began before being cut off by her cousin.

"I'm sorry. But I read my flight wrong, and it's earlier than I thought, so I'll be leaving before you get up. I need to bring over your birthday present before I go."

"You didn't have to get me anything."

"Of course I was going to get you something. Heck, I'm feeling guilty enough you're spending your birthday and Thanksgiving alone."

"I'm okay with it. I like being alone," Shannon insisted.

"I also made you a pecan pie. You love pecan pie. It's for Thanksgiving."

SEVEN

W hen Brian and Joe walked into Lucy's Diner for lunch on Wednesday afternoon, they found all the tables occupied. At one table sat Joanne Johnson, the housekeeper for Marlow House. When she spied the two lawmen looking for somewhere to sit, she immediately waved them over to her table, inviting them to join her. They accepted. A few minutes later, Joe sat next to Joanne at the table, while Brian sat on the opposite side, facing them.

"Taking a little break from work?" Brian asked. "Heather tells me Marlow House's guests arrive today."

Joe picked up a menu and shook his head. "I still can't understand why Danielle is reopening the B and B. It's not like they need the money, and she's pregnant."

Joanne chuckled before responding, "I'm also surprised they decided to reopen, but I'm delighted. There is something exciting about meeting the new people who come to the bed-and-breakfast."

"Yeah, until they try to murder you," Joe grumbled.

"At least it's no longer just Danielle living alone at Marlow House with guests she doesn't know," Brian reminded him. "Walt's there now."

Joe gave a shrug at Brian's observation, and Joanne said, "I doubt we have to worry about this week's guests."

The next moment, the server arrived and took Joe's and Brian's orders. When he left the table, Brian asked, "Have they arrived yet?"

"I don't know. They're supposed to get there this afternoon. But I'm not going in today. I finished getting the house ready yesterday. And while I normally enjoy being there when the guests arrive, it will be less awkward for Danielle if she greets these guests herself, without an audience."

"Isn't Walt there?" Brian asked.

"Yes, which will be awkward enough." Joanne picked up her beverage and took a drink.

"Are you going to be there tomorrow?" Brian asked.

Joanne flashed him a smile. "Yes. I'm helping Danielle with the Thanksgiving dinner."

THE ONLY SOUND in Marlow House's living room came from the fireplace crackling as the flames danced and flickered. The rain had stopped hours earlier, and outside, blue skies competed with the gray for its share of the overhead landscape. Walt sat on one of the easy chairs in the living room, reading a book, while Danielle lounged on the sofa, reading hers. Periodically she glanced toward the window after imagining she had heard a car drive up.

Walt closed his book, set it on his lap, and looked over at Danielle. "I don't think you've turned a page in thirty minutes."

Danielle peeked over her book at Walt. "I can't focus. But if you know I haven't been turning any pages, I don't imagine you've gotten much reading done yourself."

Walt grinned and tossed his book on the end table. "No. I haven't."

With a sigh, Danielle closed her book, sat up on the sofa, and placed the book on the coffee table. "I wish they would just get here."

"Hello!" a new voice boomed. A moment later, the ghost of Marie Nichols materialized, standing in the middle of the room between Walt and Danielle. Although Marie had been in her nineties at the time of her murder, she preferred to present herself as she looked in her eighties. The decade difference was only a subtle change, yet one Marie preferred. She would have gone much younger, yet those who could see her would not have recognized a much younger version of herself.

"Afternoon, Marie," Walt said at the same time as Danielle said, "Hi, Marie."

"I believe your guests have arrived," Marie announced. A moment later, they heard a car door slam, confirming Marie's suspicion.

Danielle felt a fluttering in the pit of her stomach, and she didn't believe it was the baby. She stood up, placed a hand on her belly, and let out a deep breath.

Getting to his feet, Walt looked at his wife with concern. "Are you okay?"

"I'm just nervous. I'll be fine... I think." Danielle looked to the open doorway leading to the entrance hall. She took a deep cleansing breath, exhaled, smiled, walked to Walt, took his hand, and with him, headed toward the doorway.

Marie vanished before they stepped from the room, yet Walt and Danielle found her waiting for them by the front door, standing several feet in front of it.

"If this medium is the real deal, he'll assume I'm just a nosy old woman greeting the guests with you," Marie told Walt and Danielle as they approached.

"And if he is not the real deal?" Walt asked.

"Then I expect him to walk through me."

The doorbell rang. Walt and Danielle paused a moment, looked at each other, and Danielle said, "Let's get this over with."

Danielle opened the front door, while Walt stood several feet behind her, next to Marie.

"Danielle!" the woman standing on the front porch with her traveling companion greeted her. Without waiting for a reply, the woman rushed to Danielle and gave her a warm hug. Danielle returned the hug, feeling some of her nervousness melt away. After the hug ended, the two women parted and stood in the doorway. They looked each other up and down.

Danielle didn't think Madeline had aged. In fact, her former mother-in-law looked younger than she had when they last saw each other. Danielle attributed that to the fact Madeline had been so weighed down by grief after Lucas's death. *Constant tears will age a person,* Danielle thought.

"You look wonderful!" Madeline gushed. She reached up and brushed her hand along Danielle's right cheek. "I wondered if you still wore your hair in the braid."

Danielle grinned at Madeline. "I cut my hair a while back, stopped wearing the braid. But when I let it grow back, I fell into old habits."

"Well, it looks lovely on you," Madeline insisted.

A cough from Madeline's traveling companion broke into the intimate reunion. The women turned to him, and Madeline said, "Oh, Danielle, I would like you to meet my friend Finn Walsh. Finn, this is Danielle."

Finn stood behind Madeline to her right, holding two suitcases.

"Hello, and please come in, both of you!" Danielle grinned. "Let's go inside where it's warmer!"

Danielle opened the door wider and stood to the side while Madeline and Finn walked into the house, Finn still carrying the two suitcases, and Madeline carrying just her purse. After they entered the house, Danielle watched as Finn walked through Marie, stopped, and set the suitcases on the floor. He looked at Walt and smiled and then glanced back at the women.

"I suppose that answered our question," Marie said. "The rude man just walked through me!" Marie stepped back, out of Finn's way, as he had just placed one suitcase through her feet.

Danielle forced a smile while trying to focus on the live people in the room. "I'd like you to meet my husband, Walt Marlow. Walt, this is Madeline Saunders and Finn Walsh."

Marie thought the smile Madeline gave Walt looked rather sad. Yet Madeline graciously held out her hand and said, "Hello, Walt, it is so nice to meet you."

Walt accepted the handshake, returned the greeting, and then exchanged greetings with Finn.

"Did you drive in from California?" Danielle asked. "Or fly to Portland?"

"No. We were in Hawaii," Madeline said.

Danielle's eyes widened. "Hawaii?"

"We flew into the Portland airport and then rented a car," Finn explained.

Danielle glanced from Madeline to Finn and back to Madeline. "You must be exhausted!"

Madeline smiled weakly. "Yes, it was a long trip."

Walt reached down and picked up the suitcases Finn had been carrying. "Let me take you to your rooms so you can freshen up, and when you come downstairs, you can have something to eat if you're hungry."

MARIE FOLLOWED THE GUESTS UPSTAIRS, curious to eavesdrop. But after Walt showed them to their rooms, they disappointed her by each going to their own rooms—which meant there would be no conversation between them to overhear. Yet, instead of going back downstairs with Walt, Marie decided to give Finn another test. Perhaps he had seen her and didn't want to say anything in front of Walt and Danielle at their first meeting. She knew Danielle typically failed to acknowledge her when nonmediums were around. Yet if that proved to be the case, Marie had a few words or two for Finn Walsh. How rude to walk through her and put a suitcase on her feet if he saw her standing there!

Marie walked through the closed bedroom door into Finn's room and found him unpacking a suitcase.

"Hello!" Marie greeted him.

Finn did not look up but continued to unpack his suitcase.

Marie moved closer to Finn and stuck her face in front of his and yelled, "Boo!"

He did not flinch or acknowledge her presence. She tried a few more times to get his attention, but when he failed to respond, she decided to go back downstairs to tell Walt and Danielle Finn was undoubtably a fake. But before she left the room, a knock came at the door, and she decided to stick around.

Finn stopped what he was doing, walked to the door, and opened it. Madeline stood in the hallway.

"I thought you were going to take a nap." Finn opened his door wider. "I know I'm tired."

"Did you want to take a nap?" Madeline stepped into his room.

"If you don't mind." He closed the door behind her.

"Of course not. After all, I slept on the flight, and you had to do all the driving from the airport. Plus, I'm just too anxious to take a

41

nap." Madeline smiled sheepishly. "I want to go downstairs and talk with Danielle."

"Certainly, I understand." Finn reached out and patted Madeline's shoulder. "I want you to know Lucas is here."

"He is?" Madeline looked around anxiously.

"He's standing right next to you. In fact, he just kissed your right cheek."

Madeline's right hand moved quickly to her face, touching the spot she imagined Lucas had kissed.

"Oh, phooey," Marie snarked, now sitting on the bed. "The only ghost in this room is me, and you can't even see me. You fake."

"Lucas wants you to remember he will be with you when you talk to Danielle. You won't be alone," Finn promised.

"Thank you, Finn," Madeline whispered. She leaned over and quickly kissed Finn's lips, turned, and rushed from the room.

"Don't forget to take Lucas with you!" Marie called after Madeline before letting out a snort. The next moment, she vanished from the room, joining Walt and Danielle in the kitchen.

"Your mother-in-law is on her way down," Marie announced. She then recapped what she'd observed upstairs.

"I was right. He is a con man," Danielle muttered. "And you say she kissed him?"

"On the lips," Marie chirped.

"What do you think his angle is?" Walt wondered aloud.

"Madeline is not rich, but she is financially stable. At least, she was. I imagine he has substantially more money than her, considering what I've read about him. In the last ten years, he's become somewhat famous, and according to the online articles, his shows are always booked. He has money," Danielle said.

"I suspect you and Walt have far more money than he does," Marie said. "And as you have learned, being wealthy does not mean someone won't greedily want more. Look at Chris's uncles."

"What are you suggesting?" Walt asked.

"From what they said upstairs, I have the feeling Finn is the one who convinced Danielle's former mother-in-law to come here," Marie said. "After all, he said something about Lucas being with his mother, to give her the courage to talk to Danielle. And we all know Lucas is not with his mother upstairs. It is all part of this Finn's con. I suggest you both watch your pocketbooks while they're here."

EIGHT

W hen Madeline walked into the kitchen at Marlow House a few minutes later, she found Danielle sitting at the kitchen table with Walt. While taking Madeline and Finn up to their rooms earlier, Walt had explained the layout of Marlow House so they could easily navigate the house when they came back downstairs.

Walt stood up when Madeline entered the room and excused himself so Danielle and Madeline could talk privately. Marie didn't afford the women the same consideration but stayed behind to eavesdrop.

"Would you like something to eat?" Danielle asked, now standing up.

"Oh no. I'm not hungry." Madeline glanced around the room. "This is a beautiful home. Did you have much restoration to do when you first moved in?"

"No. It was in good shape. Are you sure you don't want something to eat? I have some homemade chocolate chip cookies on the table in the cake pan." Danielle pointed to the table and added, "I could get you a cup of coffee, tea, maybe a glass of milk?"

"I would like a glass of water, if that's okay?" Madeline glanced at the table and smiled. "And I suppose you could tempt me with cookies. I remember you made rather good chocolate chip cookies."

Several minutes later, Danielle, Madeline, and Marie sat at the kitchen table. The glass of water Danielle had brought Madeline sat in front of her while she gingerly nibbled on one of Danielle's cookies.

"Walt seems like a nice man," Madeline said in a soft voice.

"Yes. He's a good person." Danielle sat at the table, her folded hands on the tabletop as her fingers fidgeted.

"I haven't read his book, but I understand it's quite good. He has another one coming out?"

Danielle nodded. "Yes, he does."

They sat in silence for a few minutes, and Madeline finally said, "This is awkward, isn't it?" She looked up at Danielle with a sad smile.

"I'm sorry for not keeping in touch." Danielle found it surprising that she actually meant it. "I suppose I wanted to start a new life, and I…"

"You don't need to explain," Madeline said quickly. "Really. I understand more than you realize."

"How have you been? You look wonderful, by the way."

"Thank you." Madeline flashed Danielle a smile. "Things are much better these days. Much better than the last time we saw each other."

"I assume you're living in the same house, since that's the address you used when you made the reservation."

"Yes, but I've spent little time there in the last six months. I've been traveling a great deal," Madeline explained.

"You mentioned you were in Hawaii?"

Madeline smiled. "Yes. It was beautiful there. Have you been?"

"That's where Walt and I had our honeymoon."

Madeline gave a nod and took another bite of her cookie.

"How long have you known Finn Walsh?" Danielle asked.

"About eight months."

"Are you… umm…" Danielle didn't finish her question. Instead, she picked up another cookie and took a bite.

"If you're wondering if he and I are more than friends, yes. We started seeing each other about a month after we met. I've been traveling with him for the last six months. He has readings all over the country; I've been going with him."

"Is that why you're in Frederickport? Does he have readings scheduled here? Or in the area?"

Madeline shook her head. "No. He came here for me. So I could see you."

"Please don't take this wrong, because I'm glad to see you again. But I wonder, why now?" Danielle asked.

Finishing her cookie, Madeline picked up a paper napkin from the table and primly wiped off her mouth, her fingers, and crunched up the paper napkin in her fist. She held it for a moment and looked at Danielle. "Lucas said I should come."

Danielle's eyes widened. "Lucas?"

Madeline released the napkin, and it dropped to the table as she reached over and took one of Danielle's hands in hers. "Please don't think I'm crazy."

"I don't think you're crazy," Danielle said unconvincingly.

"Not crazy, a pushover," Marie snarked.

"But Lucas promised me you would understand. He said if anyone would understand, you would." Madeline leaned back in her chair, no longer holding onto Danielle's hand.

"You spoke to Lucas?"

"In a manner of speaking. You do know who Finn is, right?" Madeline asked.

"He claims to be a psychic medium," Danielle said.

Madeline grinned. "He is the most respected psychic medium in the country. Have you ever watched any of his readings? You can find them on YouTube."

"Umm, no," Danielle lied. "I've heard of him, but I'm not really familiar with what he does."

"Oh, Danielle, you really need to watch some of his readings!" Madeline said excitedly. "He's changed my life. He helped me come to terms with losing Lucas. I understand so much now. Finn brings comfort and closure to so many people. What he does is inspiring. Truly."

Danielle reached over and patted Madeline's hand and said, "I am happy you've found closure, that you're at peace."

"That's why I'm here. Lucas wanted me to see you," Madeline said.

"I assume Finn told you that?" Danielle asked, no longer patting Madeline's hand.

Madeline grinned. "Yes, well, I'm not a medium nor psychic in any manner. But through Finn, I've been able to contact Lucas. He's been able to explain everything to me. Answer questions I had and put things into perspective."

Danielle studied Madeline for a moment, uncertain what to say. Finally, she asked, "What did he explain to you?"

With a sigh, Madeline said, "After the accident, after Lucas's death, there was talk that the woman in the car with him was his lover. We never discussed it."

"No, we didn't."

"I never imagined my son would do something like that. I didn't understand why you never publicly stood up to those people spreading that ugly rumor."

"Oh my, has she come here to demand you clear her poor son's reputation?" Marie wondered aloud.

"And what has Lucas told you about all this?" Danielle asked quietly.

Madeline looked Danielle in the eyes, took a deep breath and said, "That she was his lover. That you knew the truth. That he hurt you, and it was his fault. I am so sorry, Danielle. I was hurting so much back then that I didn't even consider what you were going through—not really. And I didn't understand why you gave me the engagement ring back, or why you wanted to get rid of the portrait. When you left, it was like I lost my daughter along with my son. I didn't understand."

"Oh my, I didn't see that one coming," Marie muttered.

"And now?" Danielle asked quietly.

"You had every reason to be angry with my son. Hurt. I can't even imagine how you felt back then. But Lucas told me you're happy now. That you have met your soul mate. He told me you forgave him."

"Lucas said that?"

"Oh no, Danielle, you aren't buying into all this?" Marie asked.

Danielle glanced briefly at Marie and back to Madeline.

"I'm curious," Danielle said hesitantly. "Did Lucas say how he knew I forgave him?"

Madeline's smile faded, and she asked in a wavering voice, "You haven't forgiven him?"

"Oh yes, I have," Danielle said quickly, leaning over and giving Madeline's hand a reassuring squeeze. "I just wondered how he knew. Did he say?"

"Not exactly. But I assume because he's been watching over you, like he watches over me. When our loved ones die, they become our guardian angels and watch over us," Madeline explained. "They see everything. They know things."

"And he believes Walt is my soul mate?"

Madeline nodded. "I will confess, when I first heard you had remarried, I… well, I am ashamed to admit I was angry. Back then, I felt you had simply erased Lucas from your life after he died. Erased me. And then I met Finn, and he helped me connect with Lucas. I came to understand the truth."

"Which was?" Danielle asked.

"That while Lucas loved you—and you loved him—you were not soul mates. And when Lucas moved on, it was your chance to find your soul mate. You had to come to Oregon because that's where you'd find Walt."

Danielle did not respond, but sat quietly while Marie rambled on, questioning why Madeline felt it necessary to come to Oregon and what was Finn's angle in all this. Finally, Madeline asked hesitantly, "Do you think I'm crazy?"

Danielle flashed Madeline a smile and shook her head. "No. I don't think you're crazy."

"I would never have come here, shared with you what Lucas told me, had Lucas not assured me you would understand. He said your mind was open to such things."

Danielle studied Madeline for a moment and then said, "You and Lucas were close."

"I always thought we were. Although, when I learned he had been unfaithful in his marriage, I realized there were things about my son I had refused to see. Such as his materialistic side."

Danielle arched her brow. "How do you mean?"

"I wasn't aware of it at the time. Oh, I suppose I could have seen it had I had my eyes open and been more objective. But Lucas explained how he had become caught up with material things when your business became successful. Back then, I just saw it as someone who was hardworking being able to enjoy the fruit of their labor. But it was more than that."

"When did Lucas explain all that to you?" Danielle asked.

Madeline grinned. "I guess he didn't explain it to me, exactly. But to Finn, who then passed on Lucas's message."

"You mentioned Lucas told you I would be open to all this. Umm... when I mentioned you and Lucas were close, I wondered, is this something he discussed with you before he died? My thoughts on mediums?"

Madeline frowned. "I'm not sure what you're asking."

"When he was still alive, did he tell you about my opinions on ghosts?"

"Ghosts? Finn says there are no such things as ghosts. There are spirits, but ghosts that stay behind and haunt people, no. Just legend. As for your question, no, we never discussed what you thought about ghosts. Why would we?"

"Is she suggesting I'm a figment of your imagination?" Marie asked with faux outrage.

"Umm... I was just curious if all your recent revelations involving Lucas stem from your contact with him through Finn," Danielle said.

"Yes." Madeline stood. "I think I have said enough for now. Perhaps I am tired. I'd like to try lying down for a while. Take a little nap. Later this evening, perhaps we can all talk, you, me, Finn, and your husband."

"Umm... yes... of course."

Madeline reached out and touched Danielle's hand. "I just need for you to know I always thought of you as a daughter. After Lucas died, it broke my heart when you left, and when you just dropped out of my life. I lost both you and Lucas. I didn't understand."

"I didn't mean to hurt you," Danielle said sincerely.

Madeline patted Danielle's hand. "I know that. And I didn't come here to make you feel guilty."

"Why did you come here?" Marie asked, knowing Madeline couldn't hear her.

"Lucas helped me understand what was really going on back then. He wanted me to come here—he said I needed to come. And he also believes you need it, too." Without another word, Madeline dropped a kiss on Danielle's forehead and left the room.

"What is that Finn up to?" Marie asked Danielle.

NINE

"I'm just trying to figure out why she's here," Marie said. "Or, more accurately, why Finn brought her here?" Marie sat alone with Walt and Danielle in Marlow House's library. Danielle had just recounted to Walt her conversation with Madeline.

"I find it difficult to envision Lucas referring to me as Danielle's soul mate," Walt said. "The last time we spoke, I seem to recall he told me not to interfere with her happiness. He wanted me to move on."

"Obviously, whatever Finn is up to, he doesn't want you to feel Madeline is a threat to your marriage," Marie suggested. "He's a crafty fellow."

"I suspect after Finn met Madeline, he did a little online research. He probably found those articles about Lucas's accident, and it's not too hard to imagine a mother refusing to see the harsh truth about a beloved deceased son," Danielle said. "I have no idea what Madeline might have told Finn before he started manipulating her by claiming to channel Lucas."

"I suppose we'll just have to wait and see what he's up to in all this," Marie said. "It will be interesting."

MADELINE CAME BACK DOWNSTAIRS two hours later; she had Finn with her. Danielle invited them to join her and Walt for dinner, and the two accepted the invitation after some coaxing. While Marlow House Bed-and-Breakfast provided breakfast to their guests—and occasionally a holiday supper, like Thanksgiving—they rarely served dinners. Of course, there were always exceptions.

Marie had left thirty minutes earlier, so it was just the four of them sitting around the dining room table, Madeline, Finn, Walt, and Danielle. Danielle had prepared chicken Florentine, a slow-cooker recipe she found on YouTube. She served it with a tossed green salad and dinner rolls.

"Madeline mentioned you were an excellent cook. She was right," Finn said after taking his first bite of dinner.

"Thank you." Danielle smiled and silently studied Finn, noting he was a good-looking older man, with thick, wavy white hair and a tanned complexion, probably because of his recent trip to Hawaii. She inwardly chuckled to herself when she realized he was probably just a couple of years older than Brian, who might find insult by her older-man description.

While Brian and Finn were about the same age, the two men dressed nothing alike. Finn reminded Danielle of a Vegas entertainer, with his somewhat flamboyant wardrobe and gold jewelry. Yet, technically speaking, he was a Vegas entertainer.

"I understand you are a psychic medium," Walt said, breaking the momentary silence.

Finn looked up at Walt and smiled. "Yes. Interesting, by your tone of voice, it would suggest you are a skeptic."

Walt returned the smile with a shrug.

"But I know you aren't a skeptic—I mean about mediums. Just about me, perhaps?" Finn flashed Walt a smile.

About to take a bite of salad, Walt paused a moment and looked at Finn and asked, "Why do you imagine I'm not a skeptic? I would assume many people are."

Finn shrugged. "Some people are naturally skeptical about anything supernatural. But many people believe in the possibility. And you are one of the believers. It's something Lucas told me."

"Danielle's first husband?" Walt asked. "I've never even met him."

Finn looked curiously at Walt, tilting his head slightly. "Interesting…"

"What?" Walt asked.

"Lucas insists you two met." Finn frowned.

"Lucas? Is he here now?" Walt suppressed a grin.

"Yes. He's standing behind his mother. He's been there since we came down for dinner." Finn nodded toward Madeline. If Walt's skeptical tone offended Finn, he did not show it. In fact, Finn seemed somewhat amused.

Madeline smiled at Walt. "It comforts me to know Lucas has never really left me."

"I guess sometimes a medium might misunderstand what a spirit is saying?" Danielle suggested. While still convinced Finn was a fake, she appreciated the comfort it gave Madeline, knowing her son was not really gone.

"Very true," Finn said with a nod. "But in this instance, I don't believe I'm misunderstanding. He keeps saying, 'I've met Walt.' He keeps repeating it over and over."

"Perhaps he has met Walt, and Walt doesn't remember," Madeline suggested. She looked at Walt and said, "I confess, I've read about you, how you came to Oregon on a holiday and were in a horrible accident and suffered from amnesia. I understand you never got your memory back. My son had a cousin who lived in Huntington Beach." Madeline paused and looked at Danielle. "Remember?"

"Umm… yes…" Danielle frowned, unsure where this was going.

Madeline turned a smile on Walt. "I remember from the article, you lived near Huntington Beach, so it is entirely possible you met my son when he visited his cousin, and you simply don't remember."

Walt stared at Madeline yet did not respond.

"Lucas insists both you and Danielle believe in mediums," Finn interrupted.

"Does he?" Walt smiled.

"Interesting," Finn murmured.

"What?" Madeline asked curiously.

Finn shrugged. "I have the feeling your son is keeping something from me."

Snow began falling from the ceiling. Danielle glanced up,

waiting for Eva to show herself. The spirit of the silent screen star Eva Thorndike used what excess energy she had for dramatic entrances, such as flourishes of colorful glitter or snowflakes. The next moment she materialized, Marie by her side.

"I'm curious. Are there any more spirits in the room?" Danielle asked.

"Yes." Finn grinned at Danielle.

Danielle glanced briefly at Eva and Marie and then back to Finn.

"You said he couldn't see us," Eva asked Marie.

"He can't." Marie walked over to Finn and waved her hand in front of his eyes. He didn't blink. Marie turned back to Eva. "See? I told you so."

"What other spirits are in the room?" Danielle asked.

"She says she's Walt's mother," Finn said.

"My mother?" Walt arched a brow and suppressed a grin.

"Yes, she tells me she came to you in a dream. Told you something very important was about to happen. Does that make sense?" Finn asked Walt.

Walt shrugged. "Not sure."

"Have you had any recent dreams of your mother?" Finn asked.

"Yes," Walt reluctantly admitted.

Finn smiled. "It's her way of validating she's here. Oh…" Finn looked at Danielle and smiled. "Congratulations."

Danielle frowned. "Congratulations?"

"Walt's mother tells me she's going to be a grandmother. She's very excited," Finn said.

"You're pregnant?" Madeline blurted.

Danielle looked at Madeline and back to Finn. "How did you know?"

"You are!" Madeline gushed. "When are you due?"

Danielle frowned and looked back at Madeline. "Umm… the doctor says mid-May."

"Lucas is happy for you," Finn said. "He says you are going to make a wonderful mother."

"He's quite good," Eva observed. "I can see why he makes so much money doing this."

"By Walt's and Danielle's expressions, for a minute there I thought he had them believing him," Marie grumbled.

Danielle flashed Eva and Marie a quick frown and then turned a sweet smile to Finn. She gave her stomach a pat and said, "I guess I am showing, aren't I?"

"Not at all; I had no idea. In fact, I believe you are a little trimmer than the last time I saw you," Madeline said.

Danielle looked at Walt and said, "That's just because Walt keeps pilfering my share of the cinnamon rolls."

"Cinnamon rolls?" Madeline frowned.

Danielle flashed her a weak smile.

"Someone else is here too," Finn said. "It's a man. He's standing behind Danielle."

Danielle glanced over her shoulder and didn't see anyone. She looked back at Finn and asked, "Who is he?"

"He says he's your father," Finn said.

Danielle arched a brow. "My father?"

"He wants you to know how excited he and your mother are over their first grandchild. He says he was at your wedding. Does that make sense?" Finn asked.

"My father died before I married Lucas," Danielle explained.

Finn shook his head and said, "He keeps showing me a locket."

Without thinking, Danielle touched her blouse's neckline. It concealed the locket she wore.

"A gold locket. It has an *M* engraved on it. Do you know what that means?" Finn asked.

Danielle shook her head. "I have no idea."

"Do you have a heart locket with an *M* engraved on it?" Finn asked.

Danielle didn't answer immediately. Instead, she glanced at Walt. Their eyes met briefly. She looked back at Finn and said, "Yes, I have a locket like that."

Finn smiled. "Your father is showing me the locket. He says he got it for you."

Danielle stared at Finn for a moment. Finally, she said, "Actually, a friend gave me the locket as a wedding gift when I married Walt."

"I don't know what to tell you. But your father keeps insisting he gave the locket to you." Finn frowned a moment and then said, "I think maybe he means he was there when your friend bought it. He might have helped your friend pick it out. Yes, that must be it."

"HE'S GOOD. I will give him that," Danielle said later that evening when she and Walt walked into their bedroom.

"It was interesting." Walt shut the door behind them. He sat on the edge of the bed and began taking off his shoes. "Fact is, I did meet Lucas. My mother did come to me in a dream and tell me something important was about to happen—that you are going to have a baby. And your father did give you that locket in a dream right before our wedding."

"It's how those guys work. Plus, he did his homework." Danielle sat on the bed.

"Explain it to me." Walt leaned over and finished taking off his shoes.

"Don't tell me you think he is the real deal?" Danielle asked incredulously.

"Hardly," Walt snarked. "Not with Marie and Eva there, and he had no clue. But you have to admit, if we were not intimately familiar with the spiritual world of mediums, we would have bought into what he's selling."

"What I really find annoying, he seems so nice."

"That is annoying?" Walt chuckled.

"Sure. I expect con men to be sort of slimy and creepy. But he is so personable and seems so nice. Sweet even. No wonder he is so good at his job."

"How did he do it tonight?" Walt asked.

Still sitting next to Walt on the mattress, Danielle touched the rim of her neckline and then looped the chain of her necklace around her finger. "I'm pretty sure when they arrived, I was wearing the locket outside of the blouse. He must have seen it. People like him are observant. He didn't even need to see the engraving to make an educated guess about the *M*, considering our surname. And had I said you gave it to me, instead of a friend, he probably would say Dad got you to buy it for me. He is giving me what he assumes I want to hear. A made-up moment about my father who died before my wedding. I'm sure Madeline already told him about my parents' accident. He is giving me a lovely memory I can hold in my heart."

"It's a memory you really have," Walt reminded her.

"True. But he doesn't know that. Finn's simply skilled at his trade. He observes, is a quick thinker, and he tells me something I would like to believe. He's good at what he does."

"And my mother?" Walt asked.

"It's not unusual for people to dream about their deceased parents. It was a safe bet that you had dreamed about your mother sometime. And he never said what she told you. Just that it was important. He left the door wide open to mean all sorts of things," Danielle said.

"But he knew you were pregnant."

"That might be a lucky, educated guess. And it's also possible he researched us before arriving. I imagine before any reading, he has someone doing background checks. That would take one stop at the closest diner for a cup of coffee for Carla to tell them I was pregnant."

"And about Lucas meeting me?" Walt asked.

"I'm sure Madeline is not the only one who researched you. Tossing in that bit about you and Lucas having met was probably for Madeline's sake. For whatever reason, whatever his con, it seems to depend on Madeline accepting our marriage."

TEN

Both Heather and Lily showed up at Marlow House early Thanksgiving morning, each eager to help Danielle. When they got there, the turkey was already stuffed, in the oven, and Danielle appeared to have the meal preparations under control. The three friends sat together at the kitchen table, Lily drinking coffee, Heather hot tea, and Danielle hot chocolate.

"When will Joanne be here?" Lily asked.

Danielle glanced briefly at the wall clock and then back to Lily. "I told her not to come in until noon."

"Where are your guests this morning?" Lily looked toward the door leading into the hallway. "I noticed the blue sedan parked out front earlier, but it's gone now."

"Madeline is upstairs taking a shower, and Finn took off this morning, said he had errands to run," Danielle explained.

"What errands does he have to run in Frederickport?" Heather asked.

Danielle shrugged and then told Lily and Heather all that had happened since her guests arrived.

"It's going to be interesting tonight, the fake medium having Thanksgiving with four legit mediums while he doesn't have a clue," Heather said with a chuckle.

"He might be fake, but wow, it's kind of creepy all that he told

Walt and Danielle last night," Lily said.

Danielle arched a brow at Lily. "Might be fake?"

Lily shrugged. "You know what I mean."

"The guy is obviously skilled at cold readings. If he weren't, he wouldn't be so successful," Danielle said. "And I'm not convinced it wasn't a hot reading."

Lily frowned. "What does that even mean?"

Danielle looked at Lily. "A cold reading is a technique where the medium makes educated guesses by observing whoever he is reading. Taking things into account such as their clothing, how they talk, their gender, whatever. For example, if he sees me wearing a heart locket, he might assume it's something my husband gave me."

"But he said your father gave it to you," Lily said. "And in a way, he did."

"We also have coincidences, which play into these readings," Danielle said.

Lily frowned. "I don't get it."

"It might have been a hot reading—that's when a person like Finn already knows something about the person. I'm sure he already knew both Walt and I don't have any parents. He might have researched us before we met, or Madeline already told him all about me. Not that she did it so he could use it in a reading, but just conversation. In that case, when he sees the locket, he can tell me my father gave it to me, knowing he has been gone a long time, and when I tell him he didn't, he can convincingly say my father got the person to give it to me. That's something a daughter who has lost her father would like to believe."

"What if you got that locket years before your father died?" Lily asked. "It is an antique. For all he knows, your grandmother gave it to you when you were a little girl."

"Facebook!" Heather blurted.

Both Lily and Danielle turned to Heather. "What about Facebook?" Lily asked.

"After Danielle was married, she posted a picture of the locket on Facebook, said it was a gift from the chief, who walked her down the aisle!" Heather explained.

Danielle flashed Lily a smug grin. "I forgot about that Facebook post. But that is exactly what happened. I imagine social media is a treasure trove for people like Finn."

"I suggest you ladies change the topic of conversation," Walt said as he walked into the kitchen. "I could hear you when I was out in the hallway, and I saw Madeline upstairs. She was just coming out of the bathroom and said she would be down here in a few minutes."

Walt proved to be correct. Ten minutes later, Madeline walked into the kitchen.

"Madeline, so nice to see you again," Lily greeted her.

"Lily, oh my, you haven't changed at all!" Madeline gave Lily a quick hug. When the hug ended, she said, "I understand you've been very busy since the last time I saw you. A husband and a little boy?"

Lily laughed, and then Danielle introduced Madeline to Heather. Walt poured Madeline a cup of coffee. He poured himself some too and then excused himself and left the four women in the kitchen, sitting around the table chatting.

Madeline seemed curious about Heather and began asking her questions about her job with the Glandon Foundation, which turned into a discussion on their shared love of animals and somehow shifted to a shared interest in sourdough bread baking. And from the sourdough bread conversation, they began discussing the Thanksgiving menu and then the guest list.

When asked who was coming, Danielle started naming off those on the guest list, but when she got to one name, Heather asked, "Who's that?"

"Remember, I mentioned him. He's an old friend of Joe's," Danielle explained.

"You invited Charlie Cramer for Thanksgiving?" Lily asked.

Danielle looked at Lily. "Kelly called and asked if they could invite him. She said he was going to be alone for Thanksgiving, and since he was an old friend of Joe's—"

"She probably wants to convince Joe to pick a new best man," Heather grumbled.

"Who's Kelly?" Madeline asked.

Lily turned a smile to Madeline and said, "My sister-in-law. Joe's her fiancé."

"And Joe works with my boyfriend, Brian. They're both on the local police force," Heather explained. "Joe's asked Brian to be his best man, and I don't think Kelly and her mother are happy about

58

it. I'm pretty sure Kelly would love to convince Joe to un-ask Brian and ask Charlie."

Madeline frowned at Heather. "Why doesn't she like your boyfriend?"

"Oh, I think Kelly likes Brian alright. But I don't think she or her mother like me. I don't think I'm the appropriate date for the best man," Heather explained.

Madeline scrunched up her nose in disapproval. "Well, that is ridiculous. I find you absolutely adorable!"

Heather broke into a grin. "Gosh, Danielle, I really like your mother-in-law!"

BETTY KELTY WAS SPENDING Thanksgiving alone. It wasn't that her family in Astoria hadn't invited her for the traditional feast. In fact, she had intended to go. There was even a pistachio pudding salad sitting in her refrigerator, which her sister had suggested she bring. Betty wasn't much of a cook, but the kids seemed to like the salad she tossed together for such events. All she needed to do was mix instant pistachio pudding, pineapple, Cool Whip, and little marshmallows. But her plans for Thanksgiving all changed when she woke up that morning and barfed. Since she wasn't running a temperature, she suspected it was food poisoning, not the flu.

Bored, Betty had spent the last hour spying on her neighbor across the street—Shannon Langdon. Betty, who worked at the local library, had moved into her house two years earlier. It belonged to her aunt, who moved to Florida for a warmer climate, but didn't want to sell her home, just in case she decided all that sunshine was not all it was cracked up to be. She also did not want to rent the house to strangers, nor leave it empty to fall into ruins. Which is how Betty managed to rent a lovely home in Frederickport on a librarian's salary.

When she first moved into the neighborhood, her aunt had told her all about Shannon, the neighborhood's recluse who never left her house. In the last two years, Betty had never seen Shannon step outside. The only visitor Shannon ever had, as far as Betty saw, were delivery people dropping something off on Shannon's doorstep, or

Eden Langdon, Shannon's cousin and another one of Betty's neighbors.

Unlike Shannon, Eden was a friendly, chatty neighbor. She had dropped by Betty's several days earlier to let her know she would be out of town for Thanksgiving weekend. Had Shannon not been a recluse, Betty would think the three women shared a lot in common. They were all single, about the same age, and each lived alone on the same street.

Betty had never actually met Shannon, although she once asked Eden for an introduction, believing she might be of some help to the recluse. Perhaps Shannon might want to check out some books from the library, and she could bring them to her. But Eden quickly told her Shannon preferred eBooks she downloaded online, and discouraged an introduction, insisting her cousin preferred her privacy.

Betty hadn't pushed the matter. But she found it interesting that on the first day of Eden's vacation from Frederickport, Shannon had a visitor. An hour earlier, a blue sedan had pulled up and parked in front of Shannon's house. At first, Betty thought it might be a delivery. It would not have been the first one that day. About thirty minutes before the sedan's arrival, the delivery car from Lucy's Diner had pulled up in front of Shannon's house. Betty had watched them take two sacks to the front door. Since the front door was not visible from the street, Betty didn't see if Shannon had taken the delivery inside. Nor did she see when the gentleman visitor—an older white-haired man driving the blue sedan—went into the house. Yet she assumed he had, since his car remained parked in front of Shannon's house.

Betty was about to turn from the window when the man from the blue sedan came walking back to his car. She watched as he got into the vehicle and then drove off. Betty glanced at the clock and said, "Wow, Shannon had a gentleman caller for over an hour. That's a first. I wonder who he was."

SHANNON LANGDON STOOD ALONE in her living room. She wore plaid pajama bottoms and a faded T-shirt. The T-shirt once belonged to Rusty. It was one he had purchased at a concert.

"I was hoping this Thanksgiving I would have something to be thankful about," Shannon said aloud. "I guess not." With a deep sigh, she headed to the kitchen, telling herself since she hadn't made herself breakfast, she might as well have Thanksgiving dinner now. So what that it wasn't even noon yet. Why wait? What was the point?

Once in the kitchen, Shannon opened the refrigerator. On one shelf was the pecan pie her cousin had brought her. Shannon loved pecan pie. On the shelf below it were the containers of food she had ordered from Lucy's Diner. When putting the food in the refrigerator earlier, she had almost spilled the cranberry sauce because its lid had flipped off, as if the container had not been properly sealed. Shannon thought it a miracle the cranberry sauce had made it all the way from the diner to her house without spilling, considering the lid hadn't been all the way on.

Shannon removed all the containers of take-out food from the refrigerator and set them on her kitchen table. She then removed the pecan pie, also setting it on the table. Shannon grabbed a fork and sat down. Too hungry to bother warming the food or getting out a plate, she dug a fork into the turkey dressing and took a bite.

"Not bad," she muttered, and then she began sampling the other food on the table. She had been eating for about ten minutes when she found it difficult to breathe. Dropping the fork she held, she sat rigidly at the table, gasping for air. A wave of nausea swept over her, and her head pounded. Unable to catch her breath, she stood up, and when she did, she lost her balance. Grabbing for the table, needing something to steady herself, she gripped the edge of the kitchen table—and its tablecloth. The next moment she spun around, still holding onto the tablecloth. It flew off the table, and with it all the food she had placed there. Shannon was unconscious before she hit the floor.

Minutes ticked away.

Finally, Shannon opened her eyes and looked up at the ceiling. "What just happened?" she asked while getting to her feet. She looked down at her kitchen table, now empty. Confused, she looked at the floor. It was not the containers of food, pecan pie, and broken pie dish under the kitchen table that caught her attention. It was the body of a woman sprawled out on the linoleum floor, looking up at her with dead eyes. Her eyes.

ELEVEN

Shannon had spent the last ten years thinking of death—her brother's death—so it didn't take her long to recognize what had just happened. That corpse on the floor of her kitchen was her body. Yet why did she die? Circling the grizzly scene, she tried to recall how she'd felt minutes before her death. Pausing in front of her body, she knelt and looked closer, studying the face and the arms.

"Why am I so pink?" Shannon muttered. She reached out and tried touching what had been her face, but her fingers moved through her nose. It startled her, and she let out a gasp and jumped back.

"What happened?" she muttered. And then it came to her. During her isolation following Rusty's death, she had spent a great deal of time reading. Agatha Christie was one of her favorite authors. Drawn to murder mysteries while trying to solve her brother's murder, what had Christie taught Shannon? That poison—specifically cyanide poisoning—could turn the victim's skin pink.

Standing abruptly, Shannon surveyed the rest of the scene, noting the food scattered on the floor—food she had been gobbling down just minutes before her death. She had been hungry, having skipped dinner the night before and then breakfast. Since the only other things she consumed that morning were water and coffee, Shannon asked, "How did the poison get in my food?"

"Finn," Shannon muttered while still staring down at the mess covering her kitchen floor. "I think we need to talk." She remembered he had told her he was staying at Marlow House. The last time she drove by Marlow House, it had been vacant. Some in town claimed the original Walt Marlow, who people once believed killed himself by stretching his neck from a rope in the attic, haunted the house. Yet, from what she'd read online, Marlow House's current owner claimed murder, not suicide, killed Walt Marlow.

No longer vacant, the new owner turned Marlow House into a bed-and-breakfast. Her cousin said it closed for a time yet recently reopened. And one of its current visitors was Finn Walsh.

Determined to talk to Finn, Shannon marched to the front door, but once she reached it, she froze. It had been years since she had stepped out of her house. Standing by the front door, she glanced over her shoulder, looking in the kitchen's direction.

"I can't stay here. Not with a dead body. Especially not with my dead body."

Steeling her courage, Shannon reached for the doorknob. Her hand moved through it. She paused for a moment; her gaze riveted on the doorknob, remembering how her finger had also gone through her face—the face of her dead body. After a moment, she let out a sigh.

"You're so stupid sometimes," Shannon said aloud before stepping through the front door, leaving her house for the first time in years.

"SO THIS IS one of the cinnamon rolls Danielle was talking about?" Madeline took another bite of the sticky sweet roll. She sat at the kitchen table with Danielle, Lily, and Heather, each nibbling on a cinnamon roll.

"They are decadent." Heather tore her cinnamon roll in half.

Madeline looked at Danielle. "And you didn't bake these?"

"No. We buy them at a bakery in town, Old Salts. We like to have them for our guests," Danielle said.

"For your guests?" Lily gave a snort. "The B and B was closed for over a year and a half, and I don't recall any cinnamon roll shortages at Marlow House during that time."

"Oh, shut up." Danielle laughed.

"It looks like Finn is back," Walt said as he walked into the kitchen a moment later.

FINN WASN'T the only one who pulled up in front of Marlow House and parked; Kelly Bartley arrived minutes after Finn. She came with a pumpkin pie, which she said was for tonight's dinner, and she wanted to drop it off early. Yet Lily suspected her sister-in-law had other motives. Kelly had already talked to her brother about how she would love to interview Finn for her blog, especially since he was spending Thanksgiving in Frederickport.

When Finn stepped into the house a few minutes before Kelly knocked on the door, he came carrying two bottles of wine.

"This is for tonight." Finn handed Walt the bottles of wine.

Those from the kitchen moved to the living room with Finn, which was where Danielle brought Kelly after she showed up with her pie. When Danielle returned to the living room after putting the pie in the kitchen, she found Kelly sitting on the sofa with Madeline and Finn, while Walt sat on one chair facing them, and Heather sat on the chair next to Walt.

"Where's Lily?" Danielle sat in the rocking chair.

"She went home to check on Connor and Ian," Kelly told her before turning her attention back to Finn.

"Kelly was just asking Finn the question people always ask him when they first meet," Madeline told Danielle.

"And what is that?" Danielle asked.

"If there are any spirits in the room." Madeline grinned.

"Actually, I said ghosts, but Mr. Walsh quickly informed me there are no such things as ghosts. But I guess he doesn't know about Marlow House being haunted." Kelly flashed Danielle a grin.

"I read about that," Madeline said. "I imagine it's common for houses like this to become the subject of ghosts stories, especially considering the history of Marlow House and what happened to the first Walt Marlow."

64

Danielle turned to Finn. "What's the difference between ghosts and spirits? Isn't it just semantics?"

Finn shook his head. "I don't think so. I see ghosts as troubled spirits who stick around and haunt the living."

"And no such things exist?" Walt asked.

"I have seen none," Finn said. "What some people call ghosts is likely energy left behind when the spirit moves on."

"What about the spirits? Do you see any now?" Kelly looked around the room as if she expected one to show itself to her at any moment.

Finn smiled at Kelly and looked to Heather. "Yes, as a matter of fact, there is. A man is standing behind Heather."

Heather turned and looked behind her chair. "I don't see him." She turned back to Finn.

"Who is he?" Kelly asked.

"He keeps saying he is Heather's grandfather."

Heather arched a brow. "My grandfather? Which one?"

Finn gave a shrug and said, "He keeps saying he is your grandfather. He wants to thank you for making things right. Does that make sense?"

"Oh, yes, it does!" Kelly answered for Heather. She turned to Finn. "Heather's great-grandfather was something of a serial killer."

"You needn't say that with such glee," Heather grumbled.

Ignoring Heather, Kelly said, "Her grandfather witnessed his father murdering one of his friends, and it tormented him. He wrote about it in a letter and even kept an emerald his father stole. Heather found the letter and emerald and returned the emerald to its rightful owner and exposed her great-grandfather as the killer. It tortured her grandfather's soul. I imagine that's what he is talking about."

Heather let out a sigh and turned her gaze from Kelly to Finn. "I suppose you read about it. There are a couple of articles about it online."

Finn chuckled. "Ahh, a skeptic. I understand. But the fact is, I didn't read about it, and since I didn't know you were going to be here today—or frankly that you even existed—it's not like I would have known to do an internet search on you. But I totally understand your skepticism."

Before Heather could respond, he turned to Kelly and said, "There is an older woman here. She says she is your grandmother."

"My grandmother?" Kelly perked up.

"She says you are going to be married soon," Finn said.

"Yes, that's right!" Kelly said excitedly.

From across the room, Danielle's gaze dropped to Kelly's left hand, where she wore an engagement ring—and no wedding band.

"Which grandmother?" Kelly asked.

"She says something about leaving you money," Finn said.

"Oh yes! I know which one. I'm planning to use the inheritance to buy a house."

Finn smiled at Kelly. "That's why she's here. She wants you to know she thinks you should use the money to buy a house. She wants you to know she approves."

Danielle bit her tongue so as not to insult her guests. Had Kelly said both her grandmothers were alive, Danielle figured he would have countered with she was like a grandmother to you. After Kelly confirmed she had no living grandmothers, it was a reasonable assumption that at least one had left her an inheritance. Kelly then provided the rest by openly sharing she wanted to use the inheritance for a house. Finn then gave Kelly what she wanted to hear—approval—her grandmother's approval. Danielle had no desire to challenge Madeline's friend on Thanksgiving. Yet, once Danielle figured out what the fake medium was up to, she would share that information with Madeline.

Danielle's train of thought abruptly shifted when an apparition suddenly appeared in the middle of the living room. Had it been a living woman, Danielle would guess she was about her age. She wore plaid pajama bottoms and a worn T-shirt inscribed with a logo from a rock band's concert. After materializing in the room, the spirit looked around, spied Finn on the sofa chatting with Kelly, and promptly marched up to him.

Danielle quickly looked over at Walt and then to Heather. They glanced briefly at Danielle, each making a questioning expression, and then looked back at the mystery ghost.

"Finn, we need to talk!" the ghost demanded.

With rapt curiosity, Walt, Danielle, and Heather stared at the obviously agitated spirit demanding Finn's attention. But unlike the three Beach Drive mediums, Finn did not seem to notice the apparition of a young woman now shouting at him to pay attention to her. Instead, he continued his conversation with Kelly, who said she would love to interview him for her blog.

After several minutes of shouting, as Finn, Kelly and Madeline sat oblivious to the spiritual tantrum, the ghost suddenly stopped, stepped back and then shook her head in disgust. "All this time. All those letters. I should have realized this morning what was going on," the ghost said.

Danielle and Heather exchanged glances, each wanting to tell the ghost they could see her, but with Kelly and Madeline in the room, neither felt comfortable doing so. They both hoped the ghost would stick around and explain to them what business she had with Finn.

Kelly stood up, not realizing she had just moved into the space the ghost occupied.

"Watch out!" the ghost yelled at Kelly, jumping back out of the way.

"I need to be going. It was lovely meeting you, Finn, Madeline," Kelly said sweetly. "I guess I will see you both at dinner tonight. You'll be meeting my fiancé."

"I understand Heather's boyfriend is going to be your fiancé's best man," Madeline said sweetly.

Kelly glanced briefly at Heather and then back to Madeline. "How did you know that?"

"Madeline asked who was coming tonight," Heather explained. "I mentioned my boyfriend was going to be Joe's best man."

"I'm looking forward to meeting both of them," Madeline said. "They must be special men to have such wonderful ladies."

Kelly smiled weakly at Madeline and finished saying goodbye while the ghost yelled, "Finn Walsh, I hope you someday burn in hell!" She vanished.

TWELVE

Joanne arrived earlier than expected on Thanksgiving Day. After being introduced to the current Marlow House guests, Joanne went to the kitchen with Heather and Danielle, where the three discussed the menu while Walt retreated to the library to read, and Madeline and Finn stayed in the living room, chatting.

Walt had been in the library for about thirty minutes when Madeline walked into the room, stopping inside the doorway. She gave the doorjamb a brief knock and said, "Hello, Walt, I hope I'm not disturbing you."

Walt looked up from his book and smiled. Begrudgingly, he had to admit Lucas had been a handsome man, and he had obviously inherited those looks from his mother. An attractive woman, Madeline wore her silver hair in a classic style barely touching her shoulders. Tall and slender, today she wore a beige silk blouse and tan slacks with gold earrings and a gold chain necklace. If someone had asked Walt to describe Madeline in one word, he would say classy.

"Of course not. Please come in, Mrs. Saunders." Closing his book, Walt stood up.

"Please don't get up. And it's Madeline. Remember? If I am to call you Walt, you need to call me Madeline. That Mrs. Saunders stuff makes me feel so old." Madeline walked all the way into the room.

68

"Please, Madeline, come in. Join me." Walt motioned to the sofa facing him and sat back down.

Standing a few feet inside the room, Madeline paused hesitantly, her tone noticeably shifting from cheerful to nervous. "I was hoping we could talk. Privately, you and me?"

Studying Madeline, Walt gave a nod. "Certainly."

With a sigh of relief, Madeline turned back to the door, closed it, and then turned back to Walt. Noticeably wringing her hands, she walked to the sofa and sat down.

"Is something wrong?" Walt asked gently.

"I… well… I hope you're not upset about me coming to Frederickport."

Curious, Walt absently set the book on the side table, leaned back in his chair, and asked, "Why would I be upset?"

Flashing him a nervous smile, Madeline tried to relax, yet failed. "I can't imagine it thrilled you to hear Lucas's mother was coming to stay at Marlow House. But I want you to know I don't want to do anything to cause friction between you and Danielle. I respect your marriage, and I am very happy for Danielle. But I needed to come."

"You are more than welcome. But I confess, I am curious; why did you feel the need to come?" Walt asked gently. "I understand you two have not stayed in contact."

With a sigh, Madeline stopped fidgeting with her hands. She leaned back on the sofa, crossed one leg over the opposing knee, and folded her hands on her lap. "No, we haven't been in contact. And it's something that's bothered me since she moved to Oregon. I didn't understand why Danielle cut me out of her life like that. You see, Danielle was more than a daughter-in-law; I considered her my daughter. I didn't understand her behavior after Lucas's death. And then I met Finn. Through him, I had answers from Lucas. Lucas made me understand. And I knew I needed to reach out to Danielle. My feelings for her have not changed. She is still very important to me."

Walt asked in a quiet voice, "Would you mind explaining what Lucas made you understand?"

Madeline took a deep breath and exhaled. "Certainly. As you probably already know, when Lucas died, a woman was in the car with him. At the time, I believed she was simply someone he worked with. Nothing more. If there were stories circulating about Lucas and the woman being lovers, they didn't reach my ears. I don't imagine my friends, who heard the stories, felt the need to share them with me. As Danielle might have told you, my son's death devastated me."

"Which is understandable."

"But then a few articles about the accident came out, and they clearly implied Lucas had died in the crash with his lover. It infuriated me. I thought someone should take that newspaper to task, sue them for trying to destroy my son's reputation. I wanted Danielle to do something."

"Did you talk to her about it?" Walt asked.

Madeline shook her head. "No. At the time, I couldn't broach the subject with her. Too awkward and uncomfortable. And perhaps, somewhere, in the back of my mind, I wondered if it was true. But I said nothing."

"And then she left," Walt said.

Madeline nodded. "Yes. After returning the engagement ring Lucas had given her. It had been in our family for years. I didn't want it back. I believed it belonged to Danielle, and it hurt when she didn't keep it. There was also a portrait Lucas had commissioned of the two of them. Danielle gave it to me. I didn't understand why she gave it away. She sold the business she and Lucas had built. I had just lost a son and then a daughter. Losing Danielle has been heavy on my mind. Often, I thought of writing to her, asking her why she cut me out of her life. I didn't have the courage. But about eight months ago, I met Finn. And through him, I learned those ugly stories were true. And I understood why Danielle left the way she did."

"Madeline, may I say something?" Walt interrupted.

"Yes, yes, of course."

"Danielle has told me about Lucas and what happened. She thought you were aware of Lucas's affair. Not before she did. But after he died. It was an awkward situation for her. I suspect she believed she was sparing you pain if she left and moved out of your life so you could avoid the uncomfortable conversation about Lucas's infidelity."

Madeline nodded. "Yes. Lucas told me."

Walt arched his brows. "He did?"

"Yes. He admitted what he had done, and he regretted hurting

Danielle. He said he never stopped loving her, but he had become so wrapped up in the success of their business, he lost track of priorities. But he also told me he was not Danielle's soul mate. You are."

"Really?"

"Earlier, when Finn said Lucas claimed to have met you, I was probably wrong about Lucas and you meeting when you lived in California. Finn and I discussed it before I came in here, and he suspects he misinterpreted Lucas's words. You see, Lucas has been watching over Danielle, and he's witnessed your relationship develop. I suspect that's what he meant when he said he met you. He didn't say you met him, just that he met you."

Walt arched his brows and asked with a bemused smile, "Lucas has been watching us?"

Madeline grinned. "Yes. Sometimes it sounds a little creepy, doesn't it? But Finn assures me that spirits aren't watching us in the bathroom—or bedroom. Oh, I suppose they could, but they don't. It's not their thing."

"And Lucas approves of me?"

"He didn't always," Madeline said with a grin.

"Oh?"

"In the beginning, he didn't approve of your relationship with Danielle. He said he worried you would... how did he say it?" Madeline paused for a moment, trying to recall the exact words. "Oh, I remember. He was worried you would interfere with her happiness."

Walt's smile faded. He stared at Madeline. When he and Lucas had met, back when they were both spirits, Lucas had told Walt just that. He wondered why Walt had not moved on, and worried Walt's presence in Marlow House would interfere with Danielle's happiness.

Noticing Walt's sudden change of expression, Madeline said quickly, "Oh, that was in the beginning. Lucas came to realize you and Danielle belong together in ways he and Danielle never did. He insists you are her soul mate. Lucas helped me to understand. In fact, if it makes you feel any better, while Lucas might occasionally look in on you and Danielle, he's not always hanging around, watching you two. He's confident Danielle's life is on the right course, and I suppose if he is looking after anyone these days, it's probably me. It's why I came here, at Lucas's urging. He understands I need my daughter back. I want Danielle back in my life. To do that, I needed to come to Marlow House."

CHRIS JOHNSON, aka Chris Glandon, walked down Beach Drive from his house to Marlow House, his pit bull, Hunny, by his side. He didn't bother with a leash since Walt had had a long discussion with Hunny about how she must behave when off a leash. Not wanting to get in trouble or hurt, Hunny dutifully obeyed Walt's words and kept close by Chris's side.

After reaching Marlow House, Chris walked up the front walk. Once at the front door, instead of knocking, he tried the doorknob. He found it unlocked, and he opened the door and walked in, Hunny still by his side.

"You can go find Walt," Chris told the dog after shutting the front door. The dog turned from Chris and ran down the hall, searching for his friend.

The first room Chris checked was the parlor; no one was there. When he reached the living room a few moments later, he peeked inside and saw an older gray-haired gentleman sitting on the sofa, reading a magazine.

Curious, Chris entered the room and said, "Good afternoon."

The man looked up and smiled. "Hello. Are you a new guest at Marlow House?"

Chris smiled and walked over to the sofa. "I was once. But now, just a friend and neighbor." He extended his hand to the man and said, "My name is Chris Johnson."

The man stood up and accepted the handshake. "I'm Finn Walsh. Nice to meet you, Mr. Johnson."

"Oh, call me Chris," Chris said, taking a seat on one chair facing the sofa.

"And you must call me Finn. Are you one of Walt and Danielle's guests for Thanksgiving dinner?"

"I am. I would never miss a chance to enjoy one of Danielle's holiday dinners."

"Madeline told me she is an excellent cook." Finn tossed the magazine he had been reading to the coffee table.

"Yes, she is. So you're the medium Danielle was telling me about?"

Finn grinned. "Guilty as charged. So are you a skeptic too?"

Chris shrugged. "No. Well, not about the possibility of spirits. It's living people I tend to be skeptical of." He flashed Finn a smile, showing off his straight white teeth.

"Fair enough. By the way, I need to mention there is someone standing next to you. She says she is your mother."

Chris glanced to his right and then his left. He saw nothing. He looked back at Finn. "Which mother?"

Finn smiled. "I assume your mother. She's holding a package, a gift. She keeps saying she gave it to you."

"A gift?"

"Yes. Odd." Finn frowned.

"What?" Chris asked.

Finn didn't answer immediately. Finally, he shook his head. "She left already. But she was holding this gift, kept saying she had given it to you. Does that make any sense?"

Chris shook his head. "No."

"And then she said I got one too. But mine was different. And then she left." Finn shook his head again and said, "I have no idea what that meant."

THIRTEEN

anielle walked into the parlor and closed the door behind her.
Waiting for her in the room sat Walt, Chris, Heather, and
Hunny. In a low voice, she said, "Finn and Madeline headed
upstairs to rest and freshen up before everyone else gets here, and
Joanne's setting the table."

"We just told Chris about our mystery ghost," Heather
told her.

"Do you guys have any idea who this ghost might be?" Danielle
asked as she took a seat next to Walt on the sofa. They faced Chris
and Heather, who sat in the chairs across from them, while Hunny
curled up on the floor by Chris's feet.

"Considering her T-shirt, she hasn't been dead for more than
ten years," Heather said.

"Why do you say that?" Walt asked.

"Because of the shirt she was wearing. It's from a concert that
was held about ten years ago in Portland," Heather said.

"Are you sure?" Danielle asked. "You weren't living in Oregon
ten years ago."

Heather gave a shrug. "I like the band and remember that
concert. I wanted to go, but I couldn't."

"From what you told me, it sounds like this ghost obviously had
some relationship with Walsh," Chris said.

Danielle looked at Chris. "She may not have known him personally."

"Why do you say that?" Chris frowned.

"While it's possible a ghost might decide to wear a T-shirt that wasn't around when she was alive, I kind of doubt it. My bet, Heather is right about her passing within the last ten years. So if she died within that time frame, that's during the time Walsh became famous," Danielle began.

"And?" Chris asked.

"Perhaps, after she died, she wanted to contact someone, a husband or whatever. And since most people aren't mediums and can't see ghosts, she looked for someone who was a famous medium during her life. While we know Walsh is a fake, many people think he is the real deal," Danielle said.

"She wanted him to burn in hell," Heather reminded her.

Danielle shrugged. "It could be something she said out of her frustration because he didn't hear her."

"She said something about this morning and letters," Heather added.

Danielle let out a sigh. "It's possible she saw him earlier this morning. She tried to contact him then, and when he didn't respond, she followed him here. I don't know. But if she shows up again, hopefully we can find out."

"I didn't tell you guys, Finn gave me a reading," Chris said.

They turned to Chris. He told them what Finn had said in the living room earlier.

"At least my reading made more sense." Heather went on to tell Chris about her reading, after which Walt told them what Madeline had said in the library.

"It's entirely possible Walsh did a Google search on Marlow House and came across the article on Heather's grandfather. Marlow House is mentioned because of the emerald. And his claim he didn't know she was going to be here, while that is likely true, it does not mean he didn't read about her before he came," Danielle suggested.

"As I recall, some of those articles included Heather's photo," Chris reminded them. "She has a distinctive look."

Heather glared at Chris. "What the heck is that supposed to mean?"

"You don't want to be ordinary, do you? Distinctive is good." Chris flashed Heather a grin.

Heather rolled her eyes.

"Chris has a point," Danielle said.

"Hey!" Heather frowned.

"No." Danielle chuckled. "I mean about him reading one of those online articles with your photograph. When he saw you here, he probably thought, *Jackpot! I can do a reading for her that will be convincing.* True, he didn't know you would be here. But we never said he planned to give that reading, but it worked out nicely for him. That's how guys like Finn pull off their act."

Heather shrugged. "Yeah, you have a point. I imagine that's what happened."

"I'm still trying to figure out Finn's motive for coming here. What does he expect to get from us?" Danielle said.

"Perhaps it has nothing to do with what he can get from you per se," Chris said. "He could be doing this all to give Madeline something she wants. You. You back in her life."

"But what does he get from that?" Danielle asked.

"There is this one thing about Finn that bothers me," Chris said.

"What's that?" Heather asked.

"He seems so nice. I mean genuinely nice. Likable. Even when he's giving a bogus reading, there is something about him I like. Bugs the hell out of me," Chris said.

"Me too!" Heather agreed. "Sure, he's obviously a fake, but I kinda like him."

"I agree. Which is probably one reason he's so successful. An unlikable con man wouldn't be able to convince his marks he's telling the truth," Danielle said.

"I don't know about that." Chris leaned back in his chair and stretched. "I can name a few obnoxious con men who've become successful."

Danielle shrugged. "Perhaps. But let's get back to why he brought Madeline here. If his reason is to make her happy, is it because he sincerely likes her? I mean, just because someone is a con man, it doesn't mean they never do something just to make someone else happy. It is possible he genuinely cares for Madeline. While Madeline is comfortable in her retirement, she is not wealthy, not like he is. So I don't believe he's after her money."

"Unless it is your money he's after," Chris said.

Danielle looked at Chris. "I thought you said he was doing this for her, not to get something out of us?"

Chris shrugged. "I'm just playing devil's advocate."

"Maybe he is a harmless faux medium," Heather said.

"While there is something likable about him, I can't really call him harmless. He's a liar," Danielle reminded them.

"After you told me he was coming, and you insisted he was a fake, I did some research on him," Heather said. "He does readings, which he makes money on, but there was nothing about him bilking vulnerable widows. It costs less than a hundred bucks to attend one of his events. That's where he is making his money."

"So he just steals a little from everyone, so it really hurts no one?" Chris snarked.

"Even if what he tells them is all made up, I think he may actually provide a useful service. If you watch those readings, he's giving people closure, helping them in their grief," Heather said. "That's not such a bad thing."

"Heather has a point," Walt said. "Perhaps he's doing this to help people. I suppose that might be possible."

The doorbell rang, interrupting their conversation. Danielle got up from the sofa and walked to the window. She peeked outside.

"It's Joe and Kelly and that friend of theirs," Danielle said.

"They're kind of early," Heather grumbled.

Danielle glanced at the clock. "Not really. I told everyone they were welcome to come around two, but that we would have dinner at four. It's almost two."

"Kelly just wants to get Finn Walsh alone. For her blog," Heather said.

Leaving the window, Danielle headed for the door while the others stood up to join her.

"THANK YOU FOR INVITING ME," Charlie said after they made introductions in the entry hall. They all exchanged pleasantries.

"Where are your B and B guests?" Kelly asked, glancing around.

"They're upstairs, freshening up," Danielle said. "Why don't we all go into the living room? Would you like a drink? Walt set up the bar in there."

"Sounds good to me." Chris headed toward the living room.

As the group of seven headed toward the living room, the doorbell rang again. Danielle answered it a moment later. Officer Brian Henderson had arrived.

HEATHER AND BRIAN sat together on the fireplace hearth, with Max on Heather's lap. Hunny stood with Chris and Walt at the small bar while the two poured cocktails and served drinks. They had just finished handing both Joe and Charlie a cocktail when Madeline and Finn walked into the room.

Once again, introductions were made, drinks served, and finally, everyone found a seat.

Kelly glanced at the front window. "I'm surprised Lily and Ian aren't here yet."

"Lily sent me a text a while ago. Connor fell asleep. She's going to wait for him to finish his nap before they come over," Danielle explained.

"When are your parents going to be here?" Heather asked.

"Mom said they would be here around three," Kelly said.

"Who else is coming?" Joe asked.

"I invited the chief, but they're going to his sister's. Mel and Adam are coming." Danielle paused briefly and glanced at the clock. "I'm sorta surprised they aren't here yet."

Kelly looked at Finn. "What I'm curious about, what spirits are in the room with us?"

"Kelly, let the poor man enjoy his drink," Joe chided.

"I'm sorry. But how often does someone get to visit with a genuine medium?" Kelly asked.

Danielle, Heather, Walt, and Chris exchanged glances, and Heather stifled a giggle.

"As I recall, you don't believe in ghosts anyway," Brian teased Joe.

Joe gave a shrug and smiled apologetically at Finn.

"Neither does Finn," Kelly said.

Brian arched a brow at Kelly. "He doesn't?"

"I have never encountered a ghost—just spirits," Finn corrected.

"What's the difference?" Brian asked.

"I think of a ghost as a spirit who sticks around and haunts people. That's not really what happens," Finn said.

"Hmm, interesting," Brian said, making a quick side glance at Heather before looking back at Finn.

"Heather claims to have seen ghosts," Kelly blurted.

They all turned to Heather, who only gave a shrug.

"I know people who have claimed to see ghosts. Many of those people honestly believe it. But there is always a logical explanation for those things," Charlie said.

"You sound like Joe," Brian said with a snort.

Charlie looked at Brian. "Imagine if all that was real. It would make your life and Joe's a lot easier."

"How so?" Heather asked.

"For one thing, it would be easier to solve murders," Charlie said.

Kelly looked at Finn. "Do you ever work with the police? I understand many mediums do."

Finn gave a shrug. "Sometimes. But it doesn't work like you might imagine. If someone is murdered, their spirit might tell me he was murdered, or confirm that the killer everyone suspected is guilty is in fact guilty, but if there is no suspect, they won't tell me who killed them."

Joe resisted smirking. He and Charlie exchanged glances, both thinking Finn was nothing more than a showman.

"Why not?" Brian asked.

"Because after a person dies and goes to heaven, they see things differently," Finn explained.

"So there really is a heaven?" Kelly asked.

Finn looked at Kelly. "I call it heaven. But yes, there is a place like heaven, but not with golden streets and angels sitting around playing harps."

"I'm still trying to figure out why they wouldn't name their killer," Brian said.

"Because once they pass over, they have different priorities than what they had in this lifetime. Their job—and they do have jobs in heaven—are more important than helping a detective solve their murder. They already know who did it, and they understand the killer will eventually be held accountable, even if it is not done in his lifetime."

"So I guess killers have nothing to fear from you," Charlie teased.

"No. They have more to fear from people like your friend Joe and Brian. Policemen whose job it is to solve murders and other crimes. Spirits have other priorities," Finn explained.

"What a crock," Danielle muttered under her breath.

FOURTEEN

Danielle glanced out the living room window and noticed Adam's car pulling up in front of Marlow House. By the time Adam and Melony reached the front porch, Danielle was already opening the door.

"Happy Thanksgiving," Danielle greeted them. An instant later, Marie Nichols, the spirit of Adam's deceased grandmother, stood behind the couple, waving at Danielle. Danielle flashed the ghost a grin, which both Melony and Adam assumed she meant for them.

"Hi, Danielle!" Melony held up the bottle of wine she carried. "This is for you."

Danielle's eyes widened at the familiar label. "Oh, the good stuff! Do I have to share?"

Melony only laughed in response.

"This is some greeting," Adam teased. "You had the door open before I even rang the bell."

Danielle opened the door wider and stepped aside so Adam and Melony could come inside the house. "I saw you drive up. But you could be like everyone else on Beach Drive and just walk in."

"Everyone on Beach Drive?" Melony gave Danielle a quick hug and then handed her the bottle of wine.

"Well, all our friends who live on this street. They don't seem to know how to use a doorbell or knock." Now holding the bottle,

Danielle glanced at it briefly and then smiled back at Adam and Melony. "Thanks for the wine."

"You're welcome. And no, you don't have to share the wine. Unless it's with us. And start keeping your doors locked. You should probably always keep them locked, considering some of the things that have happened at Marlow House." Adam watched Danielle shut the door behind them.

"Hey, does this mean if we buy Pearl's house, I can just walk in?" Melony asked.

"It would be nice if Adam and Melony moved next door after they get married," Marie said.

"Don't say that too loud." Adam glanced toward the living room. "I saw Joe's car parked out front. Kelly wants the house, too."

Melony let out a sigh. "I guess we probably shouldn't discuss it today."

A few moments later, Danielle led Adam and Melony into the living room. Introductions were made and more beverages served.

Adam and Melony had been in the living room for about ten minutes when Kelly asked Finn, "Did Adam and Mel come in with any spirits?"

Finn smiled weakly and said, "As a matter of fact, they did. An older woman."

The Beach Drive mediums glanced to Marie, who asked, "He can see me now?"

"She keeps pointing to Melony and says she's the mother," Finn said.

Marie chuckled and took a seat in an imaginary chair while saying, "I guess he can't."

"My mother?" Melony arched her brow.

"Yes. I assume your mother passed?" Finn asked.

Melony nodded.

"Jolene's here?" Adam choked out. "Lovely way to ruin Thanksgiving."

"Adam!" Melony gave him a playful swat on the arm.

"I take it you didn't get along with Melony's mother?" Charlie asked.

"That's an understatement," Adam grumbled.

"She says she's sorry," Finn said. "And she gives you both her blessing. You are getting married, aren't you?"

From across the room, Danielle glanced at the obvious engagement ring on Melony's left hand.

"Yes." Melony smiled at Finn. "But I'm afraid you have your spirit wires crossed. My mother would never give us her blessings."

"Perhaps it's my grandmother," Adam teased. "I could see Grandma giving her blessing. She loved Mel."

"And I give you both my blessing," Marie told deaf ears. "But this fake medium can't hear me."

"No, it's Melony's mother. At least, that's what she keeps saying. That's why she's here. She wants you to understand she's sorry for everything that happened. She wants you to be happy and for you both to forgive her," Finn said.

Melony smiled at Finn, but by her expression, Danielle didn't think she was buying the professed medium's claim.

"And there is someone else who is here," Finn said, turning his gaze to Adam. "He just barged in, pushed Melony's mother aside. He says he's your grandfather, and he wants to tell you something."

Adam arched his brows. "My grandfather?"

"Yes, he needs you to pass on a message to someone," Finn said.

"Which grandfather?" Adam asked, sounding bemused. "I had two. And they are both dead."

"He keeps showing me dominos. Does that mean anything?" Finn asked.

"Why can't this grandfather just tell Finn his name?" Danielle whispered to Walt, who suppressed a chuckle.

Adam shrugged. "My grandpa Nichols taught me how to play dominos."

Finn nodded. "Yes, it is your grandpa Nichols. It is his way of validating it's him."

"Tell Grandpa I hope he is taking good care of Grandma. I sure miss her," Adam said wistfully.

"Aww, Adam, you dear boy," Marie cooed.

"Your grandfather says this message is for your grandmother," Finn said.

Adam smiled at Finn. "Well, I think if Grandpa has a message for Grandma, it would be better if he gave it to her himself, since she died three years ago."

Melony looked at Adam. "Wow, has it really been three years?"

Adam turned to Melony and nodded. "Right before Thanksgiving, three years ago."

"Your grandfather insists he has a message to pass on to her," Finn said.

"I'm curious; what is the message?" Walt asked.

They all turned to Finn, who said, "I don't understand what any of this means. Especially if your grandmother passed away three years ago. I'm just passing on what he's telling me."

"Okay, what's the message?" Adam asked.

"He says tell her it's okay to come. He understands. Until death do us part," Finn said just as the doorbell rang.

DANIELLE OPENED the front door for Ian's parents, Walt at her side. She spied Lily, Ian, Connor, and Sadie preparing to cross the street to Marlow House.

"Happy Thanksgiving," Danielle greeted them.

"Thank you for inviting us," June said.

Walt and Ian's father, John, shook hands, and more greetings were exchanged.

"Everyone's in the living room having cocktails," Walt said.

"That sounds good." John stepped into the house.

"I'm going to wait here." June nodded toward her son and his family now crossing the street.

Instead of waiting with June or going to the living room with John and Walt, Danielle excused herself and headed to the downstairs guest bathroom.

When Ian and his family were within earshot of his mother, June asked, "Do you really think you should bring Sadie?"

"If we didn't bring Sadie, we wouldn't be welcomed," Lily told her mother-in-law.

June did not look amused by her daughter-in-law's comment.

Ian, who carried Connor, laughed at his mother's reaction. "Really, Mom, Lily is not joking. Walt and Sadie, well, they have a special bond."

June rolled her eyes. "She is a dog, Ian."

"Yes, I know, Mother." Ian dropped a kiss on her cheek and walked into the house with Connor.

WHEN DANIELLE STEPPED out of the bathroom, she found Heather waiting.

"You have to admit that was damn creepy," Heather told Danielle.

"You mean Ian's parents?" Danielle teased.

"That too." Heather let out a snort. She glanced toward the open doorway into the living room, where the sound of voices drifted out. "Ian's mother is in there all gushing over Joe's old high school pal. But I was talking about Finn's reading."

"I don't see Jolene going all forgiving with Adam. From what I recall, her ghost was kinda snotty to me," Danielle said.

"Remember, there are no such things as ghosts," Heather reminded her.

"Yeah, right," Danielle scoffed.

"But I was talking about Adam's grandfather."

Danielle grew serious and glanced to the living room and back at Heather. "Yeah. That was kind of creepy, especially since Marie's said on more than one occasion that her marital obligations ended, well, she'd say until death do us part."

"I know! Freaky! How did he know that? And from what the grandfather supposedly said, it wasn't like Marie was with him on the other side. Which we know she isn't," Heather said.

Danielle studied the open doorway to the living room and considered Heather's words. Finally, she said, "I'm thinking Finn Walsh really—and I mean really—wants us to believe he is the real deal. He obviously went to a great deal of work learning who would probably spend Thanksgiving at Marlow House."

"I don't think that would take much research," Heather said. "But how would he know about Marie saying until death do us part when discussing her marriage? That's something she said after she died."

Danielle turned to Heather. "Was it?"

Heather frowned. "What are you suggesting?"

"We don't know what Marie might have said to some of her friends over the years. Maybe she used that expression before when discussing her widowhood. It's entirely possible."

"What about Finn's comment about it's okay for her to come?" Heather asked.

Danielle considered the question for a moment and then shook her head. "I have no idea. But it makes me wonder, why has he gone to so much trouble to make us believe he is a genuine medium?"

———

HEATHER STEPPED into the guest bathroom, and Danielle returned to the living room. When she walked in, she found Joe and Charlie standing at the makeshift bar with Chris, Ian, and Walt.

"I didn't know you used to have a motorcycle," Danielle heard Ian tell Joe.

"Thank goodness he doesn't have one now," June muttered.

Kelly looked at her mother and smiled. "Just because Joe doesn't have one now doesn't mean he won't get another one someday. And I would look good wearing leather."

Joe chuckled at Kelly's comment while June flashed her daughter a scowl.

"Don't worry, June," Joe told his would-be mother-in-law. "My motorcycle days are long gone."

"Joe was never into it like Rusty and me," Charlie said. "I suspect he only bought the bike because we both had one."

"My mom wasn't any more thrilled than Kelly's with my motorcycle," Joe said.

"It's more dangerous to be a cop than to ride a motorcycle," Kelly said.

June looked at her daughter. "Being a police officer in a little town like Frederickport is nothing like it is in a big city like Portland."

"In retrospect, we should have stayed in Frederickport rather than moving to Portland," Charlie mused.

Kelly looked at her parents. "Charlie and another one of their friends opened a motorcycle shop in Portland after they got out of high school. Joe stayed here and joined the police force."

"We tried to convince Joe to go into business with us. But he was having none of it. He was smarter than us." Charlie laughed.

"What is it they say, something like 65% of all businesses fail within the first ten years?" John said.

"It wasn't just that, Dad," Kelly said. "Charlie's business partner was murdered. A robbery at their store."

"Oh no!" John looked at Charlie. "What happened?"

"Like Kelly said, it was a robbery. All they got was what was in the cash register. There had been a series of robberies in the area. This was the first time they hurt someone. The police's theory was that Rusty must have walked in on the guy, and he panicked." Charlie let out a sigh.

Finn looked at Charlie with a frown. "Rusty?"

"Rusty was the other friend," Kelly said.

"In high school, it was always the three of us, Rusty, Charlie, and me," Joe said.

"Did they catch the guy?" June asked.

Joe shook his head. "No. Had it happened now instead of ten years ago, I imagine during one of those previous robberies, they would have caught that guy on video. Everyone has surveillance cameras up these days."

"I often wonder about that," Charlie mused.

"If you will excuse me." Danielle stood. "I'm going to check on Joanne and see what else needs to be done so we can get dinner on."

Lily stood, but Danielle said, "Joanne and I can handle it."

FIFTEEN

A fter Danielle left everyone in the living room, she found Joanne in the kitchen. The housekeeper and cook had just finished mashing the potatoes and putting them in the slow cooker to keep warm and was now making the gravy.

When Joanne saw Danielle walk into the room, she looked up from stirring the gravy. "The table is all set, but I didn't see the name cards."

"Dang, I forgot. I'll go print them off. Be right back." Danielle dashed to the library computer. Ten minutes later, after printing off the name cards, she went to the dining room and placed them around the table. Earlier that day, Walt had added a leaf to the dining room table so it could comfortably accommodate all the Thanksgiving guests.

She set Walt's name tag at the head of the table, with hers facing him. To Walt's left, she placed name cards for Mel, Adam, June, John, Kelly, Joe, Charlie, and then Finn, who was to her right. On Walt's right, she set Heather, Brian, Lily, Connor, Ian, Joanne, Chris, and then Madeline, who was to her left. Joanne had already placed the filled water glasses around the table, along with empty wine-glasses.

When Danielle returned to the kitchen, she found Walt with

Joanne, with Walt slicing up the turkey and arranging the meat on the platter. Danielle left Walt and Joanne in the kitchen and returned to the living room to invite their dinner guests to come to the table.

"I'll see you later, Danielle," Marie said before vanishing, while the others made their way to the dining room.

"I CAN SIT NEXT TO CONNOR," June said when she noticed the position of the name cards.

"Mom, it works better with Connor between Lily and me," Ian told June. "You're sitting across from us so we can all visit. We asked Danielle to put Connor between us."

Begrudgingly, June took her assigned seat across the table while the rest of the dinner guests took their places. Chris poured the wine for those who wanted it; Joanne placed baskets of fresh rolls on the table, along with two gravy boats and dishes of butter. Walt carried in the platter of turkey while Danielle, Lily, and Heather brought in the various side dishes. Instead of placing the food on the table, they arranged it on the nearby buffet.

"We've found it easier with this many people to put the food on the buffet," Danielle explained. "Unfortunately, that means you have to get up to serve yourselves."

"Works for me," Brian said. "And everything looks delicious. Thanks for inviting me."

"I second that," Charlie said. "I thought I'd be spending Thanksgiving alone. Thanks again for the invitation."

"You're very welcome." Danielle smiled at the two men before going to her place at one end of the table.

A moment later, after all the food had been set on the table or buffet, everyone who had been helping took their place at the table, including Joanne.

June looked across the table at Joanne and said, "Oh, you're eating with us?"

"Of course she is," Ian said, reaching over to Joanne, who sat next to him. He patted her hand. "Joanne is Marlow House family."

"A lucky member of the family; I get to sit between these two handsome men," Joanne added, glancing from Ian to her left and Chris to her right.

June smiled sheepishly and picked up her cloth napkin, arranging it on her lap.

Danielle thanked them all for coming and asked Walt if he would say grace. After grace, Danielle invited her guests to help themselves to the food.

John looked around and asked, "Where are the dogs? Did you put them outside?"

"I would hope so," June said.

"No, they're in the house." Walt flashed June a smile. "They can go outside if they want. We have a doggy door. But they won't be coming in here."

"Are you sure? I worry about Connor with his highchair. Sadie's always right there, waiting for him to drop something." June gave a shudder.

"Hey, it's efficient, Mom," Ian said. "Sadie cleans up what Connor drops so we don't have to. A win for Sadie and a win for us."

June scowled at Ian. "But not when Danielle has gone to so much trouble to prepare such a lovely dinner. I'm sure she doesn't want Sadie under the table bothering her guests."

"Don't worry," Walt assured her. "Sadie, Hunny, and Max won't come into the dining room while we're eating. I told them not to."

June frowned at Walt. He hadn't said it in a teasing tone. He sounded serious.

Now standing up, Connor's plate in her hand, Lily said, "Walt is something of a pet whisperer. He can get the dogs and Max to do practically anything."

"I CAN'T BELIEVE THOSE ANIMALS," John said, looking through the open doorway into the entry hall. Hunny, Sadie, and Max all sat in the hallway, looking into the dining room, yet not one of them tried stepping into the room with the food.

"I told you," Lily said, handing Connor a piece of her dinner roll. "Walt has it all under control."

"I remember Danielle and Walt's wedding." Kelly picked up her cloth napkin and arranged it on her lap.

June looked at Kelly. "What about their wedding?"

"Sadie wasn't just in Lily and Ian's wedding," Kelly said. "She was in Walt and Danielle's, and so was Danielle's cat. Those two walked down the staircase like it was choreographed and sat perfectly still through the entire ceremony."

"People still talk about it," Joe said with a snort.

"I can understand training a dog, and Sadie is smart, but a cat?" June asked.

"Max is pretty smart." Danielle flashed Walt a grin and took a sip of her water.

They shared a few pet stories, and then the conversation shifted when Charlie asked Ian's parents, "I understand you recently moved to Frederickport."

"Yes, we're building a house," June said.

"Yeah, Joe told me. I hear you bought the Marymoor property," Charlie said.

"Are you familiar with it?" John asked.

"Sure, I grew up in Frederickport. We used to ride bikes down that street and talk about how that place was haunted." Charlie laughed.

"As Finn assures us, there are no such things as ghosts." June looked down the table and flashed Finn a smile. "So we have nothing to worry about."

Adam and Melony exchange glances, remembering what they had witnessed at the Marymoor site, yet said nothing.

"I assume you no longer have family here, since you say you were spending Thanksgiving alone?" June asked Charlie.

"No family. There was just my mom and me, anyway. But Mom has been gone a long time." Charlie glanced briefly at Adam and then looked at June and said, "After she passed away, I rented out her house. I had it in Adam's rental program, but I've been considering selling, and that's why I'm in town."

"You really should think about staying in Frederickport," June said. "I bet Joe would love having his old friend back in town."

"It would be nice if you stuck around," Joe agreed.

"It would," Kelly said. "You already have a house here."

Charlie laughed. "True."

The conversation bounced from topic to topic and then quieted while the dinner guests enjoyed the food. Charlie broke the momentary silence when he turned to Ian and said, "I have a question for you, Ian."

Ian looked up from his plate. "Yes?"

"First, I need to say this is quite an impressive gathering. I can tell people I shared Thanksgiving with the famous Finn Walsh," he flashed a smile at Finn and then looked to Walt and said, "at the home of the *New York Times* bestselling author Walt Marlow." He turned back to Ian and said, "And with Jon Altar. I had no idea you were Jon Altar. Kelly told me."

"Well, my sister has a big mouth," Ian teased.

Danielle glanced at Chris and thought she had to give Kelly some credit. Apparently, Kelly had not spilled the beans on Chris's identity. Either that, or she told him not to say anything.

"But I wanted to ask you; how did you pick out your pen name? I assume the first name is for your father?" Charlie watched Ian, waiting for his answer.

Ian smiled and glanced at his father, back to Charlie. "In a way. But my dad spells his name J-o-h-n while my pen name is Jon spelled J-o-n."

"My son always has to be different," June teased.

"As for the Altar, it's a name I found on our family tree. I don't know anything about that line of the family, but I liked the sound of the name," Ian explained.

"I never understood why people use pen names. Why didn't you just write under your own name, like Walt does?" Charlie asked.

"Sometimes it is nice to be incognito," Chris answered for Ian. "Especially for someone like Ian."

"I suppose." Charlie dug his fork into his stuffing.

Madeline looked at Charlie. "Isn't the stuffing wonderful?"

Charlie looked up at Madeline and smiled. "It's delicious."

"I always loved Danielle's stuffing." Madeline flashed a smile to Danielle.

"Thank you." Danielle grinned.

"Everything is delicious," Joe said. The other dinner guests concurred.

A few minutes later, Joe asked Charlie, "I have been meaning to ask. Did you ever stop in and see Shannon?"

Charlie looked up and shook his head. "No. But I was thinking of stopping over there this evening after I leave here. I know she's spending Thanksgiving alone; her cousin went to California for the weekend."

"Oh, I wish I'd known; I would have had you invite your friend," Danielle said. "I hate for people to spend holidays alone."

"Is Shannon an old girlfriend?" June asked.

"No, just a friend," Charlie told June before looking at Danielle and saying, "That's a very generous offer, but I'm afraid she wouldn't have come even if I had asked her."

"She has agoraphobia," Joe explained.

"Oh my, isn't that when someone is afraid to leave the house?" June asked.

"I've heard of that," Madeline said.

"Remember we mentioned Rusty, the friend who was murdered?" Kelly asked her mother. "Shannon is his sister."

About to take a bite of his roll, Finn momentarily froze. Without taking a bite, he set the roll back on his plate and looked over at Kelly, silently listening.

"Has she always had agoraphobia?" Madeline asked.

"Shannon was always shy," Joe explained. "She and Rusty were twins."

"When people say twins are just alike, they never met Shannon and Rusty," Charlie said with a snort.

"Why do you say that?" Danielle asked.

"Rusty was the outgoing one," Charlie explained. "Shannon was always reserved. But very close to her brother. And he was protective of her."

"While it hit all of us hard when Rusty was killed, it devastated his sister," Joe explained.

"And she lives in Frederickport?" June asked.

"Yes," Joe said.

June looked at Kelly and asked, "Have you met her?"

Kelly shook her head, and Joe said, "I never got close to Shannon. Not like her and Charlie. It's probably because she moved to Portland with Rusty when they opened the motorcycle shop."

"She and Rusty shared an apartment," Charlie explained. "But after Rusty was killed, she moved back with her folks and became more withdrawn, and then, well, after a while, she seemed unable or unwilling to leave her house."

"And then her parents both died, and from what I hear, she never leaves her house," Joe said.

"That's horrible." June looked at Kelly. "You really should reach out to this poor girl. Sounds like she could use a friend."

SIXTEEN

After everyone finished dinner, Danielle stood up and said, "Why don't you all retire to the living room? Chris and Ian have volunteered to play bartender, so if anyone would like an after-dinner drink or coffee, they can help you. And later, we'll serve dessert in the living room."

"Let me help you clean up," Madeline offered as she stood.

"Thank you, but we have this under control. Honestly," Danielle said sweetly. "And Joanne is going to the living room, too."

"Don't be silly. I need to clean up," Joanne insisted.

Danielle gently nudged Joanne to follow the rest of the guests. "I insist. Chris is already preparing you a special after-dinner drink."

"Well, in that case." Joanne grinned and followed the others to the living room.

No one else volunteered to help, but Heather, Brian, and Lily quietly stayed behind without asking. After the others left the dining room, Heather walked to where Sadie, Max and Hunny had been watching them earlier. Heather looked down the hallway, and after the guests had gone into the living room, she looked back at the table and said, "Okay, the coast is clear."

Walt stood at the dining room table while Brian stood in the doorway between the kitchen and dining room, holding the door open. Inside, Lily and Danielle waited for the dishes to arrive. Then, like a scene out of some Disney animation, the dirty dishes on the table quickly stacked themselves, after first tipping to one side to drop any silverware onto the tablecloth. The next moment, the pile of dishes floated from the table past Brian, who held the door open, to Lily and Danielle, who waited in the kitchen. They quickly placed the stack of dishes on the counter. After the dishes came the serving plates, followed by the glasses.

"We could have carried them in," Brian said as he watched Lily and Danielle hastily snatch glasses from the air before Walt could no longer see the glasses, making his telekinetic powers unable to hold them in midair.

"Sure we could." Lily laughed. "But cleaning up wouldn't be half as fun!"

After moving the dishes and glasses, Walt headed to the kitchen to help load the dishwasher while Heather and Brian stayed behind, gathering up all the silverware left on the table.

"I guess Walt didn't want to try moving these," Brian said while gathering up all the silverware and placing it in a plastic tub.

"I doubt he wanted to try moving this many small, separate pieces at once. How would he explain it if he lost focus and dropped a trail of silverware on the floor?" Heather laughed at the idea.

"You know, someone could have left the living room to use the bathroom, and then looked this way and noticed floating dishes," Brian said as he dropped the last two forks into the tub.

Heather shrugged. "True. If it had been Finn, perhaps he would rethink his opinion on ghosts."

"The guy is obviously a fake. He actually believes there is no such thing as ghosts," Brian scoffed.

Heather grinned. "Hey, look at you. All believing in ghosts and stuff. What would Joe think?"

"You ruined me," Brian teased.

Heather glanced briefly toward the hallway and then back to Brian. "Do you know who that woman is they were talking about? The one who won't leave her house."

Brian nodded. "Yes. But I don't really know her. I met her grandmother on a call once. She lived next door. After she died, she left the house to her two granddaughters. Shannon Langdon, the one they were talking about, who won't leave her house. And her cousin, Eden Langdon. Eden didn't grow up in Frederickport like

Shannon. But she moved into the house after her grandmother died."

"So this Shannon owns two houses in Frederickport?"

"One and a half. She owns the house she lives in. It was her parents' house. And the one next door, that was her grandparents', she's half owner."

"I wonder how that works out."

Brian shrugged. "Well, the last time I spoke to Eden, not terrific. She wanted to sell her grandparents' house and take her half and move somewhere else. But according to the terms of the will, she can't sell without Shannon's permission. And Shannon doesn't want to sell or rent out the house."

"Why?" Heather frowned.

"From what Joe told me once, she doesn't want strangers living in that house next door to her."

"Doesn't she have a neighbor on the other side?"

Brian laughed. "I asked Joe the same thing when he told me. But he explained, on that side, it's an older couple Shannon has known all her life. She apparently has no problem with them as neighbors, but she doesn't want strangers moving in on the other side. She wants the house empty or with her cousin in it. And Eden can't afford to maintain an empty house. Sure, there is no mortgage on it, but it still costs money to pay for repairs, utilities, and insurance."

"I understand that. But can't this Eden go to court and make her cousin at least buy out her share? Hardly seems fair."

"I agree. But that takes money, and Eden doesn't have it," Brian explained. "Plus, I suspect Eden feels responsible for her cousin. And I doubt Shannon knows how she feels."

"How do you know all this?"

"Umm... well, I sorta took Eden out a couple of times."

Heather arched her brow. "Sorta?"

IN THE LIVING ROOM, Kelly, Joe, and Charlie stood by the fireplace, away from the rest of the group. Each held a drink in hand and enjoyed the heat emanating from the nearby flames.

Charlie motioned toward the living room doorway with his

drink and said, "What's the deal with that Heather and Brian? Isn't Brian the one who works with you?"

"Yes, he's a good friend. I guess they're seeing each other." Joe shrugged.

"I like Brian, but he doesn't make the best choices with women," Kelly whispered. "He's been divorced twice. I'm just hoping he doesn't make Heather number three."

"I understand what he sees in her." Charlie took a sip of his drink before continuing, "I just don't get what she sees in him. Sure, he is a nice guy, but he's old enough to be her father. What is she, about twenty-six?"

"She might be thirty, not sure," Kelly said.

"Maybe she has a daddy complex," Charlie suggested.

Kelly frowned at Charlie. "You find her attractive?"

"Charlie always went for the bad girls." Joe chuckled.

Kelly glanced to the doorway and back to Charlie. "And Heather looks like a bad girl?"

"She doesn't look like someone you'd take home and introduce to Mom and Grandma." Charlie snickered.

"You might be disappointed," Joe said. "Despite Heather's looks, she's not what you're seeing."

Charlie took another sip of his drink and then said, "I'm just trying to figure out how those two ever got together."

Joe told Charlie about Walt, Brian, and Heather's misadventure in the mountains, which had formed a kinship between the three, especially between Brian and Heather.

Across the room, Finn, who had just spilled wine on his sleeve, got up from his place on the sofa and excused himself so he could go upstairs and change his shirt, leaving Madeline alone. But she wasn't alone for long. June quickly took a seat on the sofa next to her.

"We haven't had a chance to talk," June said. "Are you enjoying your stay in Frederickport?"

"It's a lovely little town. More rain than I like, but it is beautiful." Madeline smiled warmly.

"Not sure we would have settled here if it weren't for our children," June said, glancing briefly to Ian and then to Kelly.

"I understand wanting to be close to your kids. Especially as we get older."

"And how do you like Marlow House? We stayed here when we first moved to town."

"Danielle told me. By the way, I've always liked your daughter-in-law, Lily; she's a delightful girl, so full of life," Madeline said. "And you have such a precious little grandson. You're so lucky."

"Thank you. And I understand you're Danielle's mother-in-law."

Madeline smiled. "Yes. She was married to my Lucas."

"I'm so sorry about your son. Ian told me about how you lost him in a car accident. I can't imagine losing a child." June glanced over at her grandson, Connor, who sat in the corner on a blanket, with Sadie on one side and Hunny on the other. The young boy rolled a ball out into the room, which the dogs took turns retrieving and bringing it back to the child so he could roll it again. Momentarily distracted from her conversation with Madeline, she wondered if someone had taught the dogs that trick.

"Thank you. But I'm doing much better now. It's comforting to know Lucas is happy. Finn has helped me so much."

June looked back to Madeline. "So you actually believe Finn is a genuine medium, not just an entertainer?"

"Oh yes, he is most definitely legitimate," Madeline insisted. "But I understand if you don't believe. I didn't at first. But then I met Finn, and everything changed. And what you'll discover with Finn, he doesn't shy away from nonbelievers. In fact, he looks forward to them at his readings. He claims they're his favorite." Madeline chuckled.

"Why is that?"

"He enjoys the challenge of making them believers, which he inevitably does."

"He impressed my daughter, Kelly, with the reading he gave her earlier today when she dropped by Marlow House. She called and told me about it."

"Yes, it was about an inheritance. Your daughter has a house she wants to buy?" Madeline asked.

"She wants to buy the house next door to this one." June rolled her eyes at the idea.

"The neighbor who was murdered?"

"And it wasn't the first murder there. About a year ago, they found two bodies in the backyard," June whispered.

"I read about that online. Such a tragic story."

June glanced around the room and said in a low voice, "And Marlow House has its own tragic history, beginning with the original Walt Marlow—murdered in his attic. Kelly never understood why Danielle and Walt had their bedroom up there."

"Marlow House has an interesting history."

"I don't know why Kelly wants to move to Beach Drive. I understand she wants to be closer to her brother, but frankly, I think this street is cursed. Finn could keep himself busy in this neighborhood, considering all the murders that have taken place on this street."

"I don't believe Danielle's convinced he's the real thing," Madeline confided in a whisper. "I know her well enough to recognize that look."

"Which surprises me. Kelly tells me there was a time Danielle thought she could communicate with spirits," June said.

Madeline frowned. "I certainly have never heard that before. Perhaps Kelly misunderstood?"

June shrugged. "I don't think so."

SEVENTEEN

W hen Danielle, Walt, Lily, Heather, and Brian walked into the living room, Chris immediately poured Walt a brandy and asked the others what they would like to drink. While they quietly made their requests, Danielle got the attention of the room and told everyone they would serve dessert in about twenty minutes.

As Danielle discussed dessert, Joanne quietly slipped from the room, heading for the kitchen. She intended to finish cleaning up from dinner and get dessert ready. But when she stepped into the kitchen, expecting to find the dishes neatly stacked, and pots and pans waiting to be washed, she found the dishwasher running and no dirty pots, pans, or dishes in sight. Joanne glanced at the clock and calculated she had left the dinner table only twenty minutes earlier. How had they cleared the table, cleaned all the dishes, and put away the leftovers in such a short time?

"Wow, I'm impressed," Joanne said, glancing around the room. The only sign of Thanksgiving sat on the kitchen table—several uncut pies waiting to be eaten. She walked to the counter, reached to an overhead cabinet, and began taking down the small plates for the servings of pie.

Back in the living room, Brian told Chris he'd get his drink after he came back from the restroom. He then left the living room, heading for the downstairs bathroom. Heather set her drink on the bar so she could go visit Connor, who sat on the other side of the room, happily playing with the dogs.

When Heather reached Connor, he looked up and smiled. Connor held his arms out to her, wanting to be picked up.

"You're getting way too big for that," Heather said while taking a seat on the blanket. She reached out and tweaked Connor's cheek, and he giggled. Each dog nudged Heather with a wet nose. She absently gave them each a pat before nudging them off the blanket to give her and Connor more space.

"Whatcha doing here, buddy?" Heather asked, picking up one of the toys scattered on the blanket. She handed it to Connor. "I'm surprised Marie isn't here keeping you entertained." She glanced at the dogs, who now sat at attention, staring at her and Connor. Heather arched a brow. "But I see Walt gave childcare duty to those two."

Connor dropped the toy Heather had handed him and picked up another one—a toy truck. He gave it to Heather. She took it and began pushing it around on the blanket, making motor sounds, while Connor picked up another truck and joined her in the game.

"You like to play trucks?" A male voice interrupted the play. Heather looked up and found Charlie standing over her, cocktail in hand. Not waiting for an answer, he crouched down, now at eye level with Heather and out of earshot from the rest of the room aside from her and Connor.

"Sometimes," Heather answered.

"What else do you like to play?" Charlie asked in a low voice.

Instead of answering, Heather arched her brows.

"I grew up in Frederickport," Charlie whispered. "I understand you moved here a few years ago. Where are you from?"

"California."

Charlie grinned. "California is a big state. Where in California?"

"Riverside."

He gave a nod and said, "I bet I could show you some cool spots around here that you haven't been to. And afterwards, maybe, you could show me some of your favorite places." Not waiting for a response, he reached out and brushed his hand over her cheek, yet not before glancing around the room to make sure no one was looking their way.

Heather's eyes widened. "Did you just hit on me?"

He gave her a smile and said, "Let's just say I'm putting out an invitation. Letting you know I'm interested. I think we could have fun. You're pretty hot, by the way."

"Umm, you realize I'm here with my boyfriend, don't you?" Heather asked.

Charlie shrugged. "Yeah. But I'm only going to be here for a few weeks. He doesn't need to find out. I won't tell him."

Heather was about to respond when Charlie stood abruptly and, before turning away, whispered, "We'll have fun."

Speechless, Heather watched as Charlie walked across the room, his back now to her as he headed for the bar. Connor dropped a toy truck on Heather's lap, recapturing her attention. He picked up the truck and handed it to her. Still thinking of what had just happened, Heather found it impossible to continue playing with Connor. Fortunately, a familiar male voice came to the rescue when Ian said, "Sorry, I'm going to take your playmate to the parlor. I suspect he needs a diaper change."

Heather looked up at Ian and smiled weakly as he picked up Connor. She stumbled to her feet and glanced around the room. Brian had not returned, and Charlie stood with the others at the bar, chatting away like nothing had just happened, his back to her.

Angry, Heather marched from the room. Just as she stepped out into the hall, she saw Ian take Connor into the parlor as Brian stepped out of the bathroom. She marched to Brian, grabbed his hand, and dragged him to the parlor.

Confused, Brian asked, "What is wrong?"

He repeated the question as she pushed him into the parlor, shutting the door behind them. Ian looked up from where he was changing Connor on the sofa.

"I can't believe that guy!" Heather fumed.

"What's wrong?" Ian asked from the sofa, trying to contain a wiggling Connor.

"That friend of your future brother-in-law just hit on me!" Heather snapped.

"Charlie?" Brian and Ian asked at the same time.

Heather recounted what had happened in the living room minutes earlier, while Ian finished changing Connor's diaper.

"He is right about one thing," Brian said.

Heather narrowed her eyes at Brian. "What?"

Brian wrapped an arm around her, pulling her close. "You are hot."

"Oh, shut up," she snapped.

Brian chuckled. "You want me to talk to him?"

"No," Heather grumbled. She sat on the sofa next to Ian, who now had Connor on the opposite side. Connor crawled across Ian and climbed onto Heather's lap. She accepted the toddler's embrace and held him.

"I could slug him. That would be more satisfying," Brian said, now sitting on the sofa's arm as he absently reached over and ruffled Connor's red curls.

"No," Heather said. "But I should get Walt to do it. A good sucker punch for a sucker. He would never see it coming, or where it came from."

Both men laughed.

"I wonder what my sister would say about the guy now," Ian said.

"Kelly seems kinda impressed with him." After Heather said it, she laughed, suddenly realizing something.

Brian frowned at Heather. "What's so funny?"

"Kelly is not thrilled with me going to the wedding as the best man's date," Heather said.

"That's not true," Ian objected.

Heather looked at Ian. "Come on, Ian. I know she's your sister, and you two are close. But you have to admit it's true; she doesn't like me. And I don't think your mom particularly likes me, either. If your sister could swing it, she would get Joe to have his old high school buddy be best man."

Instead of answering, Ian and Brian exchanged glances and then looked back at Heather.

Heather laughed and said, "But now that I know Charlie is interested in me, I should help your sister's wish come true. And then, when Charlie is officially the best man, I take him up on the offer and make sure our first date is someplace Kelly sees us."

"That is my sister you are talking about," Ian said, trying to stifle a laugh.

Heather shrugged, and Brian pulled her from the sofa into his arms. "I guess this means I'll be Joe's best man."

"You already are," Heather reminded him.

"I mean, I obviously won't be turning down the honor, because if I do, you'll take Charlie up on his offer."

Heather laughed and gave Brian a playful punch in the arm.

Ian stood up with Connor. "I'm going to get some of that pie. You two stay out of trouble. And Heather, Kelly doesn't dislike you. But she might be a little jealous."

Heather frowned at Ian. "Jealous, why?"

"For one thing, her only nephew adores you." Ian flashed Heather a grin and headed to the door, but before opening it, he turned to the pair one last time and asked in a serious tone, "Do you want me to say anything to Kelly or Joe about what happened in there?"

Heather shook her head. "No. I just needed to vent. The guy won't be around that long. Joe doesn't need to know what a jerk his old friend is. I imagine this would bother Joe more than it does me."

Ian gave them a nod and then left the parlor with Connor, closing the door behind him.

Brian sat on the sofa next to Heather, wrapping an arm around her as she leaned against his shoulder.

"You know, when I first moved to town, I had such a crush on Ian," Heather confessed.

"Hmmm…"

"Of course, he was with Lily, and I did not have a chance. But you know what?"

"What?" Brian asked.

"He and Lily are perfect for each other. But I do have good taste in men."

Brian chuckled. "I'll take that as a compliment instead of a reminder I was second choice."

"Nah, when it came to what's important, you did better than Ian."

"How so?" Brian asked.

"When Lily told Ian about Walt, well, he broke up with her. When you learned about Walt, that's kind of when we got together. It impressed Chris how well you accepted all this."

"In fairness to Ian, had he been stuck up on that mountain and experienced what I did, he might have accepted it sooner."

Heather shrugged. "Perhaps."

They sat in silence for a few minutes, and then Brian said in a serious tone, "Funny thing, I was considering asking Joe if he wanted to ask Charlie to be the best man. It had nothing to do with you. But I just figured Joe might have regretted asking me after realizing his best friend from high school was in town. He's talked about him and Rusty before, and I know how close they used to be. It wouldn't hurt my feelings."

"I understand. And if you decide to do it, I promise I won't ask Charlie out."

Brian grinned and gave Heather a little squeeze. "Good, because I really don't want to arrest you."

"Arrest me?" Heather frowned.

"Yeah, I figure the way he acted, you might end up killing him, knowing you."

WHEN HEATHER and Brian returned to the living room a few minutes later, Heather stopped in her tracks when she spied Charlie standing on the other side of the room, talking to Joe, while a woman stood between them.

Heather grabbed Brian's hand and said in a whisper, "She's here!"

"Who?" Brian glanced around the living room and didn't see anyone new.

"The mystery ghost," Heather said. "The one who knew Finn. She's here, standing over there with Joe and Charlie."

"Now is your chance. You can find out who she is," Brian suggested.

Heather rolled her eyes. "Yeah, right, with Ian's family here."

EIGHTEEN

"Excuse me!" Joanne's voice called out. Heather and Brian, who stood in the doorway leading into the living room, turned around and found Joanne standing in the hallway, carrying a large tray with plates of pie.

"Let me take that," Brian offered, reaching for the tray.

"That's okay. I've got this. But I need you two to move," Joanne said with a laugh. "But if you want to help, there's another tray in the kitchen that needs to be brought out."

"I'll get it," Brian said as he and Heather quickly moved completely out of Joanne's way as she took the tray of dessert into the living room. Brian left for the kitchen, leaving Heather alone by the living room entrance. Heather looked over at Joe and Charlie and then glanced around the room. Once again, the ghost had vanished.

Hesitantly, Heather entered the room. She noticed some people now had coffee, and she assumed either Danielle or Joanne had served it while she had been in the parlor. The non-mediums continued to chatter, now discussing their choice of pie—pecan, apple, or pumpkin—as Joanne set the tray on the coffee table. But the mediums were silent and exchanging glances, and when Chris's gaze met Heather's and then Walt's and Danielle's, Heather knew they too had noticed the uninvited guest. Heather made her way to the bar, where Chris now stood alone.

"She's back, and now she's gone," Heather told Chris in a low voice. Standing side by side, they both looked out into the room.

"Where's Brian?" Chris asked. "I saw him leaving earlier, and he didn't come back. Did something happen?"

Heather shook her head. "No, he went to the bathroom, and then I had to tell him something." She glared across the room at Charlie and Joe, who now stood with Kelly, each with a piece of pie.

Chris noticed Heather's scowl. "Is something wrong?"

"He hit on me," Heather hissed.

"Who hit on you?" Chris asked.

"Charlie. Right there in the middle of the living room while I was playing with Connor."

"Are you sure? Maybe he was being friendly?"

Heather turned her glare on Chris. "I know when a guy hits on me. It's kinda obvious when they get a little too close, start talking about how hot you are and what a good time you'll have. And what really cinches it is when they promise not to tell your boyfriend."

Chris arched his brows. "Seriously?"

"Are you saying I'm making it up?" she snapped.

"Of course not."

"Then don't ask stupid questions." Now crossing her arms across her chest, she looked back into the room.

Chris took a deep breath, let out a sigh, and asked, "Did you tell Brian?"

"Yeah. He offered to slug him for me."

Chris smiled. "Did you take him up on his offer?"

"No. I told him I would rather Walt do it."

Chris chuckled.

Heather let out a sigh, dropped her arms to her sides, and turned a weak smile to Chris. "I'm sorry I was bitchy."

"Hey, you were just being you."

DANIELLE SAT NEXT TO MADELINE, a plate with a slice of pecan pie in hand. The two sat alone, while the other people in the room gathered in small clusters, each involved with his or her own private conversations.

"The pumpkin pie was delicious," Madeline told Danielle. She had just taken her last bite of pie when Danielle sat down. Danielle took the empty plate from Madeline, only a fork and some crumbs remained on it, and set it on the coffee table while still holding her plate in the other hand. "You were always an excellent baker."

"Thank you, Madeline. But I must confess, Kelly brought the pumpkin pie. She told me she picked it up at Old Salts. That's where we get the cinnamon rolls."

"I'm afraid if I lived so close to such a good bakery, I'd need to buy a new wardrobe in a significantly larger size!"

Danielle took a bite of her pie after saying, "It can be a challenge, that's for sure."

"Danielle, I wanted to ask you something," Madeline said in a low voice.

Danielle set her fork on her plate with the partially eaten piece of pie and looked at Madeline. "Certainly."

"I didn't want to discuss this with you until after Thanksgiving. Oh, I know it's still Thanksgiving; I just meant while you were so busy preparing tonight's dinner. Which was delicious, by the way. Everything was so good."

"I'm glad you enjoyed it. It was nice sharing a Thanksgiving with you again."

Madeline reached out and patted Danielle's knee. "It was."

"So what did you want to ask me?"

"It's the primary reason I'm here," Madeline said.

"Okay…" Danielle waited for Madeline to continue.

"Tomorrow, would you mind joining Finn and me for a reading? I would also like Walt to be there."

"A reading?"

Madeline nodded. "Lucas wants to talk to you both. He has some things he needs to say."

Danielle arched her brows. "Oh…"

"I can tell you are a skeptic," Madeline said in a gentle voice. "I understand."

"I suppose I am, a little." Danielle silently thought, *I'm not a skeptic; I just know he's a fake.*

Madeline glanced over to June, who now stood across the room.

She looked back at Danielle and said, "June said something odd to me."

"What was that?"

"She said there was a time you claimed to communicate with spirits. I don't remember you ever saying that. At least, not to me. And Lucas never mentioned it."

"Really…" Danielle muttered, glancing briefly to June and back to Madeline.

"June said her daughter told her," Madeline explained.

"Well, Kelly has an active imagination," Danielle said.

"Kelly obviously likes to talk about ghosts. She also told Finn that Heather has claimed to see ghosts."

Danielle smiled. "Well, many people have made similar claims. Lily's mother, Tammy, insists her mother came to her after she died, told her she was fine and to go on with life and be happy."

"And Tammy might very well have seen her mother. It's very similar to what Finn experiences. He says many people possess psychic powers like he does, in varying degrees."

"I'm sure Walt would sit in on a reading tomorrow. I'm interested to hear what Lucas has to say." Danielle smiled sweetly.

———

JOANNE WALKED around the room with a tray, collecting the plates. In one corner stood Charlie, Joe, Kelly, Adam, and Mel. When Joanne walked up to the group, Charlie set his plate on the tray and said, "That was delicious pie."

"Glad you enjoyed it," Joanne said as the others added their plates to the tray. Walt walked up to the small group with Ian and John as Joanne walked away. June sat across the room with Kelly on the blanket with Connor, while Finn joined Madeline and Danielle on the sofa. By the bar, Brian had joined Chris and Heather, and the three chatted.

Adam briefly glanced at the sofa and said, "The restless spirits seemed to have left Finn alone during dinner. I wonder if he has some arrangement with them not to bother him while he's eating."

"Don't be such a skeptic," Kelly teased.

Adam replied with a shrug.

"Joe, remember that psychic medium Rusty took Shannon to? It was for their birthday," Charlie asked.

"I remember, right before he was killed," Joe said.

"I thought later, if the guy had been a real psychic, why didn't he warn Rusty not to go into work the next day?" Charlie said.

"A psychic medium is not the same thing as a fortune-teller," Ian reminded them. "They can't see into the future."

"Neither can a fortune-teller," Joe said with a snort.

"Who was it?" Kelly asked.

"I don't know. But it reminds me of something else." Charlie pulled his cellphone out of his back pocket. He looked at Joe and said, "I'm going to give Shannon a call. When I leave here later, I'd like to stop by and see her. I hate thinking of her spending Thanksgiving alone. But I understand. There is no way I'm going to pry her from that house."

"You're more than welcome to take a plate of food to her," Walt offered. "We have plenty of leftovers."

Charlie smiled at Walt. "Thanks, that's nice of you to offer. But when I spoke to Eden, she told me Shannon had ordered dinner from Lucy's Diner."

"Lucy's delivers?" Ian asked with a frown.

"Yes," Joe said. "They've been offering Thanksgiving dinner as takeout for about five years now. They typically close early on Thanksgiving, so they make their deliveries before noon."

"I've heard it's pretty good," Adam said.

Charlie looked at Joe. "I thought cops were only up on the schedule of donut shops."

"Ha, ha," Joe said dryly. "Donut jokes. You were never very original."

Charlie laughed and then excused himself and walked away while looking at his phone.

"You should go with him," Kelly told Joe.

"Go with who?" Joe frowned.

"Charlie. I know you and Shannon weren't close, but she was the sister of one of your best friends. And it sounds like she needs some friends," Kelly said.

"In the beginning, I tried to keep in touch," Joe told Kelly. "Shannon made it clear she did not want me bothering her."

"But—" Kelly began, only to be cut off by her brother.

"While your heart is in the right place," Ian began, "I don't think a friend is what she needs. Sounds to me like she needs some professional help."

"I agree," Adam chimed in. "It's not exactly normal for someone to stay in her house for years without going outside."

"When did she become a shut-in?" Ian asked.

"She moved back with her parents after her brother's death, and while she stayed home most of the time, I wouldn't exactly have called her a shut-in back then. More an introvert, which she always was to some extent," Joe explained.

"So it was after her parents died that she became a shut-in?" Melony asked.

Joe considered the question a moment before saying, "Her father died first. Within a year after Rusty. Then a couple of years later, her mother died, and then a few weeks after that, her grandmother passed away. She lived next door to Shannon. Eden came to town for the funeral, and Shannon talked her into moving into their grandmother's house for a while."

"And Eden stayed," Kelly said.

Joe shrugged. "I think Eden knew she couldn't leave her cousin alone, not after seeing her."

Their discussion stopped when Charlie rejoined the group. He tucked the phone back in his pocket and said, "She doesn't answer her phone. I called her this morning too. She didn't answer then, either."

"Do you think she's alright?" Kelly asked.

Charlie shrugged. "She's probably just not answering her phone. Since she doesn't have caller ID, I won't take it personally."

"Everyone has caller ID these days," Melony said. "Unless she doesn't have your number in her contacts."

Charlie grinned. "She doesn't have a cellphone, only a landline."

"She doesn't have a cellphone?" Melony thought everyone had a cellphone.

"Landlines can have caller ID," Joe reminded them.

"True, but I don't think hers does," Charlie said.

"What are you going to do?" Kelly asked. "Are you stopping over there anyway?"

The mystery ghost appeared in the middle of the group. Walt's eyes widened in surprise, but he said nothing.

"Charlie, you're still here!" the spirit blurted. "I wish you could see me, hear me!" She turned to Joe and waved her hand in front of his face. "Joe, it's me, Shannon. Rusty's sister. Please see me!"

NINETEEN

G etting no response from Joe or Charlie, the spirit again
vanished. Walt quietly excused himself from the group and
walked to his wife, who sat on one end of the sofa, chatting with
Madeline and Finn. Her back had been to him when the ghost
made her reappearance. He stepped up to the sofa, leaned toward
Danielle, and whispered something into her ear. Afterwards, he gave
Madeline and Finn a nod and smile before turning to the bar and
walking away.

"What was she saying?" Heather asked when Walt walked up to
the bar.

"I know who she is now," Walt said in a quiet voice.

Before giving the answer, he waited for Danielle to join them.

"She was here again?" Danielle asked when she reached Walt
and the others.

Heather looked at Danielle. "You didn't see her?"

Danielle shook her head.

"Walt says he knows who she is," Chris said. They all turned to
Walt, waiting for his answer.

"Her exact words to Joe, 'Joe, it's me, Shannon. Rusty's sister.
Please see me!'" Walt repeated.

"You mean that girl who won't leave her house?" Heather asked.

"She's obviously left it," Walt said with a shrug.

Brian groaned. "Does this mean she's dead?"

"Either that or having an out-of-body experience," Walt quipped.

Danielle rolled her eyes. "I seriously doubt that."

"My bet, she's dead," Chris said. He looked at Walt and asked, "You saw her close up? Any bullet holes? Stab wound? Bruises around her neck?"

Brian frowned at Chris and glanced at the other mediums surrounding him. None looked horrified at the turn of events. "You people are sick. You know that? We just find out a young woman is dead and—"

"And likely murdered," Heather interrupted. "Or perhaps suicide. I bet it was suicide. Who would murder her? The poor girl never left her house."

Again, Brian groaned and shook his head.

Danielle looked at Brian sympathetically and patted his arm. "Brian, it's not that we are insensitive. But, to begin with, we've never met her. And if we started getting emotional over every ghost we stumble over, well, we'd go nuts."

"I'm not talking about her ghost. I'm talking about a dead woman whose body is probably lying alone in her house. And no one even knows she's dead," Brian said.

"We know she's dead. And every ghost comes with a dead body," Heather said dryly. "So I'm not sure what your point is."

"Charlie was talking about going over there," Walt said.

Danielle cringed. "Someone needs to go with him."

"Yeah, I agree. It sucks finding a dead body," Heather said.

"Coming from someone skilled at finding corpses," Chris quipped.

Heather shrugged. "At least I'm rarely familiar with the ones I find."

Brian groaned again.

"Do you need a drink?" Chris asked Brian.

Walt looked over at Ian, who still stood with Joe and the others. "Perhaps I should have a talk with Ian."

"Why?" Danielle asked.

"When Charlie was off calling Shannon to tell her he wanted to come over, Kelly was trying to get Joe to offer to go with him. Not sure if she wanted to go too, but she wanted him to go. I'm sure Kelly felt sorry for her," Walt explained.

"Kelly is just being a busybody," Heather grumbled.

"Perhaps, but Kelly is not without empathy," Danielle said. "This poor Shannon girl is… or was… about our age. And it seems like her last ten years have been rather lonely."

"You're right. But Charlie obviously didn't get Shannon on the phone," Heather said.

"He thought nothing was wrong, just that Shannon didn't want to answer the phone," Walt explained.

"Ahh, she didn't want to talk to him?" Heather snickered. "I can understand that."

Danielle looked at Heather. "Why do you say that?"

"According to Charlie, she doesn't have caller ID, so she didn't know who was calling. He didn't take it personally," Walt said.

"She wasn't ignoring the call. Ghosts can't answer the phone," Brian muttered.

"Marie could," Heather chirped. "Of course, if she talked into it, no one would hear."

"So is he still going over?" Chris asked.

"I'm not sure, but I think so," Walt said.

"You still didn't explain why you need to talk to Ian," Danielle reminded them.

Walt flashed Danielle a smile and said, "No, I didn't. What I was going to say, when Kelly talked about Joe going over there and how Shannon needed friends, Ian said something about her needing professional help instead of friends."

"Which she obviously did, if she killed herself," Heather said.

"Ian seemed to be telling his sister not to push it," Walt said. "Instead of encouraging Joe to go with Charlie, to back off."

"Ahh, and you think Ian should go in the other direction? Agreeing with Kelly that Joe should tag along?" Heather said.

"It might be a good idea if Charlie has a police officer with him when he finds the body," Walt said.

"Yeah, but if she died inside her house, they probably aren't going to break in. Will they?" Danielle looked at Brian.

Brian considered the question for a moment. "Not sure.

Normally in a case like this, when you know someone is home, they are alone, and not answering, you might break in."

"Like you guys did with Pearl," Danielle said.

"I was fairly certain Pearl was dead," Brian reminded them. "But in this case, Joe doesn't know if Shannon is in her house hurt, or in her bathroom soaking in her tub with her earpods on, listening to music."

"True," Danielle said.

———

MARLOW HOUSE'S Thanksgiving guests prepared to go home. Walt spied Ian heading out into the hallway; he assumed going to the bathroom. When Ian stepped out of the restroom a few minutes later, Walt was in the hallway waiting. He asked Ian to go into the parlor with him so they could talk in private.

"Shannon is dead?" Ian said after Walt explained about the visiting ghost.

"It looks that way. And she never leaves her house, so we assume she died there, and she hasn't been discovered. Is Charlie still planning to go over there after he leaves here?"

"Yes. And I'm glad Kelly didn't press Joe to go with Charlie; she would have gone," Ian said.

"We think it would be a good idea if Joe went along. If he doesn't, then she's likely not going to be found. At least not until her cousin comes back from vacation," Walt said.

———

SINCE ADAM PLANNED to work on Friday, he and Melony left first. Joanne had finished up the dessert dishes and now stood in the entry hall with the rest of Marlow House's Thanksgiving guests, many of whom were preparing to leave. June, who stood with her husband, John, by her side, said, "That was a lovely dinner, Danielle. We want to thank you and Walt for inviting us."

"You are most welcome, June. We're glad you came," Danielle said.

June glanced over at Finn, who stood with Madeline, saying goodbye to the dinner guests. She looked back at Danielle. "It was quite fascinating meeting Finn Walsh. I have to say, I was never much of a believer in all that stuff, but he makes me wonder." She then added in a whisper, "He gave me a message from my mother, and it was uncanny! It was like she was actually here in the room!"

Danielle smiled. "I'm glad you enjoyed yourself."

"Oh, and your mother-in-law is such a dear!" June then flashed an apologetic smile to Walt and looked back at Danielle. "Although Kelly tells me the correct term is former mother-in-law. She seems rather fond of you."

"Madeline is a good person," Danielle agreed. "I was lucky to have her as a mother-in-law."

June glanced briefly at Charlie and said in a loud voice, "And I enjoyed getting to meet my future son-in-law's dear friend."

"And I enjoyed meeting the family Joe will be joining," Charlie returned with a grin.

"You really need to come to that wedding! I hope you're in town then," June said.

"I'm not sure how I could miss my best buddy's wedding." Charlie gave Joe a hearty pat on the back.

June beamed at the response, and then she and John exchanged a few parting words with the others before stepping out of the house.

"I need to get going if I intend to stop by and see Shannon. I don't think anyone should be completely alone for Thanksgiving." Charlie then looked at Walt and Danielle and said, "Thanks again for inviting me. I really appreciate it. Dinner was great and so was the company."

"You're welcome," Danielle said.

"Is Joe going with you?" Ian asked.

Kelly glanced at her brother.

Charlie grinned at Ian. "You know, that is a great idea." He looked at Joe. "Why don't you come with me? I bet Shannon would love to see you."

Joe shrugged. "I don't think so. Shannon and I were never that close, and after Rusty died, she didn't seem interested in maintaining a friendship."

"Oh, come on," Charlie urged. "It might be just what Shannon needs. She's been on my mind a lot lately. We need to help her. I keep thinking about how we've let Rusty down, not doing more to get her back into the world. Maybe it's time."

"I agree with Charlie," Kelly said. "You need to go."

"Kelly can stay here with us," Ian offered. "Lily and I aren't leaving right away."

"I can go with them," Kelly said. "I'll stay in the car if she doesn't feel comfortable with a stranger. And who knows, she might like a girlfriend."

Ian started to object but was cut off when Heather said, "I think that is really sweet of Kelly."

———

UPSTAIRS, Madeline and Finn had retreated to their rooms to rest, while the residents of Beach Drive sat in the living room of Marlow House. Joanne, Charlie, Joe, and Kelly had left minutes earlier.

"Thanks a lot, Heather," Ian grumbled as he took a seat on the sofa with Lily, Connor playing by their feet on the floor.

"Hey, I've found my share of dead bodies, and I'm doing okay." Heather took a seat on Brian's lap after he sat on one of the chairs facing the sofa.

"Dead bodies? What am I missing?" Lily asked.

Walt and Heather then told Lily all that she had missed. Right as they finished the telling, Marie and Eva appeared in the living room, a flurry of snowflakes falling around them before vanishing.

"Where have you two been?" Danielle asked. For the non-mediums, Danielle added, "Marie and Eva just got here."

"We've been here and there," Eva said.

"We could have used you to talk to a spirit who kept showing up here," Danielle said.

"You couldn't talk to the spirit?" Marie asked.

Danielle then told Eva and Marie all that had happened regarding Shannon's ghost.

"We hope Joe finds her body; unfortunately they probably won't go into the house. But it would be better if Joe finds her, since he's a cop. I feel sorry for her cousin, because that's probably who's going to find her, and by that time she's going to be really stinky, if she isn't already." Heather wrinkled her nose.

"I suppose we might be able to help," Marie said.

"Help, how?" Danielle asked.

Marie smiled. "We'll convince Joe and his friend to go into the house."

Danielle repeated what Marie said, and Ian replied with, "Just as long as Kelly doesn't go into the house. She doesn't need to find the body."

TWENTY

Darkness blanketed Frederickport, and with it came the rain. Joe sat in the passenger side of Kelly's car as they followed Charlie's vehicle from Marlow House to Shannon's. Kelly glanced at Joe and said, "I like Charlie. He seems like a nice guy."

"It's good seeing him again."

"You think he will come to the wedding?" Kelly asked.

"Sounds like he's going to try. Yet I imagine it'll depend on what he does with his mother's house. That's where he stays when he's in town. Of course, before, it was typically rented, which I suspect is one reason he rarely came back for visits."

"You know, he can always stay at Marlow House if it sells," Kelly suggested.

"Might be cheaper to stay at the Seahorse," Joe said. "That's if his mother's house sells and he wants to come to the wedding."

"You sure didn't talk to Brian much tonight," Kelly noted.

Joe shrugged. "We spend enough time together at work, and he was with Heather."

Kelly let out a sigh. "I still don't understand those two."

"You and me both."

THE GHOSTS of Eva Thorndike and Marie Nicholas arrived minutes before Charlie pulled his car up in front of Shannon's house. It looked as if someone was home because lights were on inside. The two spirits had just enough time to survey the property around the house before he parked. If not for the floodlights installed around the yard that came on at dusk, it would have been difficult for Eva and Marie to see without a flashlight. While they found nothing suspicious in the yard, and certainly no body, they expected if they found something, it would be inside the house.

Eva and Marie stood on the front porch and watched as Kelly pulled up behind Charlie's parked car, Joe in her passenger seat. Charlie hadn't gotten out of his vehicle yet. Eva looked at Marie and said, "We should get inside and see what we find."

The next minute, the ghosts went through the house, each taking different rooms to get the job done quicker. They didn't want Charlie and Joe to knock on the door and then leave when no one answered. But first, they wanted to see what they might find inside.

When Marie moved through the wall from the living room to the kitchen, the first thing she noticed were the open containers of food scattered on the floor. It wasn't until she moved closer to the table that Marie saw the body of a lifeless young woman sprawled out on the kitchen floor. Marie assumed it must be the body of Shannon Langdon. The last time she had seen the woman had been at the funeral of Shannon's grandmother. Marie didn't know Shannon personally, but she had known her grandmother.

"Eva, she's in here!" Marie called out. "In the kitchen!"

The next moment, Eva appeared in the room with Marie.

"Oh my. Is that who they thought we'd find?" Eva asked, standing over the body.

"I assume it's Shannon; that's whose ghost was over at Marlow House, trying to talk to Joe. And this is her house. I've seen Shannon before, yet it's been years. But it looks like her. Thinner than I remember, and her hair is much longer," Marie said as she walked around the body, examining it from various angles.

"Shannon, are you here?" Eva called out. "If you are, show yourself! Marie and I can see and hear you!"

Marie and Eva stood in silence, waiting for Shannon to respond. Nothing. Eva called out again, but instead of Shannon's voice answering her, a doorbell rang.

MARIE LEFT Eva in the house, still calling out for Shannon's ghost. When she walked through the front wall in the living room onto the front porch, she found Joe and his friend standing there ringing the doorbell while Kelly waited in her car. The porch's overhang protected both men from the rain.

"Lights are on," Joe observed as they waited for someone to answer the door.

Marie tried to remember the name of Joe's friend. Finally, it came to her. "It's Charlie!"

After a few minutes, Charlie rang the bell again. When no one came to the door, he stepped off the patio, pulled the hood of his jacket over his head, and looked into the living room window.

"Don't make me arrest you for being a peeping tom," Joe teased.

Ignoring the rain and Joe's comment, Charlie continued to peer in the window. "No one is in the living room, but the lights are on."

Charlie returned to the cover of the porch and pulled out his cellphone.

"Are you calling her?" Joe asked.

"Yes. She might answer her phone this time. I really wish she at least had an answering machine," Charlie grumbled. A few moments later, as Charlie held the phone to his ear, the sound of a phone ringing came from inside the house. It rang and rang until Charlie finally hung up and shoved his phone back into his pocket.

"I don't have a good feeling about this," Charlie said. "Let's look in the other windows."

"Maybe she's in the bathroom," Joe suggested. "Or in her bedroom, and she just doesn't want to answer the door. It's dark out, and she doesn't know who it is. A single woman living alone. We should come back tomorrow, during the day."

In response, Charlie started knocking loudly on the front door while calling out, "Shannon! It's Charlie and Joe! Please answer the door! Shannon!"

As Charlie continued to knock loudly and shout Shannon's name, Marie let out a sigh and said, "Let's hurry this up, shall we?"

The next moment, Marie moved back through the wall into the living room. Focusing her energy on the front door, she unlocked the deadbolt and then the doorknob. As Charlie continued to knock, she willed the doorknob to turn, and just as she hoped would happen, the front door eased open a little with Charlie's knock. To speed up the process, Marie again focused her energy, and the door flew all the way open.

Outside, Charlie startled at the suddenly opened door.

"It must not have been shut all the way," Charlie stammered nervously as he hesitantly stepped into the house and looked around. Joe followed him inside as Charlie called out for Shannon while leaving the front door wide open.

Marie followed the two men as they hesitantly walked through the house while calling out for the occupant.

KELLY SAT IN HER CAR, waiting for Joe. Since she couldn't see the front door, she wondered what was taking them so long. Had they gone inside, or were they still standing on Shannon's front porch ringing the doorbell?

After glancing at her watch, Kelly removed the key from the ignition, unfastened her seatbelt, and opened the car door. The rain had stopped, so she didn't bother pulling the hood of her jacket up over her head when she got out of the vehicle. Slamming the door shut behind her, Kelly headed for the front porch.

Once standing at the open doorway, she looked inside the house, but no one was in the living room. She stepped inside and was about to call out when she noticed voices coming from another part of the house. Without thinking, she closed the door behind her and started toward the voices.

Just as she reached the open doorway into the kitchen, she spied Joe standing by the sink, talking on his cellphone, while Charlie stood on the other side of the room, staring down at the floor. She couldn't hear what Joe was saying or why he was on the phone. With a frown, she walked into the room.

"What's going on?" Kelly asked. "Where's Shannon?"

Startled by Kelly's voice, Joe, still on the phone, looked at her and put his palm up, giving her a hand motion to stop. But Kelly failed to heed Joe's instruction and continued into the kitchen, wanting to see what had captured Charlie's attention.

"I don't think she's going to be a very obedient wife." Marie snickered. She and Eva sat on the kitchen counter, watching the scene unfold.

When Joe and Charlie first found the body, Joe had reached Shannon first, checking for vitals. After finding no pulse and pronouncing Shannon dead, he looked up to find Charlie in a daze, stumbling around the kitchen, picking up the food containers off the floor and setting them on the table, as if putting the room in order might bring their friend back to life. Joe had yelled at Charlie not to touch anything else, ordered him to go stand by the counter, and then called the station.

"Oh my god, is she dead!" Kelly gasped when she spied the body.

"Kelly, don't touch anything!" Joe snapped. She froze and did not move.

"Look at that. She actually obeyed his order," Marie mused.

"And you were an obedient wife?" Eva teased.

Marie shrugged. "Far more obedient than I should have been. But that was a different time."

Joe finished his phone call and said, "We should all go outside. You can both wait in the car. They'll be here in a few minutes."

"What happened to her?" Kelly asked, inching closer to the body to have a closer look. "Did she always have such red skin?"

"I can't believe she's dead," Charlie muttered.

"Looks like she's been dead for a few hours," Joe said. He looked over at the empty sacks sitting on the counter with Lucy's Diner's logo, and then at the scattered food containers. "We can safely say the time of death was after they delivered the food. We'll have to talk to the diner and see when that was."

"How did she die?" Kelly asked, now crouching closer to the body and looking at Shannon's face.

"And to think Ian was worried finding a dead body would traumatize the poor girl." Marie snickered. "It wouldn't surprise me if she pulled out her cellphone and snapped a picture."

While Marie commented on Kelly's fascination over the dead body, Joe told Kelly they would have to wait for the coroner to find out the cause of death.

Again, Joe urged Kelly and Charlie to leave the room. Charlie gave Joe an absent nod and then made his way from the kitchen into the living room as Kelly slowly trailed behind him. Just as they reached the front door, they heard sirens.

Joe looked at Kelly, placed his hands on her shoulders, and looked her in the eyes. "Go home. I'll get a ride."

"No. I'm not leaving," Kelly said stubbornly.

Joe let out a sigh and said, "Okay. But at least wait in the car."

"Come on, Joe, I don't want to wait in the car," Kelly whined. "I'll stay out of the way."

The sirens grew louder.

"Can I leave?" Charlie asked. "Not sure what good I'll be. I'll just get in the way."

Joe considered the question a moment and then said, "Okay, but I'll need you to stop by the station in the morning."

"Certainly," Charlie said with a nod.

Charlie was just driving away as the responders parked their vehicles. Kelly stood in the corner of the living room and silently watched, while Eva and Marie returned to Marlow House.

TWENTY-ONE

When Eva and Marie returned to Marlow House, they found Finn and Madeline still upstairs in their rooms, and all the others who had been at Marlow House when they had left for Shannon's were still in the living room.

The first question Danielle asked of the returning ghosts was, "Did you find her spirit?"

Before they responded, Heather whispered to Brian, "Marie and Eva are here."

"No, and we called out for her," Marie said, taking a seat on an imaginary chair. "But we found her body, and so did Joe."

"Yes, we heard," Danielle said. "We called the chief right after you left to give him the heads-up. The chief wants Brian to meet him at the station, but after he talks to you."

"I assume Edward called you to tell you they found the body?" Marie asked.

"Yes. And Kelly texted her brother about it," Danielle said.

Upon hearing Danielle mention Kelly's name, and not being able to hear or see Marie or Eva, Ian asked, "How is Kelly? Is she very upset?"

Marie arched a brow to Ian. "Upset? I wouldn't describe her reaction that way."

"How would you describe it?" Danielle asked.

Marie considered the question for a moment and then said, "More like a no-nonsense lady reporter. Or perhaps a private detective. More curious than horrified."

Danielle repeated Marie's words for the non-mediums.

"Really?" Ian frowned and slumped back in his seat, considering what Marie had said.

Danielle looked at Marie and Eva and asked, "Can you tell me everything that happened before Brian leaves so he can tell the chief?"

Marie recounted for Danielle the events at Shannon's, including unlocking the door for Charlie and opening it. Danielle repeated Marie's words for Brian.

"I need to get over there." Brian stood. "Thanks. I'll keep you guys updated." He gave Heather a quick kiss and thanked Walt and Danielle for dinner.

"Sometimes I wonder if aliens abducted Brian and sent someone to replace him," Chris said while standing at the front window of the living room, watching Brian drive away five minutes later.

"Why?" Heather asked.

Chris shrugged, turned his back to the window, and faced his friends. "Just not the same hardheaded jerk I met when I first came to town."

Danielle chuckled and looked at Heather. "It's amazing what love can do."

"Oh, please," Heather said with a snort. "His change has nothing to do with our relationship. It's just that he sees the world through new eyes now that he knows…" Heather paused, looked at Marie and Eva and then Walt, and then said, "… about you."

"COME ON, CHIEF," Joe argued. "This is my case. I found the body, and Shannon was one of my best friend's sisters."

"You're too close," the chief explained. "Surely you see that."

"How? I haven't seen Shannon in years. That's enough distance," Joe said.

"You're good friends with at least one suspect, and technically, you're a suspect, too."

Joe stood abruptly. "What are you talking about? You know I didn't kill Shannon, and Charlie hasn't seen her much more than I have."

Edward MacDonald motioned to the chair Joe had been sitting in. "Joe, sit back down."

Reluctantly, Joe returned to his chair.

"Everyone close to Shannon is a suspect. And from what you tell me, in the last ten years, she hasn't been close to anyone. We need to start somewhere."

A knock at the door interrupted their conversation.

"Come in," the chief called out.

The next moment, the door opened, and Brian walked into the room.

"Thanks for coming down." The chief motioned to the empty chair next to Joe.

"You want Brian to take over the case?" Joe grumbled.

"I still need you on it, but I think it would be best if Brian takes the lead," the chief said. "And I'd like you to call your friend Charlie —see if he can get down here. We can start with him."

Brian flashed Joe a sheepish smile and watched as he left the room. After the door shut again and Brian was alone with the chief, Brian asked, "Is it really necessary for me to take the lead?"

"He's too close to the case. And it's possible we might come across a suspect who's a friend of Joe's. He may not be objective."

"Come on, Chief, don't tell me you forgot about Danielle?"

"Danielle?" The chief frowned.

"Uh, yeah. Considering Joe's feeling toward Danielle after she first moved to town, I don't think you can say he's the type who lets personal feelings impede his job. He arrested her for murder," Brian reminded him.

The chief shrugged. "Perhaps. But I believe this is for the best."

Brian reluctantly conceded and then told the chief all that Marie had told Danielle. When he finished, the chief said, "Joe seemed to think there was significance in the house being unlocked and the door not shut all the way."

"Which isn't the case."

"And we can't tell Joe. Another reason I need you to be lead on this. I can't have Joe follow useless clues because of something Marie does," the chief said.

Brian chuckled. "You think perhaps our job was easier before we had all this help?"

"In some ways."

"What's the cause of death?" Brian asked.

"We won't know until the coroner finishes his report. But it looks like poisoning. The way the food fell on the kitchen floor, and how the body landed, it looks like she may have been reacting to the poison and, in doing so, inadvertently pulled off the tablecloth. And it doesn't look like anyone else was in the kitchen at the time, considering the only footprints in all that mess belonged to the victim. Nothing to indicate someone else was in the kitchen before Joe and Charlie arrived."

"The food was poisoned?" Brian asked.

"They're bagging it up and taking it to the lab. But the way some of the food landed, it may be difficult to pinpoint which food had the poison, if that's what happened."

"Or did someone doctor her medication like with Rachel Moore?" Brian asked, referring to the cause of death in a recent homicide.

The chief's desk phone rang. He answered it, talked a moment, and when he hung up, he looked at Brian. "That was Joe. He got a hold of Charlie. He's coming down to the station now. I'd like you to interview him."

"You want me to do it? Maybe that might not be a good idea."

The chief frowned. "Why?"

"I may not be impartial. At Marlow House today, he hit on Heather."

The chief arched a brow. "Seriously?"

"Heather was not amused. I offered to slug him, but she said she'd rather have Walt do it."

The chief grinned. "Oh, one of those sucker punches where you never see it coming—nor see who gave it to you."

"Yeah. I got one of those once." Brian chuckled. "You want to interview Charlie instead of me?"

"Does he know you know? About hitting on Heather?"

Brian shook his head. "No. She didn't want me to say anything."

"Does Joe know?"

"No."

"Then I don't see what the problem is." The chief glanced

briefly at the clock and then looked back at Brian. "He should be here in about fifteen minutes."

BRIAN AND CHARLIE sat in the interrogation room alone, Brian on one side of the table and Charlie on the other, while the chief and Joe stood in the adjacent office observing the pair through the one-way mirror. In Brian's hand he held an ink pen, while a yellow legal pad lay before him on the tabletop.

"When we were having Thanksgiving dinner earlier today, I certainly didn't think we would be sitting here tonight," Charlie said after he first sat down. He clasped his hands together, resting them on the tabletop before him, his thumbs fidgeting, fencing against each other.

"No, neither did I," Brian agreed. "I'm sorry about your friend, by the way."

Charlie shook his head. "It's such a shock. Hard for me to fathom."

"When was the last time you saw Shannon?" Brian asked.

"Last time I was in town. Five years ago."

"Since then, have you kept in touch with her? Phone calls, emails?" Brian hoped Charlie might know something about Shannon's recent life that would lead them to whoever wanted her dead.

"An occasional phone call, but we exchanged emails about every week."

"I didn't realize you were closer to Shannon than Joe," Brian said without thinking. He remembered Joe saying he and his old friend hadn't kept in touch, yet according to what Charlie was now telling him, he had kept in touch with Shannon.

"Not really. But you have to understand how close I was to her brother, Rusty. Heck, he was like my brother, too. We went into business together. And when he died, well, it was rough for all of us. It really hit Shannon the hardest. They were so close, and well, she never got over his death. She had always been an introvert, but after Rusty died, she completely withdrew from the world. I just felt it was important to keep in contact with her. But it wasn't always easy."

"How do you mean?" Brian asked.

"It was hard seeing her withdraw more and more each year.

When we talked on the phone, all she wanted to talk about was some new idea she had to find Rusty's killer. It's why the phone calls tapered off, and I kept to short, brief emails. I wanted to let her know I was still there for her, but I needed to move on after Rusty's murder. I wanted her to move on, too. It was like reliving his death with every phone call. The police had no leads; the case had gone cold. But Shannon just kept rehashing it and rehashing it. I wanted to be there for her, but I am not a counselor, and honestly, that's what she needed."

Brian nodded. "I can understand that. Is there anyone who would want to hurt Shannon?"

"Wait a minute, you aren't suggesting someone murdered her? That's absurd. No one would want to hurt Shannon."

"How do you think she died?" Brian asked.

Charlie shrugged and said, "I assumed she had some sort of seizure or something, considering the way the kitchen looked, like she'd lost control of herself."

"Joe said it looked like poisoning."

"Yeah, Joe mentioned something like that when we were over there. But that makes little sense. I just can't imagine anyone would have a reason to kill her. If someone told me she died from poison, I would assume she took it herself."

Brian studied Charlie. "You think she killed herself?"

"Not by how the kitchen looked. I figure if someone uses poison to commit suicide, you'd find them in bed or on a sofa, like they were sleeping. Not on the floor in the middle of what looks like a food fight."

TWENTY-TWO

On Friday morning Lily slipped over to Marlow House and entered through the kitchen door, where she found Walt and Danielle sitting at the table, Walt drinking coffee and Danielle hot chocolate.

"Morning, Lily," both Danielle and Walt chimed, neither getting up from the table.

"Morning. Where are your guests?" Lily asked in a low voice after shutting the door behind her.

"Madeline's upstairs in her bedroom, and Finn's in his room," Danielle explained while Lily poured herself a cup of coffee.

"Have you figured out what the deal is with those two?" Lily brought her steaming mug to the table and joined Walt and Danielle.

"You mean, is he just her medium, friend or lover?" Danielle asked.

"Something like that," Lily said before taking a sip.

"Marie saw them kissing after they first arrived. And from what Madeline told me, they are a couple. But they did get separate rooms," Danielle said.

"I imagine it would be awkward staying at your former daughter-in-law's house with your boyfriend. Plus, you haven't seen each other since you moved." Lily gave a shrug and took another sip of coffee.

"And from what I understand, the acceptance of cohabitation of unmarried couples has only occurred in recent times. Considering Madeline's age, it might be uncomfortable for her to openly share a room with her lover," Walt said.

About to take a sip of her coffee, Lily paused a moment, looked at Walt, and said, "So you think they are lovers?"

"Most definitely," Walt said. "It's not only the kiss Marie witnessed. It's how they look at each other."

"Do I look that way at Ian?" Lily asked.

Walt turned to Lily and grinned. "You looked that way at Ian the first time you saw him through my spotting scope in the attic."

Lily giggled and set her coffee mug on the table. "So what did they say about the possible murder?"

"I didn't tell them what happened," Danielle said. "They never came back down last night, and this morning when I saw Madeline upstairs, it didn't seem the best greeting before coffee."

"You should tell them. Finn can channel that poor woman and find out what happened," Lily snarked.

Danielle started to say something and then froze as if a new thought had occurred to her. By Walt's expression, something had just occurred to him, too. They turned to each other, Danielle's eyes widening at the thought.

"We need to tell the chief," Danielle said, knowing Walt was thinking the same thing.

"Tell the chief what?" Lily asked. She frowned at Walt and Danielle, looking from one to another. "What is it?"

"The ghost we saw when Finn first arrived. It was Shannon Langdon," Danielle said.

"Umm, yeah, you guys said that last night," Lily said.

"But we didn't think about what we heard her tell Finn that first time," Danielle said.

"What are you talking about?" Lily asked. "Do you two suddenly read each other's minds?"

"By what Shannon said to Finn, she knew him," Walt said.

UPON ARRIVING at the police station on Friday morning, Brian grabbed a cup of coffee in the break room and headed to the chief's office. He found him there on the phone. After taking a seat in a chair facing the desk, he waited for the chief to finish his phone call. When MacDonald finally hung up, he picked up his cup of coffee, looked over his desk to Brian, and said, "It was poison. I need to tell Joe."

MacDonald took a drink of his coffee, set the mug back on his desk, and made another phone call.

"How was it administered?" Brian asked after the chief finished his call.

"It's between the pecan pie and cranberry sauce," the chief said, and then he took a drink of his coffee.

"They were both poisoned?" Brian asked.

The chief set his cup on the desk and leaned back in the chair. "When the food landed on the floor, the pecan pie landed first, with the cranberry sauce on top of it. They can't really tell if one contaminated the other, or if they both contained poison before they fell, especially since the victim walked through it before falling. She had some of the pecan pie and cranberry sauce on her shoes."

"We have another twist in this case," Brian said.

"What's that?"

"It appears Shannon and the medium staying at Marlow House might have been acquainted. And it's possible he saw her yesterday morning," Brian said.

"Really? How did you find that out?"

"Heather called me after Danielle called her." Brian then told him of the ghost who'd visited Marlow House and tried talking to Finn, and how they now realized it had been Shannon's ghost. "Danielle was going to call you, but she called Heather first, who said she'd pass it on to me, and I'd tell you."

"Before we interview this medium—" the chief began, only to be cut off by Brian.

"Heather insists he's a fake, not a real medium," Brian said.

"Which is why we need to get a little more information before we interview our fake medium. At the moment, the only thing linking him to our victim is the victim's ghost."

"When she first showed up and started talking to him, they assumed it probably wasn't someone he knew personally, but a spirit reaching out to a famous medium. Maybe she had followed him here. But if she recently died, how did she find him? And something she said made it sound like they might have seen each other that morning."

The next moment, a knock came at the office door. The chief shouted, "Come in."

The door opened. Joe walked into the office and said, "I finally got ahold of Eden."

"How did she take it?" the chief asked.

"Honestly, she didn't sound that surprised," Joe said as he sat down. "I guess I expected a different reaction."

"From what I remember of Eden Langdon, she kept things close to the vest. I wouldn't read too much into it," Brian said.

"Considering her cousin's age, I would think her death would come as a shock," the chief said.

"When I told her the cause of death was poisoning, she immediately jumped to the conclusion she committed suicide. She even said she had worried something like this would happen."

"WHERE'S LILY?" Kelly asked when she walked into Ian's living room with him on Friday morning, Sadie trailing behind them, her tail wagging.

"She's across the street at Marlow House. Want a cup of coffee?"

"No, thanks. I'm coffee'd out." Kelly sat on the sofa next to where Connor played on the floor with his trucks. He handed her a toy truck.

"How are you doing after last night?" Ian asked as he sat down in his chair.

Kelly moved to the floor with Connor and began pushing around toy trucks while she talked to Ian. "I felt sorry for Joe. He wasn't close to Shannon, even so, she had been the twin sister of one of his best friends. And poor Charlie, Joe said he was in total shock after they walked into the kitchen and found her."

"Not surprising."

"He just started doing random things, like trying to clean up the mess."

"From what I understand, they suspect foul play. Certainly, Joe didn't let him compromise the evidence."

"Of course not," Kelly snapped. "As soon as Joe realized what he was doing, he told him to stay put. The poor guy wasn't thinking straight. Joe says Charlie felt responsible for Shannon, like a big brother."

"How did you handle all this? Must not have been a pretty scene," Ian said.

"I had never met her, so it wasn't like I found a friend, like for Joe and Charlie. This may sound horrible, but I found it rather fascinating. It could make an interesting piece. A who-done-it. Recluse murdered in her own home, and why?"

"Are you going to blog about it?" Ian asked.

Kelly shrugged. "Not sure. But you know what sucks?"

"You mean besides a young woman being murdered?"

"The chief made Brian lead on the case, not Joe. He says Joe is too close to it."

Ian shrugged. "He has a point."

"Brian's too close to the case too," Kelly countered.

"How do you figure that?"

"Because he used to date one of the suspects," Kelly said. "Joe told me last night."

"Who did he date?" Ian asked.

"Her cousin, Eden Langdon. She's the prime suspect. After all, she has the most to gain by her cousin's death. The house she lives in belongs to her and Shannon. What do you want to bet Eden is Shannon's sole beneficiary? With her cousin gone, Eden now owns not just a hundred percent of the house she lives in, but now she owns the house next door. And I know what houses go for in Frederickport these days. That is a lot of money. Who else would have a motive? And what about opportunity? From what I understand, she was the only person Shannon regularly saw. Eden had access to Shannon's house; she could easily poison something in her refrigerator that she knew she would eat over Thanksgiving. And then, while she is out of town, establishing an alibi, her cousin conveniently dies."

"If all that is true, I don't think leaving town would be much of an alibi."

"Exactly!" Kelly said.

LATER, on Friday morning, Walt, Danielle, Finn, and Madeline sat around the dining room table at Marlow House, preparing to eat breakfast. Earlier that morning, before the guests came downstairs, Walt had removed two leaves from the dining room table, making it considerably smaller.

Danielle served quiche she'd prepared the day before, which only required reheating in the oven before serving. Side dishes included fruit and Old Salts cinnamon rolls. They enjoyed small talk during the meal, and it wasn't until they began eating a dessert of cinnamon rolls while some at the table enjoyed a second cup of coffee before the topic of the murder came up.

"Your breakfast was as delicious as your Thanksgiving feast," Madeline said as she pulled a cinnamon roll in half. "But last night, I didn't realize how tired I was. After I came upstairs, I lay down, thinking it would just be a few minutes, and I fell fast asleep. When I woke up, it was after ten!"

"I know what you mean," Finn agreed. "I did the same thing. I suspect we were more tired than we realized after that flight from Hawaii on Wednesday."

Madeline nodded in agreement and took a bite of her roll.

"Last night, after you retired to your room, I'm afraid we had a sad turn of events," Danielle said.

"What happened?" Madeline asked.

"After Joe and Kelly left here, they went with Charlie to visit an old high school friend of Charlie's and Joe's. When they got to her house, they found her in the kitchen. Dead."

"Dead?" Madeline gasped.

"Oh my, what happened?" Finn asked as he picked up his cup of coffee to take a sip.

Danielle looked at Finn. "We don't know yet. Her name was Shannon Langdon."

Finn choked on his coffee.

TWENTY-THREE

After breakfast on Friday morning, Danielle was halfway up the stairs to the attic when she remembered they had recently moved to the master bedroom on the second floor. Inwardly groaning, she turned around and started back to the second floor. When she got there, she found Walt standing by their bedroom door, looking at her curiously.

"I thought you said you were going to our bedroom?" Walt asked.

Walking toward Walt, Danielle shook her head in disgust. "I was. That was the second time I've done that."

"You forgot we changed rooms?" Walt teased as he opened their bedroom door for her.

"I can't believe I did that," Danielle grumbled as she walked into their room, Walt following. He closed the door.

"If it makes you feel any better, I've done it myself."

"Really?" Danielle looked up into Walt's twinkling blue eyes.

He smiled down at her. "No, but if it makes you feel any better…"

"Oh, you!" Danielle giggled. She gave him a playful swat on the arm and didn't resist when he kissed her.

After the kiss ended, he said, "I lied. I actually did do it. Three times."

"Three times?"

Walt shrugged. "But you have to remember, that attic was basically my bedroom for over a century."

"True." Danielle let out a sigh, snatched up her cellphone off the dresser, and flopped down on the bed, kicking her shoes off as she did. They had made the bed that morning, yet she had no aversion to rumpling the bedspread and scrunching up the pillows along the headboard.

"Say hi to Edward for me," Walt said as he made his way to their private bathroom.

Now alone in the bedroom while Walt retreated to the bathroom with the door shut, Danielle called the chief as she leaned against the pile of pillows.

"Anything new, Chief?" Danielle asked after he answered the phone.

"Brian and Joe are going over to talk to Lucy's Diner. That's where some of the food came from," the chief said.

"I remember Charlie saying she ordered Thanksgiving dinner from Lucy's," Danielle said.

"Any chance you've seen her ghost again?" MacDonald asked.

"No. I assume Brian passed on Heather's message?" Danielle asked.

"You mean about our victim's ghost visiting your guest on Thanksgiving morning?" the chief asked.

"Yes. At first, we assumed they probably didn't know each other. He may not be legit, but he's a famous medium. Well, a famous fake one, but his fans believe he's real. Anyway, we thought it might be a case of a spirit searching out a medium to pass on a message, and since he's famous, she picked him. And because he couldn't really see her, she got angry."

"And now you think they might have known each other?" the chief asked.

"This morning at breakfast, I mentioned what happened last night. Madeline and Finn had gone up to bed before hearing about it. So it wasn't until breakfast this morning that I told them about Joe and Charlie finding an old high school friend's body."

"And how did he react?" the chief asked.

"After I mentioned her name, he spit coffee on my tablecloth."

"He spit on your tablecloth?"

"After he started choking on his coffee. This was after I told them what had happened and mentioned her name. He never said he knew her or that the name was familiar. But clearly hearing that name shook him up. Yet it also tells me if he knew her, he wasn't responsible for her death."

"Why do you say that?"

"Because it obviously surprised him."

"How did he explain the reaction?" the chief asked.

"He just said his coffee went down wrong."

"If he knows her, especially if he saw her yesterday morning, then he moves up on the suspect list despite his reaction," the chief asked.

"I think he knows something."

"Unfortunately, at the moment, the only connection between those two is from the victim's ghost. But I'll ask Brian to dig deeper into a link between our victim and your fake medium. In the meantime, the prime suspect is Eden Langdon."

"The cousin?"

"Yes. But it's early in the investigation."

"Madeline wants Finn to do a reading with Walt and me later this afternoon. We'll take that opportunity to see what we can find out about him, and if he's ever been in this area before. Remember, Shannon hasn't left that house in the last decade. So if they ever met prior to his visit to Marlow House, it had to have been before Rusty's death."

BRIAN AND JOE sat in a booth at Lucy's Diner, talking to the restaurant's manager, Rod Wilks. Joe and Brian sat quietly while Rod inspected photographs the officers had handed him.

"That looks like our containers. That's our logo," Rod said, shaking his head in disbelief. He looked through the photos again before restacking the pictures and handing them back to Joe. "You say she was poisoned?"

Joe nodded. "Yes. We found poison in the pecan pie and the cranberry sauce."

"Shannon didn't order pecan pie from us. But she did order cranberry sauce." Again, Rod shook his head in disbelief. "It couldn't be the cranberry sauce. At least, not what she got from us."

"The only cranberry sauce at the house came from the container with your logo," Brian said.

"You said it was also in the pecan pie? I don't understand." Rod frowned.

"As you can see in those photos, the food fell on the floor, and the cranberry sauce landed in the pecan pie. After they removed it for the lab, it's hard to tell where the poison originated," Brian explained. "When the autopsy is complete, they may have a more definitive answer."

"Like I said, it wasn't from the cranberry sauce. We have nothing on the premises that contains any kind of poison. You are welcome to look," Rod said.

"We will," Joe said.

"In fact, we only use all natural cleaning products. Nothing toxic."

"What about rat or ant poison?" Brian asked.

"Nope. We never buy that stuff. We use peppermint oil."

"Peppermint oil?" Joe frowned.

Brian looked at Joe and said, "Peppermint oil helps keep critters away. Heather uses it."

Joe looked back to Rod and asked, "Did Shannon order food here a lot?"

"Probably once a week. Sometimes her cousin, Eden, would pick it up, and sometimes we'd deliver it."

"Who delivered Shannon's Thanksgiving order?" Brian asked.

"I did. And I'm the one who put the order together. So if she got poisoned from our food, I'm the one who did it."

"Are you confessing to murdering Shannon Langdon?" Brian asked.

"Of course not," Rod snapped. "All I meant, she wasn't poisoned from our food because I prepared her order and took it to her. And I sure as heck didn't put anything in her cranberry sauce. Aside from our breakfast orders, the only thing we prepared yesterday was a traditional Thanksgiving dinner. You know, with turkey, stuffing, the works. Something like that is not prepared one order at a time. The cranberry sauce I put in the container for Shannon, it came from the same batch that went out to all our other

Thanksgiving customers yesterday. Have you heard of anyone else being poisoned in town?"

"No," Brian admitted. "How well do you know Shannon Langdon?"

Rod shrugged. "I didn't. Not really. I moved to Frederickport six years ago."

"That was after Shannon stopped leaving her house," Joe noted.

Rod nodded. "Her cousin, Eden, comes in here. After I first moved to town, she told me about Shannon. I felt sorry for her. But I've never met her."

"Are you saying yesterday was the first time you delivered food to her?" Brian asked.

Rod shook his head. "No. I've dropped orders off at her house many times. But when she orders something, she puts it on her credit card. Her instructions are for us to drop it off by her front door, ring her bell, and then leave. That's what I did yesterday. Like I always do."

"And she didn't open her door while you were there?" Joe asked.

"No. I dropped it off and drove away. I suppose she could have opened her door and took the food inside when I walked back to my car. But you can't see her front door from the street, so I have no idea when she brought the food in her house."

MADELINE HAD WANTED Danielle and Walt to meet with her and Finn right after breakfast for the reading. But Danielle used the excuse Walt needed to email his agent that morning. Danielle wished to delay the reading. They then agreed to meet in the Marlow House library at noon. This gave Danielle time to call the chief, and for her and Walt to discuss their game plan to find out as much as they could about Finn and if he had a link to Shannon Langdon.

When Walt and Danielle first walked into the library, they found their two guests standing in front of the portraits of Walt and Angela Marlow. While Madeline and Finn had already seen the portraits, this was the first opportunity they had to give them a close look.

Madeline glanced over at Walt and Danielle as they walked into the room. "It really is uncanny how much you look like him," Madeline told Walt.

"Those are the reproductions," Danielle said. "The original portraits are in the local museum." She and Walt now stood next to Madeline and Finn, their gaze also on the two portraits.

"Yes, I read all about it before coming here," Madeline said. "I can't believe how much has happened to you since you moved to Oregon."

Danielle glanced at Walt and smiled. "Yes, it has been a constant adventure."

"She was beautiful," Finn noted, giving a nod to the portrait of Angela.

"From what I read, it was only skin deep." Madeline looked at Danielle and asked, "Do you really believe she conspired with her brother to murder the original Walt Marlow?"

"Yes, I do," Danielle said.

Madeline looked back at the portraits and said, "I asked Finn if he could feel Walt Marlow's spirit here. Wouldn't it be exciting if he came through?"

"Yes… yes it would." Danielle looked curiously at Finn, wondering if he would suddenly start channeling Walt.

"I don't believe Walt Marlow and his wife have anything to say," Finn said.

"How do you know?" Danielle asked.

Finn turned from the portraits and shrugged. "I can't just summon up spirits at will. I don't do seances, and I heartily discourage Ouija boards. Spirits only come through if they have a message they need to convey."

"So Walt Marlow has nothing to say?" Walt asked.

Finn grinned at Walt. "Not that Walt Marlow. I don't know about you."

Walt returned Finn's grin and then motioned to the nearby loveseat and chairs. "Why don't we sit down?"

A moment later, the four each took a seat, with Walt and Danielle in the love seat and Finn and Madeline sitting in the chairs facing them.

"This isn't your first visit to Oregon, is it?" Danielle asked Finn.

"Finn's career started in Oregon," Madeline answered for him.

Finn flashed a smile to Madeline and looked back at Walt and Danielle.

"Does this mean you're from Oregon?" Danielle asked.

Finn shook his head. "No. In the beginning I gave readings to close friends, but it wasn't my job. In fact, I never imagined this would become the career it has. I had just quit my job in California when a friend convinced me to come stay with him in Oregon. He arranged some small gatherings where I gave readings, and well, one thing led to another, and here I am."

"How long did you stay in Oregon?" Danielle asked.

"Just about five months. Things took off, got a little crazy, and before I knew it, I had bookings in other states."

"How long ago was this?" Walt asked. "When you lived in Oregon?"

"I can't really say I lived in Oregon. I just stayed here for a few months. But it has been about ten years since I was last here."

"Where about in Oregon?" Danielle asked.

"Portland. This is the first opportunity I've had to visit your charming town. In fact, when I was in Oregon, I saw little outside of Portland."

TWENTY-FOUR

"There is someone here impatiently waiting for us to finish what he calls small talk," Finn said with a chuckle.

Madeline looked at Finn. "A spirit is here?"

"He's been here most of the time." Finn flashed Madeline a gentle smile.

"Lucas?" Madeline asked.

Finn nodded.

Madeline looked at Walt and said, "I hope this doesn't make you uncomfortable."

"I find it rather interesting," Walt said.

Madeline looked at Finn. "Before you begin, I would like to say something to Walt and Danielle." She turned to Walt and Danielle, took a deep breath, exhaled, and said, "One reason we came was because of Lucas. It was something he wanted—to reach out not just to Danielle, but to Walt." She looked back at Finn and smiled, as if telling him he could now continue.

Finn looked to Walt and Danielle and said, "Lucas is telling me he wanted his mother to come here because he felt it was important to bring her and Danielle back into each other's lives. He says Danielle was always like a daughter to his mother."

"It's true," Madeline whispered as she dabbed the corners of her eyes with a piece of tissue.

"He tells me that because of the circumstances of his death, it caused a rift between Danielle and his mother, which was not their fault, but his. Does that make sense?" Finn asked.

"There wasn't a rift between us," Danielle argued.

Finn smiled and said, "Lucas tells me you were always particular about choosing the right words. He says it's something you obsessed over in your business. Does that make sense?" Finn asked Danielle.

"Well, he did used to say that." Danielle looked at Madeline and said, "I'm sure you used to hear him say that a lot."

Finn chuckled. "I didn't bring that up as a validation that he is, in fact, here. And while Madeline never mentioned that to me—"

"I didn't," Madeline insisted.

"The reason I bring it up is that Lucas finds amusement that you take offense to the word rift. He says it's very typical of you," Finn said.

Danielle frowned but did not reply.

"Lucas said he didn't mean a rift like you two had an argument. He just meant that because of his actions, you two drifted apart," Finn explained.

"Okay…" Danielle muttered.

"Lucas says you need each other. His mother lost her only child, and both Danielle and Walt have lost both their parents. He hopes you can be part of each other's lives in a significant way."

Madeline looked sheepishly at Walt and Danielle. "I am touched by Lucas's intentions, but I promise I don't intend to intrude on your life more than I already have this weekend. Lucas was so insistent we come here, and he wanted a reading. But I understand you two are starting a new life together, with a baby on the way, and I imagine the last thing you want is Danielle's former mother-in-law to impose on your life. It really is enough that we can share this weekend."

"Your son is rolling his eyes at you," Finn said.

"He rolls his eyes too?" Walt asked, looking over to Danielle.

"He tells me he picked up the habit from Danielle," Finn told Walt. "He's telling me that Walt and Danielle need Madeline as much as she needs them. He says his mother has a lot of love to give."

"Oh my." Madeline sniffled and dabbed the corners of her eyes again with the tissue.

Finn looked at Danielle. "Lucas knows you have forgiven him. He also knows that Walt is your soul mate, and he's okay with that. And he is also telling me he knows Walt's secret, but he is not free to disclose it to me or his mother. He tells me only a small circle of your friends know the secret. Does that make any sense to you?" Finn asked.

ACROSS TOWN, Charlie and Joe sat together at Beach Taco, waiting for their order. Charlie had called Joe earlier that day, asking if Joe could get away from work during lunchtime and meet with him.

"Any news on Shannon?" Charlie asked.

"She was definitely poisoned."

"Oh my God," Charlie muttered, shaking his head in disbelief. "Have you gotten in touch with Eden? I did what you said and didn't try contacting her. I left it to you."

"Yes. She's flying into Portland this afternoon and then driving back to Frederickport. She initially assumed it was suicide when I told her."

"That's understandable, considering Shannon's mental state. Yet considering the condition of that kitchen, it looks like someone was with her when she died. That would suggest murder, not suicide, but it also takes Eden off the suspect list since she was in California," Charlie said. "That's assuming the coroner has the time of death sometime on Thanksgiving Day."

"We don't think it's suicide, but we suspect she was alone when she died," Joe said.

Charlie frowned. "How can you say that?"

"The only footprints in any of that mess were Shannon's and ours," Joe explained. "The only fingerprints on any of the to-go containers were Shannon's and the manager of Lucy's Diner, who prepared and delivered the order. Considering the amount of food on the floor in the kitchen, there should have been some other footprints had there been someone with Shannon, but there wasn't. Nothing suggests someone recently wiped up the floor."

"So she just threw the food on the floor?" Charlie frowned and added, "But I suppose it could mean it was suicide after all."

"Why do you say that?" Joe asked.

Charlie shrugged. "Someone takes their own life. It's like screw this world. They are angry. And angry people throw things. It could just be part of it all."

Joe shook his head. "No. We don't think that's what happened. The coroner says it looks like Shannon went into convulsions before she died, and she reached out to hold on to something, grabbed hold of the tablecloth instead of the table, and ended up pulling all the food onto the floor."

"How did she get the poison? What was it in?" Charlie asked.

"We have two potential sources, but I'm afraid I can't say at this time."

Charlie nodded. "I understand. I guess this means Eden isn't off the suspect list. She could have tampered with something in Shannon's refrigerator before she left for California."

"True. But if the coroner can make a final determination on which food someone tampered with, we can narrow down potential suspects."

"You say that like you actually have suspects."

"The person closest to the victim is always scrutinized. That would be Eden. But if the tests prove the poison came from the food delivered on Thursday, that would eliminate Eden. Unless, of course, she had an accomplice."

Charlie leaned back in his chair and sighed. "Honestly, I don't see Eden as the killer. On the surface she has motive, but considering how she has always looked after Shannon since their grandmother died, and she's a nice lady. No, she had nothing to do with Shannon's death. I can't believe it."

"What do you mean motive?" Joe asked.

Charlie shrugged. "No more motive than I had for killing my mother."

"Your mother died of cancer," Joe reminded him.

"True. But I was going to inherit her house. Does that mean I killed Mom? Of course not. And if someone else had killed Mom instead of the cancer, it still wouldn't mean it was me, even with me inheriting her house."

"So you're saying Eden inherits Shannon's house?" Charlie asked.

"Yes, I don't imagine it's a big secret. She also inherits the other half of the house she and Shannon inherited from their grand-mother. But there is no way Eden would kill someone for money. She's not that type of person."

"We found two sets of fingerprints in the kitchen—specifically on the refrigerator—that did not belong to Shannon or to us. I assume one set belongs to Eden, since she was practically the only person to visit Shannon. But it's possible someone like a repairman recently visited the house, which we need to discuss with Eden."

"Or the other set belongs to the killer," Charlie suggested.

"Possibly. But would a killer really be so careless to leave finger-prints on the refrigerator if he somehow got into the house and poisoned her food?"

Charlie let out a deep sigh and said, "No one would hurt Shan-non. I mean, why?"

"That's what we must find out. But hopefully there will be some-thing on Shannon's computer that will help."

The next moment, someone at the counter called out their order number. Joe and Charlie walked up to the counter, picked up their orders, and then returned to the table.

Charlie was just adding salsa to his taco when he said, "When you mentioned Shannon's computer, I remembered something."

Joe looked up from his food. "What?"

"A couple of days ago, I received an email from Shannon. I didn't think it had anything to do with all this. Perhaps it does. I don't know," Charlie said.

"What kind of email?" Joe asked.

Charlie set his taco back on its wrapper and reached for his cell-phone. "Let me get it. I'm sure I didn't delete it."

A few moments later, Charlie handed his phone to Joe and told him to read it.

Hi. It's me. Tomorrow is my birthday. Of course, that means it's Rusty's birthday too. Can you believe it has been ten years since his death? Ten long years, not knowing who was responsible. That is finally going to change. I thought you would want to know.

I will be meeting someone on Friday. He'll be able to give me the answers. I can't say who he is, and why he hasn't come forward until now, but you might say he was there the day Rusty was killed. He holds the key to what really happened. The reason he hasn't come forward before, he didn't realize what he knew. I've been trying to contact him for a long time now, and he's finally gotten back to me and agreed to meet me. He doesn't know why I need to see him, and I hope when I tell him, it doesn't scare him away. But I have faith this will all work out. Rusty will finally get justice. As soon as I see him, I'll let you know what he says. Shannon.

"Shannon's murder is linked to Rusty's?" Joe said aloud, more to himself than to Charlie.

Charlie shook his head. "I don't know what to think."

"Why didn't you give this to me yesterday?" Joe asked.

"Honestly? I didn't think about it. You didn't keep in touch with Shannon like I did. You have no idea how delusional she had become over the years. This email is nothing new. And I really didn't think it meant anything. And it probably doesn't."

"Any idea who this person is she was talking about?"

"I have no clue."

"According to this email, he was supposed to show up today."

"I'm sorry, Joe. I honestly did not even think about it until just a few minutes ago. And chances are there was no person coming over."

"Why do you say that?"

"Like I said, she'd become more and more delusional over the years. It is entirely possible this person with all the answers is a figment of her imagination. And I really can't imagine anyone killing Shannon. If that kitchen got that way because Shannon had some sort of convulsion as a reaction from the poison, then who's to say the reaction wasn't something that occurred after she voluntarily took it? I hate to say it, and I feel guilty because maybe I could have prevented it, but I believe she took her own life."

TWENTY-FIVE

Twilight turned to darkness before she reached Frederickport. When she pulled up in front of Shannon's house, the full moon overhead lit up the street, yet no lights came from inside the house. After parking and turning off the ignition, she sat in the car and stared up at the dark building. A few moments later, she unfastened her seatbelt and reached for her purse sitting on the passenger seat. From it she retrieved her cellphone. After tossing the purse back on the seat, she fiddled with the phone, looking for the flashlight app. Once she found it, she opened the car door and got from the vehicle, cellphone and keys in hand.

When she reached the front porch, she immediately noticed the crime tape blocking the entrance. She pushed the tape aside and fitted the key into the doorknob. After unlocking the door, she stepped inside the house, but instead of turning on the overhead light, she used the flashlight app to light the way.

She closed the door behind her and stood in the dark living room, pointing the light from the phone toward the kitchen doorway. She made her way into the kitchen by following the light of her phone. Unlike the living room, it was not totally dark without a flashlight. A twinkling night light by the kitchen sink provided dim illumination. She walked to the refrigerator and opened the door.

The refrigerator's light turned on. Holding the refrigerator door open, she looked into the brightly lit area.

The next moment, the overhead light flashed on, flooding the room in brightness. She gasped in surprise and twirled around to see who had turned on the light.

"Eden?"

"Brian?"

They said at the same time.

Eden let out a sigh of relief, closed the refrigerator, and faced Brian. "Damn, you scared the crap out of me."

"This is a crime scene. What are you doing here?" Brian asked.

Eden glared at Brian. "First off, I didn't see any no-trespassing signs. And I have every right to come in here. And the second thing, the last time we talked, you said the cause of death had not been determined. So how can you call it a crime scene if it ends up being ruled a suicide, which I suspect it will be?"

"That's the third thing," Brian corrected.

Eden frowned. "What are you talking about?"

"The list you just gave me. You said the second thing, but it was the third thing," Brian returned.

"Why are you harassing me, Brian?" Eden asked.

"I'm not harassing you. You're the one who ignored the sign not to enter the crime scene."

"I didn't see any sign," she argued.

"You saw the tape. It was right in front of the door you came through."

She shrugged. "So? I just figured your people left it there, forgot to pick it up when they were done."

"There is a sign."

"It's dark outside."

"There's a full moon," Brian reminded her.

"What's the big deal?"

"I'm trying to figure out why you felt it necessary to come straight to Shannon's house after you got back in town instead of going home. And instead of turning on the lights when you got inside, you wandered through the dark house."

"I was using my flashlight app." She held up her phone for him to see.

"Why didn't you turn on one of the overhead lights?" he asked.

"Why does it matter? And how do you know I didn't go home first?"

"Because I've been parked across the street for over an hour watching this house. And from what you told me on the phone, I figured you should arrive back in town about now."

"You were sitting out there waiting for me?" she asked.

"No. I was watching Shannon's house."

"Why?"

"Because your cousin was murdered," Brian snapped.

"Seems like a waste of time to watch it now. Maybe you should have been watching it before someone murdered her."

"Now you agree it was murder, not suicide?"

"God, you're as irritating as I remember," Eden snapped.

"Why did you come over here?" Brian demanded.

Eden let out a deep sigh and looked Brian in the eyes. "This morning Joe call's and tells me Shannon is dead. I've gotten used to worrying about Shannon, and frankly when he called, I thought she had finally done it. She finally took her life. But on the phone, he suggests it might be murder. That is just too much to comprehend. So when I got back in town and pulled up our street, I found myself parking in front of Shannon's house, not mine. I... I couldn't believe she was really gone. That she is really dead. It had to be some horrible mistake, and if I just went into her house, I would find her here. Still alive."

"And you thought you'd find her in the refrigerator?"

AFTER BRIAN ESCORTED Eden from the house, he made her promise to come down to the police station in the morning for an official interview. She agreed and got into her car and drove it to the garage next door while Brian remained in the vehicle across the street, watching Shannon's house.

When they escorted Eden to the interrogation room on Saturday morning, she found Police Chief MacDonald waiting to interview her, not Brian Henderson.

"I assumed Brian would be here," Eden said when she took a seat at the table across from the chief. "Is he coming?"

"No."

Eden shrugged at his reply and leaned back in the seat. "Can I ask you a question before you start with your questions?"

The chief nodded. "Certainly."

"Brian said someone poisoned Shannon, claims it was murder. But are you sure? It had to have been suicide."

"Why do you say that?" the chief asked.

"Because no one would want to murder Shannon. At least not someone who's going to figure out a way to poison her. Unless it's some psycho stranger tampering with capsules at the pharmacy, and they don't care who they kill. But it isn't as easy to tamper with medicine off the store shelves as it used to be."

"Why are you so certain no one would want to kill her?" the chief asked.

"Isn't it obvious? She's been a recluse for years. Refuses to leave the house, distanced herself from all her old friends. She saw no one. She doesn't know anyone who would want to kill her like that."

"Tell me, when Shannon dies, who inherits her house?"

Eden's eyes widened. She stared at the chief a moment before saying, "I certainly did not murder my cousin. I wasn't even in town when she died."

"But you have to agree you had a motive," the chief said.

"You certainly don't intend to arrest me for my cousin's murder just because I might be in her will?" Eden asked.

"I am trying to get as much information about your cousin as I can, and the motives of those around her, so we can find out what happened," the chief said in a calm voice.

"As for my motives, I honestly don't know who Shannon's leaving her house to. It could be me, but knowing Shannon, it could be some charity like the March of Dimes or Saint Jude's. Now, she did own half of the house I live in. Our grandmother left it to both of us, and Shannon never made me pay any rent on her half. It was sort of a deal we had since she didn't want me to sell the house. Her half goes to me. But I certainly wouldn't kill my cousin for half equity. No way."

"If someone murdered her, and it wasn't you, then who do you think it could be?"

Eden had no immediate response and sat speechless for a few minutes while her hands fidgeted nervously on the tabletop. Finally, she said, "I suppose there were people in her life, sort of. But I can't imagine they would want her dead."

"For example?"

"There was Fred Skinner."

"Who is Fred Skinner?" the chief asked.

Eden shrugged. "I never met him. He's just someone Shannon knew in high school, and they sort of became pen pals a few years back. She never told me much about him, but it wasn't like they ever saw each other in person. He was just some guy she exchanged emails with."

"Anyone else?" the chief asked.

"There was Charlie Cramer. I understand he was with Joe when they found her body. Charlie was Rusty's best friend and business partner. Rusty was Shannon's twin. He was murdered ten years ago."

"Yes, I'm familiar with the case. Anyone else?"

Eden considered the question a moment before saying, "She'd have me mail letters to different people. Some wrote back. I know because I'd bring her mail in for her."

"Like who?"

Eden shrugged. "Different people. An occasional birthday card to someone she used to know, inquiry to the police in Portland to see if anything new had come up on Rusty's case, stuff like that."

"Did anyone visit her?"

"After Rusty's murder, Charlie used to come around and check on her. She became too much for him. Shannon could be intense."

"Intense how?" the chief asked.

"Always talking about Rusty and finding his killer. Not sure how she planned to do that by holing up in her house all these years. But she did spend a lot of time on her computer. Anyway, after a while, Charlie's visits became less and less frequent. I know they continued to exchange emails. And he'd stop in and see her when he came to town. I guess that's what he was doing when they found her."

"There was food all over the floor when they found her. We know most of the food came from Lucy's Diner. The food Shannon ordered for Thanksgiving. But there was also a pecan pie. They told me they didn't deliver a pecan pie."

Eden shook her head. "No. I brought Shannon the pecan pie on Wednesday before I left."

"SO YOU DIDN'T INTERVIEW your old girlfriend?" Heather asked Brian Saturday afternoon. The two sat together in a booth at Pier Café, waiting for Carla to bring their lunch order.

"She was never my girlfriend," Brian corrected. "We dated a few times. As it is, it does not thrill Joe that the chief put me lead on this case under the guise he's too close. It wouldn't look good if I then interview the prime suspect, whom I took out a few times."

"We both know the chief didn't make you lead because of any conflict of interest. It was about you knowing about us," Heather said.

"It annoyed Joe that the chief didn't ask Eden if Shannon had a habit of leaving her front door unlocked or not all the way closed," Brian said.

"Which would have been pointless since Marie opened that door."

Brian nodded. "Exactly."

"Is she really the prime suspect?"

"Unless we find something on this Fred Skinner, or something on Shannon's computer or old emails, I think Eden should get a good lawyer."

"And you don't believe it's possible she killed herself?" Heather asked. "She was a troubled girl."

"If she put something in her own food, then where is the source? We found no containers of poison in her house. No empty containers in her trash. It had to come from somewhere. But where?"

"I wish her ghost would show up again, and I could ask her," Heather said.

"Eden admitted to one thing," Brian said.

"What was that?"

"She said she made Shannon a pecan pie and gave it to her before she left for California."

Heather cringed. "Didn't the pecan pie have traces of poison?"

"I think that's what Eden was looking for in the refrigerator, the pecan pie."

"I think Eden needs an attorney," Heather added.

TWENTY-SIX

Carla had recently cut her hair and now wore it spiky on top. Instead of pastels, streaks of orange and red colored the top of her head, reminding Brian of a bird's crest. Heather assumed the new color scheme was in theme with fall or Thanksgiving, like her own nail polish.

"She looks like a bird trying to attract a mate," Brian told Heather as they watched Carla walk toward them, lunch plates in hand.

"Shh, she might hear you," Heather whispered with a giggle. "And it's the male who uses colorful plumage to attract the females, not the female."

Brian shrugged but made no further comment, as Carla was now within earshot.

"Okay, you have the turkey sandwich," Carla said to Heather as she set the plate in front of her. She then placed the other plate she had been carrying in front of Brian. "And you have the burger."

"Thanks, Carla," Heather said as she removed one slice of bread to add some of the mayonnaise to the sandwich.

"Only the tourists order turkey sandwiches Thanksgiving weekend. Or me since I didn't cook a turkey. Didn't you make a turkey?" Carla stood over the pair, her hands now resting on her hips.

Heather looked up at Carla and smiled. "Nope. We had

Thanksgiving dinner at Marlow House, so no turkey leftovers in the fridge. If Danielle didn't have guests this weekend at the B and B, I could have probably snagged some leftovers."

Without asking permission, Carla sat in the booth next to Brian, giving him a little nudge with her hip to move down the bench. Without comment, Brian rolled his eyes but quietly pushed his lunch plate down the table as he moved away from Carla, making room for her to sit down.

"I guess Marlow House reopened this weekend," Carla said excitedly as she propped her elbows on the tabletop and rested her chin on balled fists. She looked across the table at Heather.

"Yep, the B and B is officially reopened," Heather said as she put her sandwich back together.

"And I heard about Shannon Langdon. How someone killed her, and Joe and some other guy found her after they left Marlow House." She turned to Brian. "Do you know who did it yet?"

"It's still under investigation," Brian said, picking up his burger.

"I guess it all worked out for Eden." Carla leaned back in the booth. "Not that she meant for it to happen this way, but I guess she really will be moving."

"What are you talking about?" Heather asked.

"It's no secret Eden never wanted to settle in Frederickport, but Shannon was so stubborn, didn't want strangers living next door, and Eden couldn't afford to let the house sit vacant. She still had to come up with half the expenses," Carla said.

"I don't understand how Shannon could stop her cousin from selling her share of the house," Heather said.

"Because of the terms of their grandmother's will," Brian reminded her.

Carla looked at Brian and smiled. "That's right, you used to date Eden."

"We went out a couple of times, that's all," Brian said before taking a bite of his burger.

Carla looked back to Heather and said, "Eden always said if she had the money, she'd hire an attorney and challenge the terms in her grandmother's will. But she couldn't really afford to do that on a bookkeeper's salary. At least, not on what that construction company pays her."

"But you said something about it all working out for Eden?"

Heather said. "You mean because her cousin died, and she can now move?"

"Yeah, in a way. Last week Eden came in for lunch, and she told me she was going to California to spend Thanksgiving with a friend, and if it all worked out, she would come back and be packing her things and get out of the rain for good. She doesn't like Oregon. Too wet for her."

"She knew her cousin would be murdered?" Heather asked.

Carla's eyes widened as she stared at Heather. "Of course not! I like Eden. She wouldn't kill her cousin. She just had another plan to get out of here."

"Another plan?" Brian asked.

"Yeah. She's been trying to figure out how to get out of Frederickport without walking away from the equity in her house. That's a lot of money. She's had different ideas, but they never worked out before. I'm not sure how she was going to swing it this time, but it doesn't really matter, because Shannon's dead."

INSTEAD OF RETURNING to the station after lunch on Saturday, Brian met Joe over at the chief's house. Brian, Joe, and MacDonald sat at the kitchen table while Eddy Junior and Evan played video games in the living room.

"I can't believe if Eden planned to poison her cousin while she was out of town, she'd be telling people about it. Especially Carla," the chief said.

"She obviously didn't say she was poisoning her, just that she would move from Frederickport. Which I assume she can do now once her cousin's estate is settled," Brian said.

"Unless she's in prison," Joe quipped.

"We need to talk to Eden again," Brian said. "Find out what she meant when she told Carla she'd be moving."

"While you were at lunch, I found Fred Skinner. I thought the name was familiar," Joe said.

"Does he live in Frederickport?" Brian asked.

"Used to. He went to school with us, and he and Shannon dated briefly in our junior year. He was a couple of years ahead of us. But now he lives in Seaside, is married, and has two kids," Joe explained.

Brian arched his brow. "He's married?"

"Yeah, I got his number from Craig. Fred works for a company Craig uses. I talked to him for about twenty minutes. He was not happy when I called, and he begged me not to tell his wife he and Shannon had been pen pals. I believe his exact words were, what is the point of getting my wife all upset now that Shannon is dead?" Joe shook his head in disgust.

"Did you finish reading the emails they got off Shannon's computer?" Brian asked Joe.

"Yeah, pretty much," Joe said.

"How good of pen pals were they?" the chief asked.

"Doesn't sound like he was broken up over Shannon's death," Brian said.

Joe shrugged. "It was hard to tell on the phone. And he had already heard about her murder when I got ahold of him."

"So what about the emails between him and Shannon?" the chief prodded.

"From what I can tell, he sent the first email about five years ago. Said he had just found out about Rusty and wanted to give his condolences. He had been living in California and had just moved back to Oregon and settled in Seaside. After that first contact, they started exchanging emails several times a week. He never once mentioned his wife or kids. And Shannon never asked. They didn't sound like lovers in the emails, more like good friends sharing their innermost thoughts and fears," Joe explained.

"You can do that without mentioning you have a wife and kids at home?" Brian asked.

Joe gave another shrug and said, "But he has an alibi. His wife is from California, and they spent all last week at his in-laws' and just got back to Seaside late last night," Joe explained.

"Does he have any idea who might have wanted her dead?" Brian asked.

"He claims they never talked on the phone. Only exchanged emails. And I read all those. There is nothing. The only people Shannon ever mentioned to Fred were Eden and Charlie, and it was never anything negative," Joe said.

"We need to talk to Eden again," the chief said.

LATE SATURDAY AFTERNOON, Eden sat with Joe in the interrogation room.

"Yes, I said if things worked out, I would move after Thanksgiving. But I wasn't talking about Shannon dying. Heavens no! You can't seriously believe I killed my cousin. I took care of her all these years. I brought her groceries, shopped for her when she couldn't order something online. I spent time with her so she wouldn't be alone. I tried to get her help, but I would never kill her."

"What did you mean when you said if things worked out?" Joe asked.

Eden took a deep breath, exhaled, and then leaned back in the chair. She looked across the table at Joe. "An old friend from California invited me to spend Thanksgiving with her. She's been trying to get me to move back to California for a few years now, but she knows I can't afford to hire an attorney to contest the terms of my grandmother's will. But she knew someone who might help me, and she was going to introduce me to him. He's an attorney and the brother of her boyfriend."

"And what did he say?" Joe asked.

Eden shrugged. "I didn't meet him. We were supposed to go over to his house tonight, but I ended up coming back here. And frankly, I'm not sure he could have helped me, anyway."

"Why do you say that?" Joe asked.

Eden looked directly into Joe's eyes. "Because I'm not sure I could have dragged Shannon into court. Oh, I confess her refusal to let me sell Grandma's house drove me insane. But I also knew she couldn't help it. Shannon was broken, and I loved her." Eden looked down at her hands now folded on the tabletop. Momentarily closing her eyes, she took a deep breath.

"What was your relationship like, yours and Shannon's?" Joe asked.

Eden looked up to Joe. "I didn't grow up in Frederickport, but I loved visiting my grandmother here. And Shannon and Rusty lived next door. We'd play together when I came for a visit. We had so much fun back then. I didn't come as much when I was in high school. Like most teenagers, I wanted to stay home and hang out with my friends. Shannon and I sorta drifted apart. And then, well, after I moved to Frederickport, Shannon and I got to know each other again. I felt responsible for her. I never had a sibling. Our parents were gone, Rusty and Grandma were gone, and Shannon was practically my sister. As much as I loved her, it doesn't mean I didn't want my own life again. And it doesn't mean I killed her."

The door opened, and Chief MacDonald walked in.

"Joe, I need to talk to you a moment."

After telling Eden he would be right back, Joe left the room, shutting the door behind him.

"What's going on?" Joe asked. "I thought you said you weren't coming in today."

"I dropped the boys off at my sister's because I got a call from the coroner. I don't think Eden is the killer."

Joe glanced briefly to the closed door leading to the interrogation room and then back to the chief. "Why do you say that?"

"Because Shannon never ate the pecan pie."

"I thought the lab results showed traces of poison in the pie?" Joe asked.

"Yes. But it looks like it got contaminated after it fell on the floor. The results are back on Shannon's stomach contents. The coroner called me at home. No traces of pecan pie in her body."

Joe glanced at the closed door again. "Any news on those fingerprints we found in the kitchen?"

There had been two sets of fingerprints found in Shannon's kitchen after they found the body, and neither one belonged to Shannon or any of the people who had showed up when the body had been found. After Eden's return to Frederickport, they identified one set as belonging to her, and she had no idea who the second set of fingerprints might belong to.

"Nothing came up on the other set," the chief said.

"When we get a hit on those fingerprints, we'll have our killer," Joe said.

TWENTY-SEVEN

"Am I under arrest?" Eden asked when Police Chief MacDonald and Joe Morelli walked back into the interrogation room. She stood by the chair she had been sitting in a moment earlier.

"No," the chief said. "Thank you for coming in to talk to us again. I know none of this has been easy for you. We are very sorry for your loss."

Eden stared at the chief. Finally, she said, "Umm, thank you. I understand you're only doing your job."

"If you remember anything that might help us, please call," Joe asked.

Eden nodded. "Definitely. If someone murdered Shannon, I want her killer caught."

Together, Joe and the chief walked Eden down the hall toward the front exit. When they reached the front of the office, a woman walking from the entrance called out, "Eden!"

"Betty!" Eden called out before rushing to meet the other woman. When she reached her, they hugged.

"I am so sorry about Shannon," Betty Kelty said as the hug ended.

"Thank you. It was such a shock," Eden said.

When the two officers reached the women, Eden looked up and said, "This is my neighbor, Betty Kelty."

"Yes, I've met Ms. Kelty," the chief said.

"Hello, Chief, Officer Morelli," Betty greeted them.

"We stopped by your house," Joe began.

Betty turned to the officers. "Karen, my next-door neighbor, told me you talked to everyone in the neighborhood."

"Those who were home," Joe corrected.

"That's why I'm here. I just got back into town, talked to Karen, and thought I should come right down. If there is any way I can help."

BRIAN HENDERSON ARRIVED BACK at the station just as Eden was leaving and before they took Betty to the interrogation room. The chief left Brian and Joe to interview the librarian while he watched from the next room.

"On Thursday morning, I was supposed to go to Astoria to spend Thanksgiving with my parents. My sister and her family were coming down from Seattle and planning to stay for a few days." Betty sat at the table across from the two officers. "But when I woke up Thanksgiving morning, I had the worst case of food poisoning. On Friday morning I felt pretty good, so I packed up and drove to Astoria to my parents'. I didn't know Shannon had been murdered the night before."

"You didn't wonder about the police cars parked in front of her house on Thursday night?" Brian asked.

"My bedroom is in the back of the house, and I turned in early." She pointed to her right ear. "I wear hearing aids, but I had taken them off. A dozen sirens could have come down the street, and I wouldn't have heard them."

"When did you find out about Shannon?" Joe asked.

"I got back to Frederickport about an hour ago. Karen, from next door, came over to tell me what had happened after I pulled into the garage. I was shocked, especially because I had been home all day on Thursday." Betty paused a moment and then asked, "Are you sure it was murder and not suicide? Karen said she died from poisoning, and while I never met Shannon personally, well, the girl was obviously troubled."

"I'm afraid it looks like foul play," Brian said.

"There was that visitor she had. Shannon never had visitors except for Eden. But this wasn't Eden."

Both Brian and Joe perked up. "Someone was over at Shannon's house on Thursday?"

Betty nodded. "Yes. In fact, she had a couple of visitors that day if you count the delivery guy from Lucy's Diner. Shannon gets... got... a lot of deliveries."

"Please try to remember everything you saw on Thursday. Start from the beginning and take your time," Brian urged.

"I was sitting by my kitchen window, looking outside, debating if I could handle a cup of coffee. If I skip my coffee in the morning, I always get a headache. But I didn't want to throw up again. That's not any fun either." Betty let out a sigh and continued, "I noticed the guy from Lucy's Diner pull up. He's been there before, dropping off food. He walked up to the front door, and he left a few minutes later."

"Did Shannon answer the door?" Brian asked.

Betty shrugged. "I don't know. The front door isn't visible from the street. In fact, when Karen told me what happened, I walked across the street. Oh, I touched nothing, promise. But I was curious to have a look. I noticed the crime tape by the door. I couldn't see it from my house."

"Then what happened?" Brian asked.

"After the guy left the food, I took a shower. When I came back into the kitchen, about thirty minutes later, I poured myself a glass of water and looked outside again. Another car pulled up and parked in front of Shannon's house. A blue sedan. An older gentleman gets out. He's alone. He heads up the walk leading to the front door. I assume Shannon let him into the house. About an hour later, he comes back out, gets into his car, and drives off."

"Have you ever seen this man before?" Joe asked.

Betty shrugged. "Not sure. I didn't get that good a look at him. He had gray hair, tall, slender. The car wasn't familiar."

"Are you sure he was there for an hour?" Brian asked.

Betty blushed. "I confess, I was kinda curious. It isn't every day, or every year, Shannon had a visitor outside of her cousin. I waited and watched by the window." Betty's eyes widened, and she let out a gasp. She looked at Joe and then Brian and asked, "Am I in danger? Did I witness my neighbor's murder? Is he going to come after me next? I'd better go back to my parents'!"

AFTER BETTY LEFT the police station, Brian stepped into the break room and made a phone call.

"Hello, Brian," Danielle said when she answered her cellphone.

"Can you go somewhere where your guests can't hear this call?" Brian asked.

"I'm with Walt in the parlor. Madeline and Finn went out. What's up?"

"What kind of car are they driving?" Brian asked.

"Umm, a rental. It's a blue sedan. Why?"

Brian told Danielle about the conversation with Betty.

Danielle groaned. "It's bad enough Madeline hooked up with a con man; please don't let him be a killer."

"We have nothing to bring him in on. The neighbor didn't get a look at his face, only a tall man with gray hair. And even his car is not unique."

"Then he probably had nothing to do with Shannon," Danielle said hopefully.

"Except I can't stop thinking about Shannon's ghost," Brian said.

Again, Danielle groaned.

"Danielle, one way we might figure this out without bothering your guests is if we could get Finn's fingerprints."

"His fingerprints?"

"There were a set of unidentified fingerprints in Shannon's kitchen. If they belong to Finn, we know he's the man the neighbor saw, and we bring him in for questioning. You could give him a glass of water and then save the glass, bag it up, and let me have it," Brian suggested.

"Is that legal?" Danielle asked.

"It's your glass. I can't just take it. But you can give it to me."

While Danielle considered Brian's suggestion for a moment, she glanced around the parlor. When doing so, she saw it. Two coffee cups sitting on the end table by the sofa. "Where are you?"

"The station," Brian said.

"I think I already have his prints. I'll bring them to you."

"HEY, JOE, ANY NEWS ON SHANNON?" Charlie asked when Joe showed up at Charlie's Frederickport house on Saturday evening. He opened the door wider, welcoming his old friend inside.

"We have some developments." Joe walked inside, and Charlie shut the door behind him.

"Please tell me you arrested someone," Charlie said.

Joe followed Charlie into the living room. "We might be close."

"So what's going on?" Charlie motioned to a chair for Joe to sit on.

After both men sat down, Joe said, "You will not believe this, but those fingerprints we found in Shannon's kitchen, the ones we couldn't identify?"

"The ones on the refrigerator?"

"Yes. We found who they belong to. Finn Walsh."

Charlie frowned. "The medium?"

"Yep."

"What does Walsh say?"

"We haven't been able to talk to him yet. He and Madeline are out for the evening. And they won't be back until late tonight. Danielle says they went to Astoria. The chief prefers they not call Finn and ask him to come back early. It will give him too much time to come up with an alibi or leave the state."

"I can understand that. What do you need from me?"

"Can you think of any connection between Walsh and Shannon? Anything? According to Danielle, he lived in Portland for a few months around the time Shannon was still there."

Charlie leaned back in his chair and considered the question. "Actually, I can. I said nothing about it because I didn't imagine it had anything to do with her death."

"What?"

"I don't know if you remember me mentioning the other night

how Rusty took Shannon out to see a medium for her birthday right before he was killed."

"Yes, what about it?"

"After meeting Walsh, I was curious, so I got on my computer to do a little search. I wanted to see what medium they'd gone to that night. Don't know why, but it was bugging me. I remembered when they saw him and where it was held. It turns out my hunch was right; it was Walsh."

"Any other connection? It's been ten years since that reading," Joe asked.

Charlie considered the question and shook his head. "I remember afterwards, both Shannon and Rusty were impressed. They had gotten a reading. Not everyone does when they go to those things. Rusty was going to meet him for another reading, but then he got killed, and with all that happened, I just forgot about Walsh."

"Thanks, Charlie. Something obviously happened back then."

Charlie looked up at Joe and frowned. "You don't think this guy had something to do with Rusty's death, do you?"

"Didn't the police back then say his death was likely linked to a series of break-ins, and after they killed him, the break-ins stopped?"

"Yes. Are you suggesting Walsh was somehow involved in the break-ins? I can't believe this is anything other than some coincidence."

Joe glanced at his watch and then stood up. "I need to get going. I promised Kelly I'd be home for dinner."

"What about Walsh?"

"Danielle called Madeline, asking her when they thought they might be back. She made the pretense she was meeting friends at Pearl Cove and wanted to make sure Finn and Madeline could get back into the house when they returned to Frederickport. They said not to worry, they wouldn't be back until after ten. They were going to a movie."

"I guess Danielle isn't really going to Pearl Cove," Charlie said.

"No, they are. With Danielle's money, they can go out to dinner every night. I still don't understand why they reopened the B and B."

TWENTY-EIGHT

"At least we now know why Finn wanted Madeline to come to Frederickport," Walt said. "It had nothing to do with us." He sat in a booth next to Danielle while Chris and Heather sat across from them at Pearl Cove.

"Because he wanted a cover while coming to Frederickport so he could murder poor Shannon?" Heather said.

Walt gave a nod, and Chris said, "It sure looks that way. But why did he murder her?"

"That's what Brian would like to know. I wish her ghost would show up again," Heather grumbled.

"Eva and Marie looked for her spirit after they found the body," Danielle said. "And Eva's out looking for her now. But it's possible she moved on."

"I hope they find her; I'd really like to know why he killed her," Heather said.

"I'm just worried about Madeline. She's having dinner and a movie with a killer," Danielle said.

"Heather told me Marie was with Madeline," Chris said.

"Yeah. Not long after we found out those were Finn's fingerprints, Marie and Eva showed up. Finn and Madeline had already taken off for Astoria. So they went to find them. Once they did, Marie stayed with them, just in case Madeline needed her help, and

Eva came back to tell us they found them. Then Eva left for the cemetery. She was going to see if anyone saw Shannon's spirit lingering around her brother's grave," Danielle explained.

"This has to have something to do with the brother's death," Heather said. "That's what Brian thinks."

"Where is ol' Brian tonight?" Chris asked. "I figured he'd be joining us."

"Ol' Brian is working," Heather said. "He's doing some research on Finn for the interrogation in the morning."

"I'm surprised they're waiting," Chris said.

"They wouldn't have if Finn and Madeline hadn't already left for Astoria," Walt said.

"Are they searching Finn's room tonight before they come home?" Chris asked.

"No, because when Finn comes back tonight, they don't want him to have any idea they're onto him. But when they take them down to the station, they will. And the chief said they will go through our trash too, because Finn and Madeline were planning to leave tomorrow afternoon. When they get up in the morning, they may start packing before the chief arrives," Danielle explained.

"You think they'll find any incriminating evidence in their rooms?" Heather asked.

Danielle shrugged. "Who knows?"

"SORRY YOU MISSED dinner at Pearl Cove," the chief told Brian. The two sat in the chief's living room on Saturday evening.

"I can't afford to eat there, anyway." Brian sipped the beer the chief had given him. Both Eddy Junior and Evan MacDonald had gone to bed before Brian arrived, leaving the two police officers alone in the living room.

"I understand Chris always insists on paying," the chief said.

"True, but…" Brian gave a shrug and didn't finish his sentence.

"I get it. But consider it a perk of Heather's job. And if your situation were reversed, well, you don't want to be accused of being sexist," MacDonald teased.

"Hey, I am a little sexist," Brian confessed.

They both laughed, and the chief said, "Thanks again for

coming over to discuss the case. I didn't want to leave the boys with my sister again, and I didn't want to call a babysitter. Eddy keeps insisting he is too old for a sitter, but I hate leaving them alone at night."

"No problem. And this is a nice change from the office." Brian took another sip of his drink and added, "And we don't have beer at the station."

Again, both men laughed. A moment later, the conversation turned serious, and the chief asked, "What did Joe find out?"

Brian told the chief about Joe's recent conversation with Charlie and then said, "Joe stopped over at Eden's and asked her if Shannon ever mentioned Finn. She said Shannon hadn't talked about him, but she had sent him letters."

"Letters?" the chief asked.

"Yes. Eden said that every few months Shannon would ask Eden to drop a letter off at the post office addressed to a Finn Walsh," Brian explained.

"Did Shannon tell Eden why she was writing him?" the chief asked.

"Not exactly. In fact, Eden didn't realize he was a medium."

"You mean that he claims to be a medium," the chief corrected.

Brian smiled. "Right."

"So what did Shannon say about the letters?" the chief asked.

"She started sending them about six or seven years ago, according to Eden. After about the third or fourth letter, Eden got curious and asked Shannon who he was. Shannon told her he was an old friend of hers and Rusty's, but she never elaborated. In fact, Eden said Shannon didn't seem to want to talk about it. Like it made her uncomfortable. So she didn't push it."

"And what did they find on Shannon's computer? Anything we can use?" the chief asked.

"Eden said Shannon spent a lot of time on her laptop, and what they found on her computer confirms that. She had been keeping files on Finn and on the robberies that had taken place around the time of her brother's death. Like the police, she believed those break-ins were linked to Rusty's murder. At least that's the impression I got from what they found on her computer."

"And Finn?" the chief asked.

"From the files and links she saved, it was as if she was tracking him. Like she wanted to know where he was, or where he was going to be," Brian explained.

"Any other interesting documents?"

"Not really. But remember how I said Shannon had been researching those break-ins and had a file about them on her computer?"

"Yes."

"Those break-ins all had the same MO. And they began a week after Finn moved to Oregon. I found out when Finn came to Oregon through my research, not Shannon's. She didn't start tracking Finn until a couple of years after her brother's murder. But she had kept information on the break-ins on her computer."

"According to Joe, the police felt Shannon's brother had been murdered by the same thieves who'd broken into other businesses in that area. They don't think murdering Rusty was part of their plan, which is why the thefts stopped so abruptly. They left the area," the chief said.

"And Walsh moved from Oregon a week after Rusty's murder," Brian said.

"You think Walsh had something to do with Rusty's murder?" the chief asked. "While he looks like he's involved in Shannon's murder, I don't know why someone like him would get involved with petty theft. Even though he's a fake medium, he makes a fortune."

"But he didn't back then," Brian said. "He wasn't making any money back when Rusty and Shannon saw him. He was just starting up. From what I've read, he was an orderly in a hospital when he quit his job and moved up to Oregon. It was a couple of years after Rusty's death that he was making significant money," Brian said.

The chief glanced at his watch. "Well, we should wrap this up. Is there anything else you should tell me before I interview Walsh in the morning?"

"Are you sure you don't want Joe or I to interview him?" Brian asked.

"I would rather the person interrogating Finn Walsh for the murder of Shannon Langdon not be someone he shared Thanksgiving dinner with."

TWENTY-NINE

"I feel so deceitful," Danielle said as she turned the strips of bacon in the skillet. Walt stood nearby, making coffee, while Marie watched.

"Why do you say that?" Marie asked.

Danielle stopped what she was doing and looked over at Marie. "First, I call Joanne and tell her not to come over today, giving some false excuse. And now I'm making enough breakfast for the four of us when Finn won't be eating here, and Madeline probably won't have an appetite after the chief arrests her friend."

"Her friend who is a killer," Marie reminded her. "Although he's quite the gentlemanly homicidal maniac. He must be one of those, what do they call them? Sociopaths?"

"Something like that," Danielle said while resuming her task.

A meow came from the open kitchen door. Walt looked down and saw Max sitting in the doorway looking at him, his black tail swishing back and forth. "Max says they're starting down the stairs."

"Showtime," Danielle muttered under her breath.

Marie smiled down at Max. "You make such a wonderful little spy."

A few minutes later, Madeline and Finn walked into the kitchen, each smiling.

"Good morning!" Finn and Madeline said cheerfully.

Walt and Danielle returned the greeting. Madeline looked at Danielle cooking bacon and said, "Oh dear, we were hoping to catch you before you started breakfast."

"You aren't leaving early, are you?" Walt asked.

"Oh, no, but we wanted to take you out to breakfast," Madeline said as Walt handed her a cup of coffee. She thanked him, and then Walt handed a cup to Finn.

"This is a bed-and-breakfast; we always serve our guests breakfast." Danielle flashed them a smile.

"What about lunch?" Finn asked. "Let us take you out to lunch before we leave today."

"That would be very nice," Walt said.

"Yes, it would." Danielle forced another smile.

The doorbell rang.

"I don't think anyone is going out to lunch today," Marie said.

Walt excused himself to answer the door. When he returned a few minutes later, Police Chief MacDonald was with him. Danielle stood at the stove, turning the sizzling bacon, while Finn and Madeline now sat at the kitchen table, drinking coffee. Marie hovered at the sidelines with Max, watching.

"Look who's here," Walt said, glancing from Danielle to their guests.

"Oh, hi, Chief," Danielle greeted him. She turned off the stove, moved the hot skillet to a cool burner, and picked up a dishtowel from the counter and began wiping off her hands. "Finn, Madeline, this is a friend of ours, Police Chief MacDonald."

Madeline and Finn each gave the chief a brief nod and hello.

"Chief, would you like to join us for breakfast?" Danielle asked, now removing the strips of bacon from the skillet to a plate covered with a sheet of paper towel.

"Sorry, Danielle, this isn't a social call. I was wondering if I could speak with one of your guests." He looked at the kitchen table and said, "Mr. Walsh, do you think I could speak privately with you in the hall?"

Neither Madeline nor Finn looked surprised at the request—nor upset. Finn stood and said, "Of course," and then walked into the hallway with the chief, leaving Madeline alone at the kitchen table.

"That happens more than you realize," Madeline said in a whisper.

"What do you mean?" Walt asked while Danielle frowned at her former mother-in-law.

"It's not the first time someone from the police has reached out to Finn for help with a homicide. Danielle told me that poor woman they found the other night had been murdered. Your friend is obviously hoping Finn can help him find clues to the murder. Unfortunately, he won't be able to help."

"Why is that?" Walt asked.

"Finn says after someone dies, they're busy with their life review, adjusting to their new reality. They aren't going to be reaching out to mediums. Too soon. And with murder, once on the other side, they see their killer in a different light."

Danielle arched her brow. "Really?" She glanced to the hallway, wondering what was going on. She assumed Marie would fill her in since she had left the kitchen with Finn.

WHEN POLICE CHIEF MacDonald asked Finn if he knew a Shannon Langdon, he expected him to deny it. He would then ask Finn if that was true, then why had they found his fingerprints in the murdered woman's kitchen?

But instead of denying knowing the woman, Finn said, "I can't say I knew her exactly, but I visited her on Thursday morning. I went over to her house."

Startled by his answer, MacDonald said nothing for a moment. Finally, he said, "You obviously know she's dead, or you would say I can't say I know her exactly, instead of knew her."

"Yes, Danielle mentioned it. So tragic."

"And you didn't think to tell Danielle or someone you had seen Ms. Langdon the morning she died?"

Finn shrugged. "I didn't see the point."

"You didn't see the point of telling someone you were one of the last people to see a murder victim? Perhaps you were the last person to see her alive."

"Are you saying she was murdered?" Finn sounded genuinely surprised.

"I'd like you to come down to the police station with me so I can ask you some more questions," the chief said.

"Certainly," Finn said, showing no reluctance to be interviewed.

FINN SAT CALMLY at the table in the interrogation room with Police Chief MacDonald while Brian and Joe watched through the one-way mirror in the next office. Madeline had wanted to accompany Finn to the station, but he had insisted she stay at Marlow House and have breakfast with Walt and Danielle. Finn felt confident he would return to Marlow House within the hour.

"Please start at the beginning," the chief said. "How did you know Shannon Langdon?"

"Like I said, I can't really say I knew her. I only met her that one time, on Thanksgiving morning."

"Why were you at her house?" the chief asked. "Why visit a perfect stranger?"

"Shannon began writing me about seven years ago. She wanted a private reading. We wrote her back and explained I only did private readings if I had an event scheduled in the area. She said she couldn't travel, and since I didn't have any plans to visit Oregon, we suggested a video reading."

"Like the ones on YouTube?" the chief asked.

Finn nodded. "But she insisted on doing it in person. Every couple of months or so, she would send us a letter requesting my current itinerary. She was persistent."

"So you finally came to the area?" the chief said.

"Yes. Frankly, I get thousands of letters a year from people who want to connect with their loved ones. My staff handles my correspondence. When I mentioned to Cameron I was going to Frederickport, he suggested I fit in a private reading. I had no events planned for my Oregon trip. This wasn't intended to be a business trip."

"Cameron?" the chief asked.

"He's my assistant. He's more familiar with my correspondence than I am. When I said we answered her letters, I was talking about my staff. I rarely read any of the letters that come in. She had mentioned she wanted to contact her twin. Cameron is also a twin. Her letters resonated with him because he's very close with his twin brother. He understood her need to talk to Rusty. So I contacted her a little over a week ago. Initially, I was to meet her on Friday, but it worked out that I could see her Thursday morning."

"And did you connect with Rusty?" the chief asked.

"First, let me say I believe my clients deserve their privacy. Connecting to a departed loved one is a highly intense and personal experience. I only share videos of clients who have agreed to share their experiences publicly. Shannon was not one who wanted to share her reading. In fact, she requested full confidentiality. Which is why I didn't mention to Danielle that I met Shannon on Thursday. At the time, I assumed she had died of natural causes, and I didn't want to violate her wishes. But now that I know she was a victim of murder, I'll tell you all I can."

"Did you connect with Rusty?" the chief repeated.

Finn shook his head. "No. He didn't come through, and that upset Shannon. Afterwards, she told me he had been murdered and that she wanted to find his killer. I explained to her that murder victims only name their killer if he or she is already a suspect."

"Certainly you knew her brother had been murdered before you saw her?" the chief asked.

Finn shook his head. "Why would I? I had never met her before we met on Thursday, and I don't do a background check on a client before a reading. And like I said, I never read any of her letters."

"Actually, you had met her before. Ten years ago, in Portland. Rusty and Shannon attended one of your readings."

"Yes, she told me. But I didn't meet them. There were probably two hundred people at that event."

"From what I understand, you did a reading for Rusty and Shannon that day and then arranged to meet Rusty later," the chief said.

Finn stared at the chief for a moment and frowned. "Not sure where you heard that, but it's not true. I'll be honest, I don't remember every person I ever read for. But when I met Shannon, she told me her brother took her to my reading as a birthday gift. When she told me when it was, I realized it was one of my first major events, so I remember it clearly. And Shannon also mentioned her disappointment at not getting a reading that day. We never met."

"Can you tell me how your fingerprints ended up on Shannon's refrigerator?"

"Certainly. When I arrived at her house, there were two paper sacks sitting on the front porch. Someone had delivered food from a restaurant. I helped her carry the sacks into the kitchen, and I opened the refrigerator for her as she put the containers away."

The chief considered Finn's answers for a moment and then asked another question. "When Danielle told you Shannon had died, why did you assume it was natural causes? She was a relatively young woman."

"While Rusty didn't come through, her mother did."

"Shannon's mother?" the chief asked.

"Yes," Finn said with a nod. "Spirits only come through if they have something they need to tell you. I don't think Rusty had anything to tell his sister. In fact, I think his silence was his way of telling her to move on. But that is only a guess on my part."

"What did Shannon's mother need to say?"

"She wanted Shannon to go to the doctor's and get a physical. From what Shannon confirmed, she hadn't seen a doctor since her brother's death. She never left the house. But Shannon's mother kept touching her left breast over and over and then showing me a hospital. I took that to mean she wanted Shannon to have a mammogram."

"Why wouldn't her mother just come out and say what she wanted to say?" the chief asked. "Why hand gestures or picture clues?"

Finn shrugged. "It's just how the spirits come through to me. It's how it works. But when Danielle told me Shannon had died, I realized what her mother was telling me was more urgent. Maybe she was trying to tell me Shannon had a heart problem. To be honest, I felt responsible for Shannon's death. I thought if I had gotten her to go to a doctor, she would still be alive. But now, now I understand it was murder."

THIRTY

Madeline helped Danielle clean up after breakfast on Sunday morning. Unbeknownst to Madeline, Walt stood behind Marlow House's garage, watching Brian and Joe sort through the rubbish. The officers intended to go through Finn's room next.

"You have disgusting trash," Brian grumbled as his gloved hands pulled another bag from the bin.

"I bet there is an easier way to do that without having to touch it." Walt snickered.

Brian scowled at Walt, both men thinking the same thing: how Walt's telekinetic powers would make the task less unpleasant. Walt flashed Brian a cheeky grin.

Joe, who leaned over a bag he'd just pulled from the bin, hadn't seen the exchange between Walt and Brian, yet he had heard Walt's comment. "I'd like to know what it is," Joe said while looking through the bag.

Walt chuckled in reply, and Brian mouthed a curse to Walt, which only earned him another chuckle.

Joe paused a moment and looked at Walt. "Danielle used to take her cans to the front of the house on Beach Drive. Certainly you don't haul the bins all the way to the street every week."

"No. When the trash company changed to these bins, they

rerouted the pickup for this side of Beach Drive, down the alley. And since we built the garage, it makes it easier," Walt said.

"I was wondering about that." Leaving the bag he had sorted on the ground, Joe looked back in the bin and spied a bundle of blue silk fabric shoved in the corner of the trash receptacle and not in one of the trash bags. He reached in and pulled it out. A moment later, he said, "I found something!"

Brian and Walt gathered around Joe as he showed them a bottle of rat poison wrapped in a silk shirt.

"I recognize that shirt," Walt said. He then let out a curse.

"Is it yours?" Brian asked.

Walt reached out and took hold of one sleeve, looking briefly at the wine stain on the fabric. "It belongs to Finn. He wore it on Thanksgiving."

Joe nodded. "I remember."

"Well, it looks like we have our murder weapon." Brian handed Joe an evidence bag.

"I really was hoping it was all some mistake," Walt said. "Madeline seems like a nice lady, and she's very fond of Finn."

"Better for her she find out now," Brian said.

THE CHIEF and Finn were still in the interrogation room when the call from Brian came. Finn sat quietly at the table across from the chief as the two lawmen talked. When the chief ended his call, he looked at Finn and said, "I'm afraid I'm going to have to hold you."

"Excuse me?" Finn frowned. He assumed the chief would take him back to Marlow House after he got off the phone.

Thirty minutes later, Finn sat in the interrogation room with Brian and the chief; he stared down at his wrinkled and stained silk shirt and the bottle of rat poison. Brian stood while the chief sat across from him. Also in the room was Marie Nichols, while Joe watched them through the one-way mirror in the adjacent office.

"That's my shirt. I spilled wine on it Thanksgiving night. I tried to get it out, but when I realized I'd stained it, I threw it away. But I've never seen that bottle of poison before."

"From what Danielle and Walt told me, and I also spoke to their housekeeper, Joanne, that bottle did not come from Marlow House,"

Brian said as he paced the room, hands on hips, his eyes never leaving the suspect.

"I certainly didn't put it there. It's true, I put the shirt in the trash, but anyone walking down the alley could have dropped that in the bin. I can promise you, you won't find my fingerprints on it."

"You're right there," Brian agreed. "You wiped the bottle clean before you wrapped it in your shirt."

"Why would I go to the trouble of wiping my prints off the bottle and then wrap it in my shirt? A shirt two Frederickport police officers saw me wearing?"

"He has a good point," Marie said from the sidelines.

"You were obviously hiding the bottle, so when someone from Marlow House put anything else into that bin, they wouldn't notice the bottle of poison," Brian explained.

"If I was the killer, why didn't I just wipe off the bottle and leave it at the scene of the crime?" Finn asked.

"I guess you didn't think of it at the time," Brian said as he sat down on the empty chair next to the chief.

Finn stared at the two officers, looking from one to the other and back. Finally, he asked, "What was my motive to kill a woman I had never met before?"

"There are some inaccuracies in your story," Brian said. "You told the chief you didn't tell anyone you saw Shannon on the day of her murder because you assumed she had died of natural causes. Yet, according to Walt and Danielle, Madeline didn't find it unusual when the chief came to talk to you today. She said the police often reach out to you, asking for help in homicide cases. Madeline was aware of Shannon's murder. How is it you weren't?"

Finn shrugged. "You'll need to ask Madeline and Danielle that question. The first time I was aware of a murder was when Chief MacDonald told me this morning."

"And according to what Shannon told a friend, you gave a reading to Shannon and her brother when you first met them ten years ago," Brian said.

"I didn't meet them ten years ago," Finn insisted.

"Why would Shannon have lied about it?" Brian asked.

"I have no idea," Finn said.

"Maybe you should ask her," Brian snarked.

Finn stared at Brian. Finally, he said, "I suppose you don't believe in mediums?"

"Oh, I believe in mediums," Brian said. "I just don't believe you're one."

"I had nothing to do with that poor woman's death," Finn insisted.

"From what I understand, when you first moved to Portland ten years ago, you didn't even have enough money to rent your own place. You stayed at a friend's, in his guest room."

"I don't understand your point," Finn said. "What does my situation back then have to do with now?"

"I think it has a lot to do with now. Right after you arrived in Oregon some ten years ago, there was a rash of break-ins close to where you were staying. They ended when you left Oregon," Brian said.

Finn frowned at Brian. "You certainly aren't talking about the break-ins Shannon felt might be linked to her brother's death?"

"So you know about that?" Brian snarked while the chief silently listened.

Finn looked at the chief. "I'll take that offer to see my attorney. This line of questioning is getting ridiculous."

WALT AND DANIELLE sat in the chief's office with him and Brian while Joe took Madeline to see Finn, with Marie tagging along.

The chief had just finished updating Walt and Danielle on his morning with Finn when Marie suddenly appeared.

"It's possible Finn didn't know about Shannon's murder. When I first told them about her death, I said nothing about murder. I assumed you didn't want that information released yet. But I told Madeline later, and it's possible she didn't tell Finn," Danielle explained.

"No way. She had to have told him," Brian insisted.

Marie looked at Brian and said, "Danielle, you need to tell Brian he was rather an ass when he was questioning poor Finn."

Danielle arched her brow at Marie. "Poor Finn?"

Since neither MacDonald nor Brian could see or hear Marie, they did not know why Danielle had just said *poor Finn*.

183

"Marie is here," Danielle explained. "She tells me Brian was rather an ass when questioning Finn."

Brian shrugged. "I was doing my job; I wasn't an ass!"

"You were too!" Marie gave Brian's right earlobe a quick pinch and tug.

"Ouch!" Brian yelped, grabbing hold of his right ear. "Dang it, Marie, that hurt! And the guy is a killer!"

"How do you know I did that?" Marie asked innocently, forgetting for a moment he could not hear her.

"Brian may be an ass, but he isn't completely stupid," Danielle told Marie.

Brian flashed Danielle a glare, and Walt snickered while the chief simply shook his head.

"Anyway, I'm not so sure Finn is a killer," Marie said. "For one thing, Finn didn't know Shannon had been murdered."

"Marie, how do you know that?" Danielle asked.

"Because I was listening to Madeline and Finn when Joe left. The two discussed it, and from what they said, she hadn't gotten around to telling him Shannon was murdered," Marie explained. "So he was telling the truth about believing she had died of natural causes."

Danielle repeated Marie's words for MacDonald and Brian. Brian silently listened, still rubbing his sore ear.

"And Finn has a point. Anyone could have put that poison in the trash after he threw the shirt away," Marie added.

"Marie, this morning you called Finn a homicidal maniac and sociopath," Walt reminded her.

Marie shrugged. "I might have been wrong."

Again, Danielle repeated Marie's words for the non-mediums in the room and then asked, "You feel he's innocent, don't you?"

"He just seems like such a nice man," Marie said. "You should have seen how he was with Madeline when he took her out to dinner and a movie. My husband could have taken lessons from him on how to treat a woman."

Again, Danielle repeated what Marie said.

"Yeah, a real lady killer," Brian snarked. He then thought better of his remark and quickly covered both ears with his hands.

"You do understand Marie could still tweak your ears even with your hands over them, right?" Danielle asked.

Frowning, Brian slowly lowered his hands and waited for another attack on one of his earlobes. It didn't come.

"Oh posh, tell Brian to stop being such a baby," Marie said.

Danielle didn't bother repeating Marie's words, and Walt asked, "So what now?"

The chief looked at Walt. "Finn has requested an attorney, and in the meantime, I'm trying to get ahold of his assistant, the one who handled all the correspondence with Shannon. If he verifies what Finn told us, we won't be able to hold him. There is no motive we can present to the DA, only speculation. Like Marie said, anyone could have put that bottle in the bin. It's all circumstantial. We'll need more before the DA would pursue this."

"He's guilty," Brian snarked. The next minute, Brian's chair flipped over, sending him to the floor.

"OH, DANIELLE, THIS IS HORRIBLE!" Madeline cried when she saw Danielle in the hallway of the police station. Danielle and Walt were just stepping out of the chief's office, and Madeline was being led down the hall by Joe after seeing Finn. The older woman rushed into Danielle's arms and received a comforting hug.

"We'll figure this out," Danielle promised after the hug ended. She gave Madeline a gentle pat on her shoulder.

"I don't understand how your friends could imagine Finn would do something like this," Madeline said. "He's such a kind and gentle man." She began to cry.

THIRTY-ONE

Danielle sat across the kitchen table from Madeline while Walt filled the kettle with water to make a pot of herb tea. He placed it on the hot burner. Marie had not come home from the police station with them but had instead stayed to see what was going on in the investigation.

"I promise I'll be here for you through this. Whatever happens," Danielle said.

Madeline's tear-rimmed eyes looked up into Danielle's hazel ones. "You think he's guilty, don't you?"

Danielle smiled softly. "I'll be honest, I don't know Finn as well as you do, so I am not sure what I think."

"He's a good man, Danielle," Madeline insisted.

"And the chief is a fair man. I'm sure he'll sort this out," Danielle said.

"That other officer, Brian Henderson, the one who was over here for Thanksgiving. He's not a very nice man. Finn told me how he questioned him. And your friend the chief just sat there and said nothing."

Walt carried two empty mugs to the table and set one by Madeline and the other by Danielle. "Ah, the good cop, bad cop?" Walt asked.

"More silent cop, bad cop," Madeline grumbled.

"Brian's not a bad guy. But when on a case, diplomacy is not his strong suit. Danielle has had her issues with him," Walt explained.

Danielle flashed Walt a smile and said, "Yeah, there was a time all I wanted to do was give Brian a good smack."

"He has Heather to do that for you now." Walt silently added, *And Marie.*

Madeline folded her hands on the tabletop. She took a deep breath, exhaled, and said, "I should probably get a motel room."

"Why?" Danielle asked.

"We obviously aren't leaving today. I'll also need to figure out what I should do about our flight."

"But why a motel? You can stay here," Danielle said.

Madeline shook her head. "No. I imagine you have other guests who've reserved the rooms."

"No, we don't have another reservation for two weeks," Danielle said. "And you will stay here, as our guest."

"I can't impose on you like that," Madeline said.

The kettle whistled. Walt picked it up from the burner, and while he filled the teapot with boiling water, he said, "Listen to her, Madeline. You will stay with us, and we'll both be here for you."

MADELINE HAD JUST GONE UPSTAIRS to take a nap when the landline rang at Marlow House. Danielle answered the call.

"May I speak to Danielle Marlow, please?" the male voice asked.

"This is Danielle Marlow; how can I help you?"

"I'd like to speak to one of your guests, Finn Walsh."

"Umm, I'm sorry. He's not here right now. Can I take a message?"

"Is Madeline Saunders there?" the man asked.

"Madeline is upstairs resting."

"Is Finn okay?" the voice asked.

"Okay?" Danielle muttered.

A noticeable sigh came from the other end of the call. "My name is Cameron Lowe; I'm Finn's assistant. I received a phone call this morning, and I never answer my calls from unknown numbers. I let them go to voicemail and screen them later. We get so many. I just went through my messages and have one from the Frederickport

Police Department saying they need to talk to me. Is Finn okay? There hasn't been an accident, has there?"

WHEN THE CHIEF and Lowe finally connected, the chief requested a video conference call; he wanted to see the man's face during questioning. Considering Brian's tendency to put witnesses on defense, and Joe's clueless nature regarding the spirits, which might impact the case, MacDonald decided it best if he interview the man. He would have preferred to interview Lowe in person. But a video conference call was his second choice.

The call would have taken place sooner had Walsh called Lowe from his cellphone, but Finn seemed quite willing to do what the chief requested, allow the chief a cold-call interview without informing Lowe of the questions. The chief figured this either meant Finn was innocent, or Lowe was in on the murder and prepared to back up Walsh. Which was why he wanted to have a video chat with the man, so he could see his expressions.

The chief began the interview with, "Tell me everything you know about Shannon Langdon."

"Shannon Langdon? Why?" Cameron asked. "I don't understand. What is going on?" Danielle hadn't told Lowe about the murder, or that they had arrested Finn. She'd just told him he needed to call the chief.

"Please just answer the question," the chief asked. "I promise, after you answer my questions, I will tell you everything."

Cameron let out a sigh, gave a nod, and then said, "She's wanted a private reading with Finn for the last seven years. Her twin brother died, and she wants to contact him."

"How did he die?" the chief asked.

Cameron shrugged. "She never said, and I didn't ask. I confess, over the years I was tempted to do a Google search on her, but if Finn found out, he'd be furious."

"Why is that?" the chief asked.

"When Finn does a reading, he doesn't want any information about the person. He says all that can really muck up a reading, and then he can misread what a spirit is saying. Plus, the less he knows about a person before a reading, then it's more difficult to be accused of faking. Although these days, with social media and how much people put out there, that's a losing cause. People always think Finn has checked the people out first. Which he doesn't."

"What else do you know about Shannon?" the chief asked.

"She told me she attended the first event he ever had. It was in Portland. That was mentioned in her first letter. She wanted to know if he was doing any more readings in Oregon, because she wanted to arrange a private reading. I wrote her back, explained how we schedule our events. But we had nothing in Oregon planned. I sent her the current schedule."

"You wrote her personally?" the chief asked.

Cameron smiled. "We get thousands of emails each month from people wanting tickets or private readings or just fan mail. We have staff who go through those emails. But we get some letters. The kind Uncle Sam's guy delivers. On actual paper. I don't normally handle those; I have staff for that. But I happened to be helping with the mail when Shannon's first letter arrived. A couple of people were out sick. I think it's because she mentioned her twin brother that got my attention. And by the way, I never told Finn Shannon had a twin."

"What did you tell her?"

"I wrote her back," Lowe explained. "I told her we had nothing planned for Oregon, but I sent her a schedule. And then a few months later, she wrote again, but this time sent the letter to my attention. Every few months she'd write me, asking the same thing, desperate to communicate with her brother, but not willing to travel. She wanted Finn to come to her. I finally realized she had agoraphobia."

"You wouldn't have saved any of those letters, would you?" the chief asked.

"Sure. We digitalize everything. You want me to send you her file?" Lowe offered.

"Yes, please. When did Finn become aware of her?"

"I never told him," Lowe explained. "Finn is very clear. Our job is to arrange readings and not to share any of the information someone has shared with us. You see, people are always so eager to talk about the loved one they want to connect with. That makes it pretty easy for the fakes out there to give convincing readings."

"You had to have told him about Shannon sometime," the chief said.

"Yeah, when I found out he was going to Frederickport. I thought, wow, that's not just in Oregon, it's in Shannon's town. I asked him to do the reading. Normally I would have arranged it, but he didn't know when he could fit her in, so he decided he would call her directly."

"Did he tell you what happened in the reading?" the chief asked.

"Sure, Finn called me when he got back that morning. He said her mother came through, not the brother. She was pretty disappointed. He also told me he understood why I was anxious for him to help her, because she wanted to connect with her twin. Finn knows how close I am to my twin brother."

"He didn't know Shannon wanted to connect with her twin brother before he saw her?"

"No, of course not. All I gave him was her name and phone number. Nothing else. He found out about the twin brother after she told him."

"According to someone who knows Shannon, she claims Finn did a reading for her and her brother at that event she attended in Oregon."

"She said that?" Cameron asked with a frown.

"Yes."

"Well, she certainly never said that to me in any of the letters. She mentioned the event she attended, and I remember it was his first major one. As for her getting a reading there, this is the first time I've heard that."

"Do you remember the event Shannon attended?"

"I started working for Finn about a year after that event."

"So you wouldn't have personal knowledge of him reading for them or not at that event?" the chief asked.

Cameron shook his head. "No. But you could watch the video."

"What video?" the chief asked.

"We always record Finn's events. You can find them on his YouTube channel. I watched all of them when I first started working for Finn. But that's been a long time ago and a lot of other events. Hard to keep them all straight."

CHIEF MACDONALD, Brian, and Joe watched the YouTube video of Finn Walsh's first major event in Portland ten years earlier. The chief had already watched the video once after going through the files Lowe had sent him.

"He didn't read for them," Joe muttered when the video ended.

"Do we know this is really the video from the event Shannon and her brother attended?" Brian asked skeptically.

"I do," Joe said as MacDonald logged out of YouTube and turned his monitor back around to face his seat while Joe and Brian sat in the chairs facing the desk.

"How can you be so sure?" Brian asked.

"Because I saw Rusty and Shannon in the audience. They were there." Joe slumped back in his seat.

"You guys can go through the file Lowe sent me. But it was just as he said. And those schedules he sent her, she obviously scanned them into PDF files, and that's what she had in her Finn file on her computer."

"But she didn't scan or keep any of the letters he sent with the schedules. At least we didn't find them on her computer or in her house," Brian noted.

"I wonder why Shannon lied about the reading," Joe asked.

Brian considered the question for a moment and finally said, "Perhaps Shannon was afraid her cousin would find the letters. Eden was already trying to persuade Shannon to get professional help. It's possible Shannon was afraid finding the letters would convince Eden she really was nuts and get her committed."

Joe frowned at Brian. "That might explain why she didn't keep the letters, but why lie about getting a reading with Rusty?"

"It wasn't a secret Rusty had taken her to see the medium before he died. Maybe she figured if she ever got the reading with Finn, the whole thing would seem less crazy if people believed she'd had her first reading before she became a recluse," the chief suggested.

THIRTY-TWO

Marie found Eva sitting on a headstone in the older section of the Frederickport Cemetery, gazing out into the distance. She wore an ankle-length gray dress of Edwardian fashion, with a prim laced collar and her hair pulled up into the style of the Gibson Girl, the drawing of Charles Dana Gibson, whom many said Eva resembled. Today Eva wore no hat or gloves or shoes.

"Eva, I knew I'd find you here," Marie said as she appeared next to the headstone.

Eva looked down at Marie and smiled. "I was about to come find you." She looked back over the cemetery landscape and said, "I was thinking of all the people buried here who've moved on."

"Has Shannon moved on? That's who you were supposed to be looking for," Marie reminded her.

Eva glanced briefly at Marie. "I looked. Unfortunately, I didn't find her. Yet one lingerer said she stopped by and visited her brother's grave. But she left before they could talk to her."

"Are they sure it was her?" Marie asked.

"They gave the same description as Danielle gave, so I have to assume it was her. Plus, the only grave she visited was Rusty Langdon's."

"Do you suppose she's moved on?"

Eva shrugged. "It's possible. And from what I understand, her brother never visited his grave."

"Are you sure?" Marie asked.

"According to those lingering spirits who take it upon themselves to greet new neighbors, they insist he never stopped by."

"Well, I suppose that happens."

Eva moved from the headstone to Marie's side. A moment later, the two spirits sat on a nearby bench. Marie told Eva all that had happened regarding the investigation of Shannon's murder.

"You seem to have a soft spot for our fake medium," Eva teased.

Marie let out a sigh. "I don't believe he's Shannon's killer, and I don't think the chief does either."

"I can't imagine he does if he's letting him go."

"Edward's no longer holding him, but he asked Finn not to leave town," Marie said.

"Can he make him stay in Frederickport?"

Marie shrugged. "I don't know, but Finn agreed, and they will stay on at Marlow House."

"Now tell me, why have you developed such a soft spot for our fake medium? Surely, it's not just because you're now convinced he didn't kill anyone."

"After I spent time with them the other night, I noticed how he treated Madeline with such respect and concern. And he has a charming sense of humor. While he may be a fake medium, his messages to Madeline comfort her. Is that really such a bad thing?"

"Marie, I find your sudden shift extremely out of character."

"Why do you say that?"

"You tend to be more... cynical. Unless, of course, we're discussing that grandson of yours."

Marie rolled her eyes. "Oh posh. You don't know what you're talking about."

"Shall we return to Marlow House so I can get a better look at this man?" The next moment, Marie and Eva vanished.

WHEN MARIE and Eva arrived at Marlow House, they found Finn and Madeline sitting at the kitchen table with Walt, while Danielle made a turkey sandwich at the counter.

"I really could have done that for you," Madeline said from the table, looking with concern over at Danielle.

"I'm fine. This is no problem at all," Danielle insisted. She cut the sandwich in half, set it on a clean plate, and added a handful of potato chips from a nearby bag. A moment later, she carried the sandwich to Finn and set the plate before him.

"Thank you, Danielle. It looks delicious." Finn picked up the sandwich and took a bite.

Danielle sat down in the empty chair between Madeline and Walt. It was then she noticed the two spirits who had entered the room—without a hint of glitter or snow. She flashed them a smile.

"You poor thing, they were going to starve you!" Madeline said, giving Finn a pat on one shoulder.

After swallowing his bite, Finn flashed Madeline a smile and said, "They weren't going to starve me. Chief MacDonald wanted to get me something to eat. I assumed I would be back sooner, so I didn't accept his offer." He took another bite after telling Danielle, "This is delicious, thank you."

"I still can't fathom they actually thought you killed that poor woman," Madeline said.

Finn set his partially eaten sandwich on the plate and looked over to Madeline. "When Chief MacDonald drove me back from the station, he was very kind. And I thought about everything more objectively, and I realized I can't blame them. After all, I was with her on the morning of her murder, and I told no one in Frederickport I had gone over there, not even after I heard she had died."

"Why didn't you tell anyone?" Walt asked.

Finn looked to Walt. "When I give someone a private reading, one not shared on my website or YouTube, I respect my client's privacy. A reading can be intensely personal. If I thought Shannon had been murdered, I would have gone to the police. There might have been something I saw that could help them find her killer. But I assumed she died of natural causes because of what her mother told me."

After Finn finished his sandwich, they all had chocolate chip cookies and then went into the library, the two spirits following them. Madeline and Finn sat on the small sofa, with Walt and Danielle across from them on the two chairs, and Marie and Eva sat nearby on imaginary chairs.

Madeline looked at the portraits and said, "I still can't believe how much Walt looks like his cousin."

"Yes, it is uncanny." Danielle flashed her husband a smile.

"I really would love to see the original portraits. Do they look much different?" Madeline asked.

"No, I doubt you could tell them apart. But since it looks like you're going to be here a few more days, you can go to the museum and see them," Danielle suggested.

Madeline smiled. "I would love that."

"Oh my," Finn blurted. Sitting up a little straighter, he stared across the room at Walt and Danielle. "This is… interesting."

Madeline turned to Finn. "What is it?"

Finn pointed to the painting of Walt and Angela and said, "A spirit just joined us. A woman. She's showing me a painting. It's large, like those two, but it's of a different woman." Finn then described the woman in the painting, along with her clothing.

"That sounds like your portrait," Marie told Eva.

Eva frowned. "It does."

"She's saying it's my daughter," Finn explained. "She keeps telling me to tell her daughter that she's with her. That she watches her."

"Who's her daughter?" Madeline asked.

Finn frowned. "I assume she's talking about the woman in the painting. But considering how she's dressed, she must be wearing a costume in the painting, or maybe it's a painting of her when she was a young woman." He looked at Danielle and asked, "Is perhaps one of your neighbors an elderly woman?"

"Umm… no… not that I can think of," Danielle said.

Finn shook his head. "I don't understand…"

"What is she saying?" Madeline asked curiously.

"She's pointing to the painting and keeps saying this is how she will always look. And now she's pointing to a necklace."

"Necklace?" Danielle asked.

"Two necklaces. A string of pearls." Finn paused and said, "Maybe they aren't pearls. Instead of white, they're lavender. No, she says they're pearls. Lavender pearls? The other necklace looks like rubies. She says it's her way to show she's really here. She wants her daughter to know she loves her and will be there for her when she comes home. But she understands it will be a while."

"Oh my," Marie muttered. She looked at Eva and noted the way the other spirit stared at the medium. "Eva, what's wrong?"

"My mother?" Eva said before vanishing.

"Eva?" Marie called out before she too vanished.

"WHAT JUST HAPPENED IN HERE?" Danielle asked Walt after Madeline and Finn excused themselves to go upstairs to rest. "And why did Eva and Marie just take off like that?"

"That's what I'm trying to figure out," Walt said.

"When Finn described Eva's painting and then mentioned a necklace, I had it all figured out," Danielle said.

"How so?"

"Before coming here, in researching Marlow House, he must have seen Eva's portrait online. After all, it's at the museum with your paintings. And then when he mentioned a necklace, I figured he was going to describe the Missing Thorndike. But instead of mentioning diamonds and emeralds, he goes with lavender pearls and rubies. He obviously got his gemstones mixed up. But I'm trying to figure out where he was going with all that mother and daughter stuff."

"He didn't get the gemstones wrong," Walt said in a quiet voice.

Danielle turned a frown to Walt. "Yes, he did."

Walt shook his head. "No. The Missing Thorndike was not Eva's only necklace. I remember two necklaces given to her on her sixteenth birthday. One was a strand of lavender pearls. Freshwater pearls her father had given her. And a ruby necklace from her mother. As an adult, she never wore them, but she kept them in her jewelry box. I don't know what happened to them."

"Somehow, Finn must have found out about them," Danielle said.

"How? And if that was Eva's portrait he was describing, then it was Eva he had the message for," Walt said.

"That's impossible."

Their discussion ended when a woman walked through the wall into the room.

"Shannon!" Danielle blurted when she spied the confused spirit glancing around the library, looking for someone.

"You can see me?" Shannon asked.

"Yes, both Walt and I can. We are mediums. But if Finn or Madeline walk back in here, we'll have to pretend you aren't here, because they can't see you, and they'll think we're crazy."

"Finn is a fake," Shannon said.

"We know Finn visited you on Thanksgiving morning. Had you met him before?" Walt asked.

Shannon turned to Walt and cocked her head slightly as she studied him. "No, that was the first time we ever met. Why?"

"What about his event you attended in Portland?" Danielle asked.

Shannon turned her gaze to Danielle. "Well, I saw him there. My brother, Rusty, took me. But we didn't get a reading or even talk to each other."

"Why did you tell Charlie Cramer Finn gave you and Rusty a reading?" Danielle asked.

"What are you talking about?" Shannon frowned.

"At that event you attended with your brother. You told Charlie that Finn had given you both a reading and that Rusty was going to have another one," Danielle explained.

Shannon shook her head. "I never said that. I don't know what you're talking about. Until Thanksgiving, I had never spoken to Finn. Well, aside from when he called to tell me he was going to be in Frederickport. He spoke to me then. But I never mentioned seeing Finn to Charlie or anyone."

Danielle's cellphone rang. She stood up. "Excuse me while I answer this. Please don't leave."

When Danielle picked up her cellphone from the coffee table, she looked to see who was calling. It was Police Chief MacDonald.

"Hi, Chief, I have good news," Danielle began, her eyes still on Shannon, who now chatted quietly with Walt.

"I have news too. Finn was right," the chief said.

"Right about what?"

"Remember how he told me Shannon's mother came through, that she kept touching her left breast, and later he wondered if it was a warning for a heart attack?"

"She had a heart attack?" Danielle asked.

"No. But according to the coroner, she had a massive lump on her left breast."

THIRTY-THREE

When Danielle got off her cellphone, she found Walt still talking to Shannon.

"So someone did murder me?" Danielle overheard Shannon say to Walt.

Danielle rejoined the conversation. "Unless you accidentally ingested poison."

Shannon looked from Walt to Danielle. "I was telling him that the only thing I had to eat on Thursday was the food I ordered from Lucy's Diner. I got sick not long after I started eating it. The poison must have been in there. But it wasn't intentional. Someone at the diner must have accidentally contaminated the food."

"Why are you so sure of that?" Danielle asked. "That it was an accident?"

Shannon shrugged. "No one has a reason to kill me. I have a very limited circle."

"How about your cousin?" Danielle said.

"Eden? Eden would never hurt me. She's always been there for me."

"Who inherits your property if you die?" Danielle asked.

Shannon stared at Danielle a moment before shaking her head. "I don't care what you say; Eden would never hurt me. Yes, she inherits my house and my half of the house she lives in. But she would never kill me for it. Anyway, Eden left Frederickport on Wednesday. She wasn't even there."

"Maybe she left something for you to eat?" Danielle suggested.

"She brought me a pie, but I never had a chance to even taste it. And the food from Lucy's was delivered on Thursday morning, after Eden left. Obviously, she had nothing to do with this."

"What about Finn?" Walt asked.

"Are you suggesting he poisoned me?" Shannon asked.

"You came here, I suspect, not long after you died. But we couldn't say anything because other people in the room couldn't see you, and they wouldn't understand," Danielle explained. "We wondered why you sought Finn out. You seemed angry with him."

"Finn had no reason to kill me. I wanted to kill him at first, but that's different."

"Why did you want to kill him?" Walt asked.

Shannon smiled at Walt. "Isn't it obvious? I wanted desperately to contact my brother. Rusty took me to Finn's first major public reading. I bought into Finn's entire act, how he connected people to their departed loved ones. And after Rusty's murder, I was trying to process everything. I didn't consider how a medium might help. But a couple of years later, I was watching a talk show, and they interviewed Walsh. I recognized him as the medium Rusty and I had seen. I started wondering if he could connect me to my brother. So I started writing him."

"That's why he came to your house on Thursday?" Danielle asked.

"Yes, but it wasn't Rusty who came through. He claimed it was my mother, giving me some medical warning." Shannon rolled her eyes and said, "I didn't start thinking Finn was a fake then. But after I realized I was dead and just wanted to find out why, I wanted to talk to someone like I am now. So I came here because he told me he was staying at Marlow House. But after I found him, I realized then he was a fake. All those years I wrote him, prayed he would come to Oregon. But it was all a show. Nothing else. Yeah, I was pretty angry. But when I say I wanted to kill him, you realize it was only a figure of speech, right?"

"Finn told the police chief that in your reading, your mother kept patting her left breast and showing him an image of the hospital," Danielle said.

"Yes." Shannon let out a sigh. "Such a fake."

"Ironically, according to the coroner, there was a massive growth in your left breast," Danielle said.

Shannon's eyes widened. "Are you saying Finn isn't a fake?"

Walt cocked a brow at his wife. "Yes, Danielle, are you suggesting Finn is a medium?"

"No, I'm not. Shannon's not the only one Finn doesn't realize is here. There is also Eva and Marie."

Shannon frowned. "Who are Eva and Marie?"

Danielle looked at Shannon. "They're like you."

"If he is a fake, are you suggesting he simply guessed about my breast?"

"He is very good at what he does. During your reading, I assume you told him you hadn't been out of your house in years," Danielle said.

"Yes, I told him not long after he arrived. But he asked me not to tell him anything else unless he asked me a question."

Walt frowned at Danielle. "What are you suggesting?"

Danielle glanced at Walt and back at Shannon. "If Shannon hadn't left her house for all that time, then it's obvious she neglected her health. She's about the age of someone who should have regular mammograms. Finn is basically encouraging her to do something most women her age should do. Now if they find something, then she could tell everyone he saved her life. I read once that about fifty percent of women will develop some sort of lump in their breast. Not necessarily dangerous. But there was a chance the mammogram would have showed something, considering she had neglected her health for so long, which would have made Finn look like the real deal."

"So I was right. He is fake," Shannon said.

"Yes, but I don't think Finn is a bad guy," Danielle said. "I think in his readings he is trying to help people, give them closure. And with you, maybe he wanted to get you out of your house and start taking care of yourself."

"But we still have the matter of a killer," Walt reminded them.

"Would you be willing to help us find out how and why you died?" Danielle asked.

"Absolutely," Shannon said.

"Then perhaps we should take our discussion over to Heather's, and there you can meet a couple of our friends who are like us," Danielle suggested.

INTRODUCTIONS HAD BEEN MADE. Shannon understood the only ones in the room who could see and hear her were Walt, Danielle, Heather, and Chris. While Brian Henderson and Police Chief MacDonald couldn't, they were aware of her presence.

"What do they want to ask me?" Shannon asked.

Heather repeated the question.

Brian took out his cellphone and opened a file. He looked up at Heather, who pointed to where Shannon sat. While he didn't see the spirit, he looked her way.

"I understand from Danielle and Walt that you don't believe anyone intentionally poisoned you. You don't believe Eden, who had a motive, or Finn, who visited you that day, had anything to do with it. But we don't believe this was some accident. So we need to find out who might have wanted you dead. Charlie Cramer gave Joe a copy of an email you sent him, and I would like to read it to you.

Hi. It's me. Tomorrow is my birthday. Of course, that means it's Rusty's birthday too. Can you believe it has been ten years since his death? Ten long years, not knowing who was responsible. That is finally going to change. I thought you would want to know.

I will be meeting someone on Friday. He'll be able to give me the answers. I can't say who he is, and why he hasn't come forward until now, but you might say he was there the day Rusty was killed. He holds the key to what really happened. The reason he hasn't come forward before, he didn't realize what he knew. I've been trying to contact him for a long time now, and he's finally gotten back to me and agreed to meet me. He doesn't know why I need to see him, and I hope when I tell him, it doesn't scare him away. But I have faith this will all work out. Rusty will finally get justice. As soon as I see him, I'll let you know what he says. Shannon.

"Who were you planning to see?" Brian asked when he finished reading the letter.

"It was Finn," Shannon said. "He contacted me, and we were going to meet on Friday, but he came early."

Heather grabbed the cellphone from Brian and reread the letter. Instead of pulling the cellphone away from Heather, he let her read the letter, waiting to hear what she might say. Heather looked to Shannon and asked, "If you were talking about Finn in this letter, why did you say he was there that day Rusty was killed? That he didn't realize what he knew?"

Shannon shrugged sheepishly and said, "You might say I was taking liberties in how I phrased that. It was Rusty who was there that day, not Finn. But I couldn't tell Charlie the person I thought I would be talking to was Rusty, through a medium. As for the part about how he didn't know what he knew, well, I kinda had to throw that in because Charlie would wonder why the guy hadn't come forward before."

"Yeah, some liberties," Heather muttered as she handed the phone back to Brian before repeating Shannon's words for the non-mediums.

"I'd like to ask you something," the chief said. "According to what Charlie Cramer told Joe Morelli, you claimed to get a personal reading from Finn when you attended his show ten years ago. But Finn claims that isn't true, and the videos of that even substantiate his claim. Why would Charlie have said that?"

Shannon considered the question for a moment and then said, "First, Finn was telling the truth. We didn't get a reading that day. In fact, we didn't even get to talk to him. There were a couple of hundred people there. But... well, it was probably something Rusty said."

"What do you mean?" Danielle asked after repeating to the chief and Brian what Shannon had just said.

"Mediums and anything spiritual always fascinated me," Shannon explained. "I remember Rusty telling me that night, when we were coming home, how Charlie had given him a hard time about taking me to Finn's reading. He thought all that stuff was fake. So I suppose I could understand Rusty saying something not quite true about how we got this amazing reading. Just to shut him up. And that's why I wrote that letter that way. I wanted to tell Charlie we might finally have the truth. But I didn't want to tell him it was through a medium; he wouldn't take it seriously."

Danielle repeated Shannon's words, and then the chief said, "But Charlie claimed you said it, not Rusty."

Shannon smiled at the chief. "Well, that was a long time ago, and Charlie often got things twisted. That was just Charlie. I can remember, back when Rusty was alive, how Charlie would tell some story about something they did in high school, and Rusty would say, 'No, Charlie, that was Joe, not me.' For Charlie, he just enjoyed telling the story, but he didn't want to be bothered by the details of who actually was there."

While Danielle repeated Shannon's words, Heather looked at Shannon and asked, "Is it true you had a crush on Charlie?"

Shannon wrinkled her nose at Heather and said, "Oh gosh, when I was about twelve. How did you know?"

"It's just what I heard." Heather shrugged.

"I was always shy, even with some of Rusty's close friends. I guess it is no secret that I... I wasn't an extrovert. Actually, I find it interesting that I feel comfortable now, not afraid. Is that normal?"

"I suppose when you're dead, what else is there to be afraid of?" Heather asked.

"You are so right!" Shannon grinned.

After Heather filled the non-mediums in on what Shannon had just said, the chief asked, "Shannon, the poison you consumed was likely in the food from Lucy's Diner. Who had access to that?"

"Danielle and Walt told me you suspected Finn. While I wasn't happy with his reading or the fact he didn't see me when I came to him later that day, I don't believe he tampered with my food. Why would he? We hadn't met until Thursday. And if he tampered with the food, the only time he could have done it was before he came into the house. The food was sitting on the front porch. But I saw him drive up. He wasn't standing on the front porch for more than a few seconds before I opened the door. And the containers of food were still in the sacks."

Danielle repeated Shannon's words, and then the chief asked, "What about after you came into the house? Was he ever alone with the food?"

"No. He helped me carry the food in. But he never touched the containers. He opened the refrigerator door for me and held it open while I took the containers out of the sacks and put them in the refrigerator. We left the kitchen after I put the food away, and we both went to the living room. He didn't leave to use the bathroom. He never went back to the kitchen."

"And you never noticed anything suspicious with the food?" the chief asked after Danielle repeated Shannon's words.

"No." Shannon paused a moment before adding, "Wait, there was something. When I was putting the food away, I almost spilled the cranberry sauce when I took the container out of the sack. The lid was only partially on the container. I remember wondering how it traveled all the way from the diner to my house without getting all over the inside of the bag."

THIRTY-FOUR

K elly walked down the beach and arrived at her brother's
house just before sunset and in time to hitch a ride to their
parents' house for Sunday dinner.

"You actually walked all the way here from your place?" Lily
asked after Kelly joined her and Ian in the living room. Sadie trailed
behind the new arrival, tail wagging, demanding attention.

"I'm trying to walk more, and it's too cold in the morning. I
don't know how Heather does it," Kelly said. "But thanks for letting
me ride with you to Mom and Dad's."

"No problem." Lily sat back on the sofa with Ian.

"Where's Connor?" Kelly asked as she sat on the floor with
Sadie, scratching the golden retriever behind her ears.

"He's taking a nap. I'm hoping he wakes up soon, so I don't
have to wake him up. He's always so grumpy when I do," Lily said.

"Isn't Joe coming?" Ian asked Kelly.

"Yes, but he's meeting us over there. He's been putting in long
hours ever since we found Shannon's body. That's why I figured I'd
get in a walk and then hitch a ride to Mom and Dad's with you
guys."

"Any news on the case?" Ian asked.

"I'm sure you heard they brought Finn Walsh in for questioning.
They were even holding him, but they let him go. I can't imagine

why someone as respectable as Finn Walsh would kill anyone. He didn't even know her."

"Respectable?" Lily asked with a snort.

"Sure. He's a good friend of Danielle's former mother-in-law, and he's super famous. Gosh, I read online they were talking about him getting his own reality show." Kelly looked down at Sadie, who had just rolled over on her back, demanding a belly rub.

With Kelly's attention briefly focused on the golden retriever, Lily and Ian exchanged knowing glances. While the couple found Finn charming and personable, neither could bring themselves to characterize him as respectable, since they felt his readings were fake.

Thirty minutes later, Kelly sat in the back of Ian's car with Connor in the car seat, while Lily sat in the front in the passenger seat. Looking across the street at Marlow House, Kelly didn't see any lights on downstairs or in the attic bedroom, but there were lights on in the bedrooms on the second floor.

Kelly continued to look across the street as Ian drove south. Her gaze briefly set on Pearl's house, with all its lights off, and she imagined how that could be her home one day. But when they drove past Heather's house the next moment, her mental wanderings jolted to the present when she spied Chief MacDonald's car parked in front of Heather's house, behind Brian's vehicle. As they drove by the house, she saw what looked like Walt standing in Heather's living room by the window.

AFTER IAN and Lily arrived at Ian's parents' house with Kelly and Connor, Ian noticed an extra place setting at the table. "Who else is coming for dinner?" he asked.

"Joe's bringing his friend Charlie," June explained as she sliced fresh cucumber to add to the salad.

"Didn't I tell you?" Kelly asked Ian as she snatched a slice of cucumber from her mother's cutting board and popped it into her mouth.

"He's such a nice young man," June said. "And he really doesn't know anyone in town, and he's all alone."

"Didn't he grow up here?" Lily asked. She had joined the three in the kitchen moments earlier after leaving Connor with his grandfather in the living room.

"Sure, but he hasn't lived here for years," Kelly said. "And he's only in town while he lists his mother's house. But we're kind of hoping he stays. According to Joe, the work he does, he can do anywhere."

"Isn't he between jobs?" Ian asked.

"Which is an ideal time to relocate," Kelly said.

"I can understand Joe wanting Charlie to stay. I kinda wanted to stay after Dani moved here," Lily said.

"Didn't you stay for Ian?" Kelly teased.

"That too." Lily grinned.

"And you know who would be perfect for Charlie?" Kelly asked.

Lily looked at her sister-in-law. "Who?"

"Laura," Kelly said.

Lily frowned. "My sister?"

"I BET your sister is already making plans to play matchmaker at her wedding. She'll probably finagle for Charlie to walk Laura down the aisle," Lily said after she and Ian left the kitchen ten minutes later. They walked through the dining room and paused in the hallway so they could talk out of earshot of Ian's family.

"I doubt that is going to happen, since she's asked Laura to be her maid of honor. Brian will have to walk her down the aisle."

"Not if Joe asks Charlie to be his best man," Lily said.

"I can't imagine Joe would un-ask Brian."

Lily shrugged. "We'll see. But you didn't think she'd ask Laura to be her maid of honor either, and she did."

"Kelly doesn't have many girlfriends in Frederickport. And she told me she wanted to ask you to be her matron of honor, but she didn't want to offend Joe's sister by showing favoritism toward one sister-in-law over another. She decided it was best if she asked you both to be in the wedding and ask someone else to be the maid of honor. And you must admit, she and Laura really hit it off."

"Ian, your sister can ask whoever she wants. It's her wedding. I find it interesting how she bonded with my sister. But if she tries to get those two together, we should let her know Laura may not be his type. After all, he hit on Heather."

Ian chuckled. "While I didn't tell her about that, apparently she already knew."

"That he hit on Heather?"

"No, that he was attracted to Heather. Kelly told me he made a comment on Thanksgiving about how he found Heather hot."

Lily's eyes widened. "He said that to Kelly?"

"I got the impression he was probably talking more to Joe."

"So what did she think?"

"Kelly said something about most guys being attracted to the bad girl. But it doesn't mean they want to marry them."

Lily scrunched up her nose. "So Heather is a bad girl?"

Ian gave a shrug.

Lily turned to Ian, stood on her tiptoes, wrapped her arms around his shoulders, and before placing a kiss on his lips, whispered, "I guess Kelly forgot her brother married his bad girl."

Ian would have laughed at the comment, but he was too busy kissing his wife.

"HAVE THERE BEEN any breaks in your friend's murder investigation?" June asked Joe as they all sat at the dining room table, passing around the plates and bowls of food.

"Unfortunately, it's been one dead end after another," Joe said as he spooned mashed potatoes onto his plate.

"Guess who I saw over at Heather's on our way here," Kelly said as she snatched a piece of fried chicken from a passing platter. "The chief."

"He was at Heather's?" Joe asked.

"So was Brian. I wondered if the chief stopped by to tell him something about the case," Kelly said.

"I don't know why he wouldn't just call if something new came up," Joe said.

"I also saw Walt over there, so I assume Danielle was there too," Kelly said. "Although they have guests at the B and B, so maybe not."

Lily and Ian exchanged glances but said nothing.

"I still can't understand why Shannon lied to me about getting a reading from Finn Walsh," Charlie said after passing a bowl of vegetables down the table.

"When was this?" June asked.

"It was years ago." Charlie picked up a dinner roll from his plate and tore it in half. "She told me about it after Rusty died, claimed he had made arrangements for a private reading, but of course, that never happened; Rusty was killed. I had forgotten the name of the medium they'd seen. But when I met him on Thanksgiving, it triggered a memory. So I pulled up Walsh's website. It had a list of all his events over the years, and there it was, the time and place of the reading Rusty and Shannon attended. The medium Shannon had been talking about all those years ago was the very same one we all spent Thanksgiving with. Small world." He shook his head as he buttered his roll.

"Why do you say she lied about it?" John asked.

"We brought Finn in for questioning. He claimed it wasn't true, and after we watched the videos they'd made of the reading Rusty and Shannon attended, it verified his claim. Finn never talked to them," Joe explained.

"Just because it wasn't on that video doesn't mean it's not true," June said.

Charlie looked at June and gave a nod. "That's exactly what I thought."

"I can't believe he had anything to do with Shannon's death," Kelly said. "He's Finn Walsh, for goodness' sake."

"I heard on the radio they brought Finn in for questioning because someone saw him at her house." June turned her attention to Joe and asked, "Is that true?"

"He admitted to giving her a reading on Thursday morning," Joe said. "But he claimed he never met her before that morning."

"The entire thing is so tragic. I'm so sorry you both lost a friend. And to think someone murdered the poor girl." June shook her head at the idea.

"You shouldn't rule out suicide," Charlie said. "I hate to say it, but I think it is entirely possible she took her own life. I feel guilty for not making more of an effort with Shannon, but she has been a little unstable. For example, if Walsh is telling the truth and we can believe those videos captured the entire event that day, why did she lie to me about it back then? And from what Eden told me, she hasn't stepped out of that house since her grandmother's funeral," Charlie said.

"Unfortunately, people with agoraphobia often suffer from suicidal thoughts," Ian said.

"What was her brother like?" Lily asked.

"He was the flip side of his sister," Joe said. "I don't think there was a shy bone in his body. He could be mister social."

"Which created its own problems," Charlie said.

"What sort of problems?" Kelly asked.

Joe looked at Charlie. "What do you mean?"

Charlie set his now empty fork on his plate and looked at Joe. "You didn't go into business with Rusty. Which only proves you were smarter than me."

Joe frowned. "And?"

"Hey, I loved Rusty. But the truth was, when it came to business, he, well, he loved the social side of the business, you know, talking bikes with our customers, arranging events, but he wasn't good about figuring out how we were going to pay the bills. The business side of business wasn't Rusty's thing," Charlie explained.

WHEN CHARLIE LEFT after dinner on Sunday evening, the others lingered in the living room, chatting while Connor napped on his father's lap.

"I wonder what would have happened to Charlie and Rusty's business if Rusty hadn't died," June mused. "By what he said, I got the impression they weren't doing well."

"No, they weren't. In fact, I'm pretty sure they were getting ready to close the doors before Rusty died," Joe said.

"How soon after Rusty died did Charlie close the business?" John asked.

"They didn't close it, Dad," Kelly said. "Charlie kept it going, and he sold it a year later. It's still open."

"How did he turn it around?" June asked.

"They had keyman insurance on both of them. After Rusty's death, Charlie used the insurance money to put back into the business, and within a year, he had an offer from a buyer. He sold out. I think he did pretty well," Joe explained.

"I assume Charlie had to pay Rusty's family his share after selling the business?" June asked.

Joe shook his head. "No. They set up the business so the other partner would inherit. At the time, the only family Charlie had was his mother. I doubt Rusty wanted to find himself partners with Mrs. Cramer should something happen to Charlie. As it was, he would still be obligated to pay off the loan Charlie had taken out for the business. And Charlie didn't want to find himself partners with Rusty's parents or sister. But I imagine had one of them married, that would have changed."

THIRTY-FIVE

W hen the chief and Brian finished asking all their questions, Shannon said, "I understand you are simply doing your job, but please, you needn't question Eden further. I don't want you bothering her. There is so much she'll need to do now that I'm dead. And she can't tell you anything more than what I just did. She had nothing to do with my death. If it's true that the poison was in the cranberry sauce, it proves Eden could not be responsible. Not unless she hired someone to poison the take-out food when she was out of town. And that idea is ludicrous."

Danielle repeated Shannon's words and then said, "Eden knew you were getting takeout food from Lucy's, right?"

"Yes, but who would she hire to do something like that in Fred-erickport?" Shannon asked. "That's too sinister, and Eden is a caring person. She would never do something like that."

Danielle repeated Shannon's words for Brian and the chief.

"That's why we need your help to figure out who wanted you dead, if not Eden," Brian said.

"Like I said before, it was probably an accident at the restaurant. Some employee placed some rat poison on the wrong shelf, and someone else grabbed it by mistake. I'm sure if you take a closer look, you'll find a container of rat or ant poison that might be mistaken for some spice."

After Heather repeated Shannon's words, Brian said, "The only problem with that, they never had any poison at the restaurant."

"I'm sure they got rid of it," Shannon said. "If I worked at a restaurant and realized I accidentally poisoned a customer, I'd get rid of the poison as fast as I could."

Before Heather repeated Shannon's words, Shannon said, "I must go. I've told you all that I can."

"Are you moving on now?" Danielle asked. "You're not staying for your funeral?"

"Moving on?" Shannon shook her head. "No. I can't move on, not without Rusty. I must find him first."

"You'll find your brother when you move on," Danielle promised. "But you might want to stick around for your funeral anyway, in case the chief or Brian has any more questions before then."

"Rusty hasn't moved on. He's still here. I can feel him." Shannon vanished.

"Shannon—" the chief began.

"She's gone, Chief. She just left," Danielle said before repeating Shannon's last words.

"If she was still here, I'd have to tell her I think she was wrong about an employee tossing the poison. It was the manager who claimed they never bought the stuff, and his records confirm it. And according to all the employees we interviewed, none of them have ever seen any poison on the premises. And they all confirmed what the manager told us. They use peppermint oil for pest and ant control."

They were silent for a few minutes before Danielle asked, "Brian, didn't you say Shannon's front door isn't visible from the street?"

"Yes. That's why the neighbor had no idea how long Finn was standing by Shannon's front door after he arrived," Brian said.

"What are you thinking?" Chris asked.

Danielle glanced briefly at Chris and then back to Brian and the chief. "Shannon said the lid to the cranberry sauce hadn't been secured to the container. She said she wondered how it hadn't spilled all over the sacks when the food had been delivered."

"So?" Brian asked.

"Perhaps the lid was secured to the container when it left the

213

restaurant, which explains why the cranberry sauce hadn't spilled in the sack. And then someone removed it after they delivered it to Shannon's house." Danielle looked at the chief. "Does Shannon's house have a back-alley access like ours?"

The chief looked to Danielle. "Yes."

"You think someone poisoned it while it was still sitting on her front porch before Finn arrived?" Chris asked.

"It is entirely possible," Danielle said. "They could have walked up from the alleyway without being seen, put the poison in the cranberry sauce, and then Finn drove up, and they didn't have time to secure the lid properly."

"But who would do that?" Brian asked. "We're back to someone intentionally poisoning Shannon, but she insists there is no one who wanted her dead."

"Someone obviously wanted her dead," Chris said.

"We interviewed all the neighbors along the alley who were home. No one reported seeing anything or anyone suspicious," the chief said.

"Maybe they saw someone in the alley, but they didn't consider it suspicious," Heather suggested.

"Of all the people we talked to, no one remembered seeing anyone in the alley on Thanksgiving morning. Unfortunately, most of them admitted they hadn't been looking out there. And there are no security cameras along that area," Brian said.

"What about the people you didn't talk to?" Danielle asked. "Did you talk to everyone who lives along the alleyway?"

"All but one neighbor, but according to the people next door to them, they were spending Thanksgiving with family and won't be home until tomorrow. But I doubt they'll be of much help since they were all gone the day Shannon died," Brian said.

"Are you sure they left before Thanksgiving Day?" Danielle asked. "They might have left that morning, in time to see something."

Before Brian could answer Danielle's question, glitter fell from the ceiling. The mediums looked upwards, and Chris said, "Eva's here."

"So am I," Marie announced when she appeared the next moment, standing beside Eva.

"Marie's here too," Heather told the non-mediums.

"Eva, why did you take off like you did earlier?" Danielle asked.

All traces of glitter vanished, and Eva said, "I had to think. That reading Finn gave me was troubling."

"Troubling how?" Heather asked.

"I know how Marie or Eva might help," Brian interrupted. "If Shannon is right—which I don't think she is—I would assume there are some nervous employees over at Lucy's Diner right now. Every employee we talked to insists they never had poison at the restaurant. But if they were lying, then all of them were lying."

"And they may talk about it amongst themselves," Heather suggested.

"Covering up something like that—even if it was an accident—could weigh on someone," Brian said.

"I know another person Marie or Eva should watch," Heather said. "If Eden had someone else poison her cousin, then that means she has an accomplice."

"And the accomplice might contact her," Danielle added.

"Exactly." Heather then updated Marie and Eva on what Shannon had told them that morning.

"You want one of us to eavesdrop over at the diner, and the other over at Eden's?" Marie asked.

"I think that might be a good idea," Walt said.

Danielle looked to Eva. "First, I'd like to know what did you mean when you said you found Finn's reading troubling?"

"He talked about the lavender pearls and the ruby necklace. It's exactly something my mother might show him if she wanted me to know it was really her," Eva said.

"What's Eva talking about?" Chris asked.

"At least you can hear her talking," Brian grumbled.

Danielle then explained to the others about the earlier reading at Marlow House, when Finn mentioned a painting and two necklaces.

"You know, that is not the only bizarre reading he gave," Chris said.

"It is not bizarre," Danielle insisted. "There is a logical explanation. Finn obviously saw Eva's portrait when researching Marlow House, along with the Missing Thorndike, and he just got confused about the necklace."

Brian laughed. "You sound like Joe. Always a logical explanation." He laughed again.

"He didn't get confused," Walt said. "He described two necklaces Eva had."

"Walt is right," Eva agreed.

"And like I said, it was not his first bizarre reading," Chris said.

Heather turned to Chris. "What do you mean?"

"Remember what he told me? In my reading, he said my mother was standing there with a gift in her hand. A gift she had given me."

"Parents always give their children gifts," Danielle reminded them. "He was waiting for you to remember some special gift your mother had given you, and when you mentioned it, he would say yes, that's it, it's her way of verifying she's really here."

Chris looked at Danielle and shook his head. "No. He was more specific. He said she had given me a gift, and that Finn had been given one too, but that his was different."

Danielle frowned at Chris. "So? If you said your mom gave you a basketball, he would say his mom gave him a football."

"No, Danielle, I don't think that's what he was saying," Chris said.

"Your birth mother was a medium too!" Heather gasped. "She passed down her gift to you. And if Finn is a medium, he has the gift. But it's different because he obviously can't see Eva and Marie!"

Chris gave Heather a nod while Danielle adamantly shook her head in denial. "You guys aren't honestly suggesting that Finn might actually be a medium?"

"He alluded to my other life," Walt reminded them. "And Lucas had told me he was afraid I would interfere with your happiness."

Danielle continued to shake her head in denial. "That can't be true."

"Danielle, the Universe does not share all its secrets with us, but it does like to leave hints—tease us a bit. It keeps us on our toes," Eva said.

"Why? What is the point?" Danielle asked.

Eva shrugged. "Perhaps so we never forget we have more to learn. When we believe we have all the answers, we stop listening, stop learning."

"What are you guys talking about?" the chief asked.

216

"Tell the chief Marie and I will monitor your suspects. As for what Shannon told you about her brother not moving on, twins have a special bond, and if she feels he has not yet crossed over, she might be right. I suggest you look for her brother yourself. I suspect he might hold the key to his sister's murder. As for Finn, we can discuss that later, when we have this other problem resolved. I have a feeling Finn may indirectly have something to do with Shannon's death, but not in the way Brian and the chief initially imagined." After having her say, Eva vanished, and a second later, Marie joined her.

THIRTY-SIX

Brian spent the night at Heather's house on Sunday evening. The next morning, he sat at her kitchen table, already dressed for work, drinking his coffee while he watched Heather toast several slices of sourdough bread. Like him, Heather had already dressed for work.

In the far corner of the kitchen, Heather's petite calico cat, Bella, stood by her food bowl, deciding if she wanted to eat her breakfast or snub the offering and demand a different can. Perhaps beef instead of seafood? But then she got a whiff of the seafood and remembered she had played this game the previous night and went to bed hungry. Reluctantly, Bella began nibbling at her food.

"Do you have a big day today?" Brian asked.

Heather removed the now toasted sourdough bread from the toaster oven and cut each slice in half, buttered them with peanut butter, and then set half the slices on one plate and the other half on a second plate. She carried the plates to the table.

"We're working on some Christmas projects." Heather set one plate in front of Brian. "You?"

"On the way to the station, I plan to swing by and check on those neighbors on the other side of Shannon's alley. They should be home by now. The ones we weren't able to interview. I assume they have to go to work this morning, which means they probably got home last night."

"If that's true, they're getting ready to leave for work now."

Brian glanced at his watch. It was almost seven o'clock. "That's why as soon as I finish eating, I'd better get going."

"Sorry I didn't fix something more exciting." Heather took a bite of her peanut butter toast.

"Hey, this is more than I fix myself in the morning."

WHEN BRIAN DROVE down the alleyway behind Shannon's house twenty minutes later, he discovered the neighbors he wanted to question had not returned late Sunday evening. They were just arriving home when he pulled up. He parked his car along the back of their property as they parked inside their garage. Unlike Shannon's side, where garages faced the street, on the street behind hers, which shared her alleyway, most of their garages faced the alley.

Brian got out of his vehicle and closed the door behind him. As he walked toward the garage, its door still open, he could hear voices and the slamming of car doors. When he reached the back of the garage, he looked inside and spied a man and woman standing at the rear of the vehicle, the trunk open as the man removed suitcases, setting each one on the garage floor behind the car.

"Excuse me," Brian called out.

The couple stopped talking and turned to face Brian.

"Hello, Officer," the woman said. "Did you need something?"

"Can I talk to you a moment, please?" Brian said.

After slamming the trunk door shut, the man walked with his wife out to where Brian stood just outside their garage. "What is this about?"

Brian introduced himself and then said, "I understand you've been away all weekend?"

"Umm, yes. Has something happened?" The woman glanced at her house and said, her voice slightly rising, "Was our house broken into?"

Brian smiled and shook his head. "No, not that I'm aware of. But I need to ask you, what day did you leave?"

"We left late Thursday morning. What is this about?" the woman asked.

"On Thursday morning, did you notice anyone in the alley? Anyone going to that house?" Brian pointed across the alley.

"Shannon Langdon's house?" the woman asked.

"You know Shannon?" Brian asked.

"We've never met. Not really. We know who she is. We know her cousin, Eden. She lives one house over. Has something happened?"

"Shannon Langdon died on Thursday," Brian explained.

"Oh no!" The woman looked over at Shannon's house. "What happened?"

"That's what we're trying to find out. Did you notice anyone in the alley that morning?" Brian asked.

"We did. Are you saying she was murdered? Why else would you ask if we saw anything?" The woman's voice rose hysterically. Her husband reached over and took her hand, giving it a squeeze, and urged her to calm down and take a deep breath.

After the woman calmed herself, the man looked at Brian. "Yes, there was someone. In fact, we talked about it, because from what we understand, no one visits Shannon aside from her cousin and the deliveries she gets. This wasn't a deliveryman."

"Please tell me what you remember from that morning," Brian urged.

"We finished putting all the suitcases in the car and were getting ready to leave. I opened the garage door, and as we backed out, I noticed a man in my rearview mirror. He was just going up the back way to Shannon's house," the man explained.

"My husband said, 'I wonder who that is,'" the woman interjected. "We knew it wasn't a deliveryman because he didn't have a truck—or any vehicle with him."

"Can you describe him?" Brian said.

The man considered the question a moment before answering, "I only glimpsed him from the back. He was wearing a dark green hoody and jeans, with the hoody pulled up. Never saw his face. I suppose it could have been a woman. I just assumed it was a man."

"Anything else?" Brian asked.

"Nothing really," the man said. "I said something to my wife. We drove away after that."

Brian looked at the woman. "What did you see?"

"Pretty much the same thing. He walked up the side of Shannon's house. His back was to us the entire time. And like my husband said, we drove away."

"So you have no idea who he is?" Brian asked.

"No. But you can ask Shannon's cousin, Eden. I'm sure she knows him," the woman said.

"Why do you think that?" Brian asked.

"Eden knows everyone Shannon knows," the man said.

"That and the fact I saw Eden talking to the man on Wednesday," the woman said.

"Where was this?" Brian asked.

"It was in front of Lucy's Diner," the woman said. "I was driving down that street on Wednesday and noticed my neighbor, Eden, sitting in her parked car in front of the diner. I was about to wave, but she wasn't looking my way. And a man walked up to her car, and they started to talk. I'm pretty sure it was the same man who was in the alley, because he was wearing the same green hoody."

"Did he have a car?" Brian asked.

The woman shrugged. "If he did, I didn't notice."

"Did you see his face?" Brian asked.

"No, just the back of him, like on Thursday."

"Are you sure it was a man?" Brian asked.

"Like my husband said, I suppose it could have been a woman, but I don't think so."

"He had his hood pulled up over his head both times?" Brian asked.

The woman nodded. "Yes."

"You didn't see his hair?"

The woman shook her head. "No."

"Are you sure it was the same person? I imagine there is more than one green hoody in Frederickport," Brian said.

"I suppose it could be someone else with the same hoody. But I assumed it was the same person because of the dolphin," the woman said.

"Dolphin?" Brian asked.

"Yes. The jacket had a white dolphin on the back of it. I like dolphins." The woman smiled.

BRIAN SAT ALONE with the chief in his office. The door closed. He had just recounted the interview with Shannon's neighbors.

"Considering you once dated Eden, I should probably interview her," the chief said.

"Hey, I have no problem arresting Eden for her cousin's murder. And this looks like a murder for hire to me."

The chief let out a sigh. "We need to identify the person in the hoody first. And remember, Shannon is adamant her cousin was not responsible for her death."

Brian rolled his eyes. "She doesn't want to believe it. It can hurt when someone you love is willing to kill you, especially for money. It's not something a person wants to admit."

After discussing the topic for a few more minutes, they agreed the chief would call Eden and ask her if she could stop at the police station for a few minutes so he could go over a few more things. Brian sat quietly as the chief made the call.

"Well?" Brian asked when the chief hung up the phone.

"As you probably heard, she's in Portland and won't be home until late tonight. But she has agreed to come in first thing in the morning."

WALT AND DANIELLE met Chris and Heather at Pier Café for lunch on Monday afternoon.

"What are Finn and Madeline doing today?" Chris asked. They had already placed their order and waited for their food.

"Sightseeing," Danielle said. "They are going to the museum first. They want to see the original paintings."

"How long do you think they're going to stay?" Chris asked. "The chief can't really make them stay, can he? And from what Shannon told us, I can't imagine he's a suspect anymore."

"No," Danielle said. "But we talked about it last night, and Finn said he would like to go to Shannon's funeral. He feels he needs to go, since he saw her right before she died."

"Maybe he thinks he's going to see her again," Heather snarked.

"I don't think so," Walt said. "Finn says it's rare for a spirit to come through so soon after his or her death. They need time to adjust. You know, tend to life reviews and such."

"You almost say that like you believe it," Heather said.

Walt gave a shrug.

"Oh, stop with all the perhaps he is really a medium talk," Danielle said.

Chris flashed a smile at Danielle and leaned back in his seat. "You must admit, he has come up with interesting readings. He even has Eva wondering."

"I've been wondering about something Eva said, too. And it isn't about Finn being a medium or fake. It's about Shannon's brother, Rusty," Danielle said.

"You mean how he may not have moved on?" Heather asked.

"Yes," Walt answered for Danielle. "Eva said she doesn't feel Rusty ever visited his grave. And if Shannon's feelings are right, and he hasn't moved on, what would that normally mean?"

"That he got stuck somewhere," Heather said.

"Like where he got killed?" Chris added.

"Yes. We were wondering, will your boss let you two take tomorrow off so you can go to Portland with us?" Danielle asked.

Heather arched her brows. "You're going ghost hunting?"

"And we'd rather not do it alone. It's more fun with a couple of friends," Danielle said.

"Where are you planning to go?" Chris asked.

"To the motorcycle shop," Walt said. "From what Charlie and Joe told us, it's still open. Under new owners, but still there. I looked the address up last night."

"A haunted motorcycle shop. Sounds like fun," Chris said.

THIRTY-SEVEN

M adeline and Finn had already left to go sightseeing on Tuesday morning when Chris and Heather showed up at Marlow House. They entered together through the kitchen door, Hunny trailing behind them.

"Morning," Walt and Danielle greeted them. They sat at the kitchen table and didn't bother standing up. Max, who had been napping by Danielle's feet, looked up and watched as Hunny went directly for Walt, her butt wiggling. The cat yawned and then resumed his nap.

"We saw Finn drive away," Heather said as she helped herself to a tea bag from the pantry.

"Are you sure it's okay if I leave Hunny here?" Chris poured himself a cup of coffee.

Danielle set her mug of hot chocolate on the table and looked at Chris. "No problem. We'll probably get back before they do, but even if we don't, Madeline loves dogs. She was quite taken with Hunny when she was over here Thursday."

Standing by the microwave heating a mug of water, Heather looked over to the kitchen table, where Chris now sat with Walt and Danielle. "Did you hear they're having Shannon's funeral tomorrow?"

Danielle picked up her mug. "The chief told me last night.

224

We're going to the funeral with Finn and Madeline. And then they'll probably leave on Thursday if the chief says it's okay."

Dunking her tea bag into the now hot mug of water, Heather joined the others at the table. "Brian said the chief can't make Finn stay in town."

Danielle shrugged. "I know. But Finn says he wants to do all he can to help find Shannon's killer. He may be a fake medium, but I think basically he's a nice man."

Instead of commenting, the others at the table exchanged glances while Danielle leaned down to pet Hunny, missing their exchange.

CHRIS DROVE the four to Portland, with Walt and Danielle sitting in the back seat.

Heather leaned back in the passenger seat and looked over at Chris. "You know, we're probably wasting half the day driving to Portland. What's the chance we're really going to find Rusty's spirit still at the bike shop? And who knows, even if he is there, it's possible he'll be in a part of the shop where customers can't go. We should've asked Marie to go with us so she could look through the entire building."

"Marie and Eva are already on surveillance duty," Chris reminded her.

Danielle leaned toward the front seats, closer to Heather and Chris. "From what we know, they murdered Rusty while he stood at the cash register while closing. If he's still there, that's probably where he'll be."

Chris glanced briefly at Heather and then looked back down the road, his hands on the steering wheel. "I know this is a crapshoot, but if he's still on this side, that's where he'll most likely be. He hasn't been seen by his grave or at his family's home. If he was there, Shannon would have seen him."

"Not necessarily," Heather said.

Chris glanced briefly at Heather and then looked back down the road. "Stop being such a pessimist."

WHEN THE FOUR mediums walked into the bike shop, they discover Heather's pessimism had been unwarranted. Standing behind the cash register stood Rusty Langdon. And if it wasn't Rusty, it was a man who looked just like his sister, albeit a slightly younger version. If any of them wondered if it was simply a coincidence and the man bore a remarkable resemblance to Shannon's ghost, that thought quickly vanished when an employee of the bike shop walked through Rusty to wait on a customer.

"And you said this was a waste of time," Chris chided Heather. The four stood just inside the bike shop, looking around. Several customers browsed the displays, and two stood at the counter, talking to the store employee who now stood next to Rusty instead of standing through him. Another employee helped a customer on the other side of the shop.

"Yeah, but now what? We can't exactly march up there and say, 'Hi, Rusty,'" Heather whispered back.

"I have an idea." Danielle looked briefly to the other mediums. "Follow me." The next moment, Danielle walked to the counter, Walt, Chris, and Heather with her.

Once at the counter, the four mediums stood quietly, waiting for the employee to finish helping a customer. While they waited, all four stared at Rusty, who stared back curiously.

"How can I help you?" the man at the register finally asked after he finished waiting on his customers.

Danielle turned a smile to him while Heather kept looking at Rusty's ghost. The minute Danielle started talking, Heather winked at the curious ghost. The gesture startled Rusty, who now stared at Heather. She flashed him a quick smile and wiggled her eyebrows up and down.

"A friend of mine, her brother used to own this shop," Danielle told the man in a loud and clear voice.

"Oh really? I've only worked here a month," the man answered.

"His name was Rusty Langdon," Danielle said. "We're from Frederickport. That's where Rusty grew up."

"Name's not familiar. But like I said, I've only been here a month. How can I help you?"

"Oh, we're just window-shopping. Thanks."

The next moment the phone rang, and the man excused himself

to answer it, leaving Danielle, Walt, Chris, and Heather alone with a curious ghost.

"We can see and hear you, Rusty," Danielle whispered. "But no one else in the shop can. We need to talk to you. Please follow us." Danielle turned away from the counter and walked with the others to a rack of clothing. When they reached it, they all pretended to be looking at the leather jackets.

"You can really see me?" Rusty asked.

Heather pulled a leather jacket from the rack and held it up in front of her. She looked at Rusty and said, "Yes, we can. How do you think I'd look in this?"

"We're not here to shop," Chris reminded her.

Heather gave a shrug and put the jacket back on the rack. "I just love leather." She turned her attention back to the ghost.

"Rusty, why are you still here?" Danielle asked.

"Why can you see me?" Rusty asked.

"We're mediums," Danielle explained.

Rusty furrowed his brows and studied the four a moment. Finally, he asked, "Like Finn Walsh?"

"Umm... yeah." Danielle resisted the temptation to roll her eyes. "Why are you still here? Why haven't you moved on? You do know that... well..."

"That I'm dead?" Rusty finished for her.

"Umm, yeah."

"I watched them take my body out of here. And no one has seen me until you." Rusty sounded insulted that she assumed he would not realize the obvious. Danielle did not bother telling him it was not uncommon for a spirit to not realize he or she was dead, even though others could not hear or see them.

"Then why are you still here?" Chris asked.

Rusty glanced at Chris and then back to Danielle. "Do you all really live in Frederickport?"

"Yes," Danielle said.

Rusty frowned. "Frederickport is a small town. I lived there my entire life. At least, until I moved to Portland. None of you look familiar, and you look about my age."

"We've only lived there a few years," Walt said.

Rusty studied Walt a moment, his frown deepening. "Although

there is something familiar about you. Did you live in Frederickport when I did?"

"Why don't you come back to Frederickport with us, and we can answer all your questions," Danielle suggested. "We really can't do this here." She looked nervously at the other customers now looking her way.

"I can't leave," Rusty said.

"What do you mean, can't?" Heather asked.

"I was murdered. And I need to get the evidence to the police. My friend, Joe Morelli, he's on the Frederickport police force. He'll know what to do with it."

"How do you expect to do that by staying here?" Heather asked.

"The evidence is hidden in the shop. I can't leave while it's still here."

"Where is it?" Danielle glanced around, suspecting that if there had been evidence, it was probably gone by now.

Rusty pointed to the floor near the rack of clothing they had been looking at. "Under that floorboard. It comes up. I hid an envelope there."

"Are you sure it's still there?" Walt asked.

"Positive. I'm the one who initially pried up that section so I could hide the envelope. I knew he would never find it there."

Heather looked at the floorboard and then back at Rusty. "Who's he?"

"My killer."

PRYING up the floorboard in the bike shop while customers browsed and two employees diligently attended to said customers' needs might have been an impossible task for most people, but with Walt's telekinetic powers, it proved tricky, but not impossible.

Chris and Heather corralled the one employee who wasn't currently with a customer and relentlessly questioned him on motorcycles. Midway through the discussion, Heather began wondering if Chris intended to buy a motorcycle.

Meanwhile, Danielle stood near the loose floorboard, her large purse sitting by her feet as she compared two leather jackets, as if trying to decide which one she liked best. After Rusty explained how to move the floorboard, Walt focused his energy on the spot. It moved slightly, revealing the corner of a yellowed envelope. Walt quickly glanced around the room, and when no one was looking his way, the envelope floated up from below the floorboard and tucked itself safely into Danielle's open purse. The next moment, the floorboard repositioned itself, returning to its original place.

WHILE WALT, Danielle, Chris, and Heather were on their way to Portland to find Rusty, Police Chief MacDonald sat in the interrogation room with Eden Langdon while Joe and Brian watched from the adjacent office.

"Sorry I couldn't come in yesterday," Eden told the chief. "But I had to meet with Shannon's attorney in Portland."

The chief arched his brows. "Shannon's attorney?"

"Yes, he wanted to discuss her estate. And, with her funeral scheduled for tomorrow, I thought it best if I got that out of the way. Has there been some new development? Is that why you wanted to talk to me?"

"We have a new person of interest we would like to talk to. And we are hoping you might identify him for us," the chief explained.

Eden frowned at the chief. "Person of interest? Who?"

"That's what we're trying to find out. But we understand you talked to him on Wednesday. The day before Thanksgiving."

Eden slumped back in her chair, her frown deepening. "I spoke to many people on Wednesday. I ran errands that day. There was a lot to do before leaving for California."

"From what we've been told, you were sitting in your car in front of Lucy's Diner, talking to a man."

"Who told you that?"

"That's not important right now. I just need for you to tell me, who were you talking to?"

Eden shrugged. "I don't remember talking to anyone."

"He wore a green hoody. It had a white dolphin on the back of the jacket," the chief explained.

Eden shook her head. "I have no idea who you're talking about. They must be mistaken. It wasn't me."

"CHARLIE HAS A JACKET LIKE THAT," Joe blurted as he stared into the interrogation room through the one-way mirror.

Brian looked at Joe. "Are you sure?"

Joe let out a sigh. "Yes. Another dead end."

"Why is it a dead end?"

"Charlie obviously didn't kill Shannon, but he probably did stop and say hi to Eden, and she just doesn't remember."

"He was also seen behind Shannon's house," Brian reminded him.

Joe shrugged. "I'm sure there is a simple explanation. But this is a waste of time."

Brian took out his cellphone and sent a text.

THE CHIEF'S phone buzzed from an incoming text. He picked the phone up and looked at it. After reading the text, he set his phone back on the table and looked across to Eden. "Did you talk to Charlie Cramer in front of Lucy's Diner on Wednesday?"

Eden stared at the chief for a moment and then broke into a smile. "Oh yes! I totally forgot. I stopped to pick up some fudge at the candy shop to take to California with me. Charlie walked by; he stopped by the car and said hi. Told me he was on his way to see Adam Nichols. That was about it. I thought you meant someone saw me have a long talk with some man. But it was just a brief hello. I wasn't surprised to see him because I talked to him on the phone, and he told me he was coming to town."

THIRTY-EIGHT

On their way back to Frederickport, Rusty sat in the back seat with Walt and Danielle. Heather tried calling Brian to tell him they had found Shannon's brother, along with the identity of his killer. When Brian didn't answer his phone, she tried calling the chief, who also didn't answer. What she didn't realize, both officers were interviewing Charlie Cramer.

INSTEAD OF MEETING Charlie in the interrogation room, the chief had called and asked him to stop in his office, explaining he had a few questions. When Charlie arrived, he found Brian with the chief.

Charlie stepped into the office and glanced around. "Is Joe going to be here?"

"No." Standing up, the chief motioned to a chair. "Please, sit down."

After Charlie sat, he looked from Brian to the chief. "What did you need to ask me?"

Now sitting behind his desk, the chief leaned forward and rested his elbows on his desktop as he looked at Charlie, who sat in the chair next to Brian. "On Thanksgiving Day, did you go over to Shannon's house?"

Charlie frowned. "Of course, you know that. I was with Joe."

"I meant before that, earlier in the day."

No longer frowning, Charlie looked at the chief and shook his head. "As Brian will tell you, I spent Thanksgiving over at Marlow House."

"You didn't go over to Shannon's before you went to Marlow House?" the chief asked.

Charlie gave a shrug and leaned back in his chair. "The first and only time I saw Shannon on Thursday was when I was with Joe. I don't know what this is about, but I'll be happy to take a lie detector test to prove I'm telling the truth."

"Perhaps you didn't see Shannon, but did you go over to her house before you came to Marlow House?" Brian asked.

Charlie sat up straight and turned to Brian. "What is this about?"

"Someone places you at Shannon's Thursday morning," the chief explained. "You were seen going up to her house from the alley."

"Did they see me going into her house? I don't think so because I didn't."

"But you walked up to her house on Thursday morning, from the alley?" the chief asked.

Charlie let out a sigh and slumped back in his chair. "So what? I walked over to Shannon's house on Thursday morning. I was going to wish her a happy Thanksgiving. But I changed my mind."

"Why would you walk all the way over there and change your mind?" Brian asked.

"You need to understand. It was hard for me to visit Shannon. Hard to see her like that. But I changed my mind later and decided it was something I needed to do for Rusty."

"Why didn't you tell us you'd stopped by her house that morning?" the chief asked.

"Because I felt like a selfish jerk. I should have knocked on her door. It was like history repeating itself. If I had gone into the shop that night, Rusty might still be alive. And if I had knocked on Shannon's door, perhaps I could have somehow prevented her death. I was ashamed. Had I seen anything that day that might have helped you find her killer—assuming there is one and she didn't take her own life—then I would have said something. I promise."

"When you walked up to the door, did you notice the food Lucy's Diner delivered?" the chief asked.

"I didn't make it to the door. I got about halfway there from the alley before I changed my mind and turned around. So there might have been something sitting there, or not. I don't know."

———

SINCE HEATHER HADN'T LEFT a message on his phone, Brian assumed the trip to Portland had been a bust. When he arrived at her house later that day, she greeted him with, "We've been waiting for you. We're in the living room."

After making the statement, she left the door wide open, turned, and marched toward the living room. Brian gave a reluctant shrug, stepped into the house, closed the door behind him, and followed Heather. Once in the living room, he found Chris, Walt, and Danielle sitting on the sofa.

"Is the chief with you?" Danielle asked.

"Umm, no. Why would he be?" Brian looked over to Heather, who had just plopped down on an oversized chair in the corner, not saying a word.

"I talked to him a few minutes ago. He's on his way over here," Danielle explained.

"Where are Madeline and Finn?" Brian asked.

"They're out," Danielle said.

Brian walked toward an empty recliner. "What's going on?" He started to sit.

"Don't sit down!" Heather screeched. "You'll sit on Rusty."

Brian froze. "You found Rusty?" He looked down at what looked like an empty chair.

"If you'd called me back, you'd know that," Heather scoffed.

"You didn't tell me to call you back. You didn't even leave a message," Brian reminded her.

"I couldn't exactly leave a message like, *hey, Brian, it's Heather. We found Rusty. Call me back.* You might listen to your messages on speakerphone when you're at work. I just figured once you saw you had a missed call from me, you'd call."

"Brian, why don't you sit over there." Chris pointed to an empty chair. "We have a lot to go over, so you might want to get comfortable."

"No, don't sit there, Brian. The chief will need that chair when he gets here." Heather stood up. "Come on, I'll share my chair with you."

Marie arrived at Heather's several minutes later, and soon after that, the chief showed up. After brief introductions, the mediums explained what they had learned that day and what needed to be done.

BRIAN SAT NEXT TO HEATHER, digesting what he had just been told. "I don't think it's a good idea. Heather could get hurt."

"I'll be fine. Marie will be with me," Heather said.

"I agree; it's not ideal. But the only real evidence we have is the word of the victim. The dead victim," the chief reminded them.

"This could work," Danielle said. "Especially since Eden plans to have everyone over to Shannon's house for a wake after the church service. If she had everyone go to her house instead of Shannon's, this wouldn't work. Heather needs a logical reason to be in that house."

"Can't we just use the photographs? Do we really need to explain where they came from? We could say they arrived in the mail," Brian suggested. "Or someone dropped them off."

"No." The chief shook his head. "All they'll prove is a crime where the statutes of limitations ran out. There is much more at stake here. Our killer may be responsible for two, not just one, murders. Do we really want to settle for just ruining his reputation?"

"I can do this, Brian. Have faith. Come on, if Danielle and Chris could fake their deaths for his uncles, I can do this," Heather argued. "And remember, I convinced Beau I was an actual witch."

"Well, that's not exactly difficult to believe," Chris quipped.

Heather flashed Chris a glare, and Brian said, "Making people believe you were a witch almost got us killed." Brian shook his head in disapproval. "It all seems a little hairbrained to me."

"Do you have a better idea?" Danielle asked.

Brian considered her question for a moment and then shrugged. "No."

"WHO WEARS THAT TO A FUNERAL?" Kelly whispered to Joe. "And why is she here, anyway? She didn't know Shannon." They stood together in Shannon's living room while other mourners mingled and moved through the living room and kitchen.

Joe shrugged. "Brian must have asked her to go to the service with him."

"She's not with Brian now."

"That's just because he went home. Said he had a pounding headache. I guess she's riding home with Walt and Danielle."

"I suppose I can understand, but why would she wear something like that?"

"It's all black. Black is for a funeral, isn't it?"

Kelly scowled. "She looks like a vampire on the prowl for fresh blood."

Joe choked on his beer. When he regained his composure, he looked at Kelly. "Don't talk so loud; someone might hear you."

HEATHER FOUND Charlie standing alone in the hallway, studying the pictures on the wall. She stood beside him and glanced up at one framed photograph. It was of Rusty and Shannon's high school graduation. The twins, each in cap and gown, stood side by side smiling into the camera, each wrapping an arm around the other.

"I'm so sorry about your friend," Heather whispered.

Charlie turned to Heather and smiled. "Thank you. I'm surprised to see you here. But I guess you probably came with your boyfriend. I know he's working on the case, and don't the cops always come to the funeral of a victim, hoping to catch the killer?"

"I suppose. Brian was at the church service, but he had to go to Portland at the last minute and won't be back until late tomorrow." Heather paused a moment and cringed. "I wasn't supposed to say that. Please don't tell your buddy Joe."

"Why not?"

"Because he might tell the chief. It's for a job interview. But he told the chief he had a migraine."

"Your boyfriend might be leaving Frederickport?"

Heather looked from the framed photo of the twins to Charlie and rolled her eyes. "I seriously doubt it. You really think another department will hire Brian, at his age?"

Charlie let out a snort. "Now, is that nice?"

Heather shrugged and looked back to the photo.

"So why didn't you just go home after your boyfriend ditched you?"

Heather looked to Charlie. "I started thinking about how you must be feeling. All sad after losing your friend. I thought maybe I could offer some comfort."

Charlie's smile faded. "What do you have in mind?"

Heather smiled mischievously. "Something naughty, something nice. After all, Christmas is around the corner."

He arched his brows. "I thought you weren't interested."

"I never said I wasn't interested. You just surprised me. But I've been thinking a lot about you since your invitation. I'm going to be all alone tonight, with nothing to do, so I thought it might be the ideal time to take you up on your offer."

"You want to come to my place, and we can discuss it more thoroughly?"

"To be honest, I'd feel more comfortable at my house. After all, we just met. But I thought we could have a little sleepover." Heather grinned.

"Are you sure? What would your boyfriend say?"

Heather shrugged. "He doesn't need to know. But I would appreciate it if you parked in the back, in the alley. We don't need to get the neighbors talking."

Charlie's grin broadened. "I can't wait."

"I'll leave the side door unlocked. Just come on in. But remember, you gave me a promise," Heather purred.

"I did?"

"Yeah, you said we could have fun together. And I really want to have some fun."

"Oh, my goodness, you sounded like a tramp!" Marie scolded after Heather left Charlie and headed toward the bathroom. Marie trailed beside her.

"That was sort of the point," Heather said after she entered the bathroom. She closed the door and locked it. "Where is Eva?"

"She's sticking with Charlie. We don't want any surprises."

Heather looked into the mirror and examined her makeup. "No, we want to be the one with the surprises. I just hope he doesn't change his mind and, instead of showing up, blabs to Joe all about what I said. Shattering both my reputation and ego at the same time."

Marie smiled at Heather. "Don't worry, dear. Men like Charlie can't resist an attractive tramp."

"Ahh, Marie. Did you just call me attractive?" Heather grinned.

THIRTY-NINE

"Charlie just parked his car," Eva told Marie and Heather when she popped into Heather's living room late Wednesday afternoon.

Heather sat on the oversized chair in the corner, facing the doorway where Charlie would come through any minute. She adjusted the skirt of her long black dress with her glove-clad hands, arranging it so that the slit on the side revealed a hint of thigh. In the fireplace, she had started a fire. The flames danced and crackled. She leaned back in the chair, took a deep breath, and waited.

When Charlie walked into the room a few minutes later, Heather felt her heart race. She told herself if Danielle and Chris could fake their own deaths, she could do this. At least Charlie was not about to make her drink poison. Or was he?

"Well, hello," Charlie purred, his eyes fixed on Heather. He walked toward her and removed his jacket, tossing it on a nearby chair as he passed it by. He was about six feet from Heather when she pulled out a pistol and pointed it at him.

He did not immediately recognize what she held, not until she said, "Stop right there."

Charlie froze. His eyes widened. "What's going on?"

"We've had a slight change of plans. But don't worry, I don't intend to shoot you. At least not if you do what I want." She motioned to the recliner. "Sit there."

His stony gaze never left Heather as he backed up to the recliner and sat down.

"Is this some sort of game?" Charlie asked, not sure if he should be worried or excited.

"Oh, it's not a game," Heather promised. "I have always advocated seizing opportunities when they arise. For example, when Brian told me he was leaving for Portland and wouldn't be back until tomorrow, I figured why not take advantage of the situation? You are a handsome man."

Charlie smiled.

"But then, after we spoke yesterday, I had to visit the bathroom at Shannon's house. I've always been a curious girl, like to poke around in other people's houses. Imagine my surprise to discover a hiding place under a loose wallboard in the bathroom. And I was even more surprised to find what someone had hidden there."

Charlie's smile faded.

"I suspect Shannon never found it. I'm sure she would have said something."

"What are you talking about?" Charlie stood up, but Heather raised her pistol and motioned for him to sit back down. Reluctantly, Charlie complied.

"Perhaps we can speed this up a bit. There is an envelope on the table next to you. Please pick it up and see what's inside."

With a frown, Charlie looked at the table and spied the envelope. He picked it up, opened it, and pulled out a photograph. He stared at it. Ten years ago, he had seen a similar one.

"Tucked in that hiding place in Shannon's bathroom was an envelope containing several photographs. I didn't think you needed to see all of them. So I hid the rest."

Still holding the photograph, Charlie looked at Heather, his expression blank.

"There was also a letter." Heather reached over to the side table and picked up a sheet of paper. "Shall I read it? Your friend Rusty wrote it. It was with the photos."

"I am writing this letter in hopes that it will never be necessary. That when I return to my parents' house on my next visit, I can destroy it and the

photographs. But in case the worst happens, I am confident these will eventually be discovered since my parents have been talking about remodeling the bathroom."

"The Langdons *were* planning to remodel that bathroom," Charlie muttered, speaking more to himself than Heather.

"I guess they never got around to it after their son's murder." Heather set the letter on her lap and looked across the room to Charlie. "Why don't I just give you a quick summary? No reason to read the rest out loud. I'd let you read it yourself, but I haven't had a chance to make a copy of it, and I don't want you to do something foolish like tear it up."

"What does it say?"

"It says you were having a hard time at the bike shop, paying the bills. And miraculously, you came up with money to keep the shop open. Rusty wondered where you were getting this money. So he followed you. Took pictures. Pictures like that one of you breaking into one of the neighboring businesses. He wanted to confront you about it, and he didn't think you would hurt him. You were his friend. But since he had never imagined you would do something like breaking and entering, he wasn't certain what you would do. So he hid some photos away, along with this letter, and hoped that he could convince you to go to the police. But I guess you didn't, did you? According to what he wrote, you were meeting him that night after closing. The night he was murdered. He asked you to come, said you two needed to talk privately about something. He didn't want Shannon to know about it. That's why he wanted to meet you at the shop."

"What do you want?" Charlie asked.

Heather stood up, gun in hand. "Well, I could use a little extra money each month. I understand you did well after selling the bike shop."

"You're blackmailing me."

Heather shrugged. "I suppose I am." She circled the room, still holding the gun, seemingly overconfident, when the tip of her shoe caught on the edge of the throw rug—something that had happened to her more times than she liked to remember. The next minute she landed facedown on the floor, with the gun sliding across the room, in what seemed like a fortuitous change of luck for Charlie. The gun landed at his feet. Still sitting, he leaned down and picked up the pistol.

When Heather rolled over, still sitting on the floor, it did not surprise her to find Charlie pointing the gun at her. After all, that had been the plan.

"Well, lookie here. I have the gun." Charlie grinned. He remained seated as he aimed the pistol at Heather.

"What are you going to do now?" Heather asked.

Charlie stood up, walked past Heather, and picked up the letter. He glanced at it, noting Rusty's signature at the bottom of the typed page. He walked to the fireplace and tossed the letter into the flames.

"No!" Heather cried out.

Charlie turned to face Heather, a Cheshire cat grin on his face. "Too bad you didn't get a chance to make that copy. Now, where are those photographs?"

"I hid them in my house. But you'll never find them."

Charlie arched his brows and then briefly glanced at the nearby fireplace, its flames devouring the letter. He looked back at Heather and smiled. "I suppose we'll have to burn the house down."

"You killed Shannon, didn't you?" Heather demanded, still sitting on the floor, looking up at Charlie.

"That might have been premature. Especially now that I understand the person she planned to meet was probably Finn. Stupid woman. Thinking a medium could really help."

"How did you do it?"

Charlie shrugged. "I brought some poison along. My plan was to surprise her, tell her I wanted to wish her a happy Thanksgiving. And then offer to make us something to drink. But when I got there, I saw the food on the porch. Eden told me she was ordering it. So I changed my plans and put it in the cranberry sauce and left. Shannon always loved cranberries. And then I heard someone park in front of her house and come up the walkway. I barely got out of there without being seen. Although, I guess someone saw me."

"Now what?" Heather asked.

"If you don't want to hand over those photos, I'll guess I'll need to find some rope and tie you up before I burn this house down, with you in it."

"Hold it right there," an unexpected voice called out from the doorway.

Charlie swung around and came face-to-face with Brian.

Without thinking, Charlie pulled the trigger. Nothing happened. He looked down at the gun in confusion and tried firing again. Nothing happened.

HEATHER SAT PRIMLY at the table in the interrogation room. She faced the chief and Joe. They asked her to explain her version of what had happened.

"I attended Shannon's service with Brian. During the service, he got a headache and wanted to go home and lie down instead of going to the wake."

"So you got a ride from Walt and Danielle?" the chief said.

"I told Brian I had aspirin at home, and he could take a nap at my house, but he just wanted to lie down in his own bed. I understood. When I don't feel good, I just want to be home. I figured, no reason for him to drive out of his way to drop me at my house, not when I could hitch a ride with Walt and Danielle. Fortunately, they took the Flex and not Walt's car."

"So that's why you were at Shannon's wake?" the chief asked.

"Yes. If I had driven myself, I would have probably gone straight home. Heck, if it weren't for Brian, I wouldn't have gone at all. Anyway, when I was at Shannon's house, I used the bathroom. And when I was getting ready to leave, I tripped and hit the wall. One wallboard came off. And I saw an envelope hidden. When I opened it up, I found a bunch of photos that looked like Charlie. They were strange. I took them to show Brian when he got back."

"Why didn't you just give them to me?" Joe asked.

Heather looked at Joe. "Why would I give them to you?"

"Then what happened?" the chief asked.

Heather took a deep breath. "I wanted to get out of there, and when I was hurrying out of the bathroom, I tripped again and dropped the envelope. Some pictures fell on the floor. I was just picking them up and putting them into my purse when Charlie walked into the hallway. I didn't think he saw them. But I guess he did."

"He knew what they were?" the chief asked.

Heather shrugged. "I guess so. He followed me to my house. He entered through the alleyway, had a gun, demanded I give him the pictures. I asked him if he killed Shannon. That's when I knew he was going to kill me."

"Why do you say that?" Joe asked.

"Because he told me he killed Shannon. And he killed Rusty. He wouldn't have told me that if he planned to just take the pictures and leave. Thankfully, Brian's headache went away, and he came over to my house. He surprised Charlie and got the gun away from him. Brian is a hero. He saved my life. Charlie would have killed me, like he did Rusty and Shannon."

———

"THIS IS CRAZY!" Charlie told Joe and the chief while Brian and Heather watched from the adjacent office through the one-way mirror.

"I didn't take a gun to Heather's! It was Heather's gun," Charlie insisted.

"The only fingerprints on the gun belonged to you and Brian," the chief said.

"Heather was wearing gloves," Charlie said.

"She wasn't wearing gloves when Brian got there," the chief said, knowing she had slipped the gloves off before the rest of the police had arrived, and when Charlie wasn't looking.

"Charlie, the gun was registered to your mother, and it was loaded. What were you thinking?" Joe asked.

"No, it wasn't loaded! I tried shooting Brian, and nothing happened!"

In the adjacent office, where Brian and Heather watched, Heather cringed. "Wow, he is really coming unhinged."

"I feel a little sorry for him."

Heather frowned at Brian. "He was going to burn me alive like he was making s'mores and I was the marshmallow!" Heather said.

"Well, he didn't take the gun to your house. Marie found it at his place. And Marie put the bullets in the gun after I arrested him."

"She did good." Heather grinned.

"The one I really feel sorry for is Joe. This is difficult for him," Brian said.

Heather let out a sigh. "Yeah, I know."

WALT STEPPED into the parlor and closed the door behind him. In the living room, Madeline and Finn visited with Chris while Walt checked on Danielle, who had gone to the parlor to talk on the phone with the chief.

Danielle ended her call and looked up at Walt. "He gave a full confession. He admitted to killing Rusty and Shannon."

Walt's eyes widened. "I didn't expect that."

Danielle set her cellphone on the desk and looked at Walt. "According to the chief, he totally freaked out when he found out the gun was the one that belonged to his mother."

"I can only imagine." Walt shook his head at the thought.

"And then when the chief claimed the gun had been loaded, well, that sent him totally over the edge. He didn't just confess to what he had done, but he was adamant about how Heather had lured him over there, tried blackmailing him, and even claimed she had a letter of Rusty's that he burned."

"Of course, there was no letter." Walt chuckled.

"Not a real one, anyway. Which, of course, only made him look crazy because Heather insisted there was no letter. It's a good thing Marie stuck around after the police left and made sure there was no sign of it left in the fireplace. If Charlie had convinced them to come back and look in the fireplace to prove he was telling the truth, not sure how that would change things."

Walt shrugged. "It wouldn't make him look less guilty, just less crazy. Perhaps he'll use an insanity defense."

FORTY

Danielle fell asleep minutes after her head hit the pillow on Wednesday evening. Yet, instead of a restful sleep, she sat on a park bench at the beach. The weather felt more summer than winter, with a clear blue sky overhead and no chill in the air. She didn't see another soul on the beach, and it wasn't until she heard voices that she realized she was not alone. Someone sat on the bench with her. She turned to the right and looked into the smiling face of her cousin, Cheryl.

"Hey, Dani-Boo," Cheryl greeted her with a grin.

"Cheryl!"

"Look who else is here." Cheryl nodded to Danielle's left. Danielle turned around and looked into the twinkling eyes of her late husband.

"Lucas?" Danielle's eyes widened.

"Hello, Dani," Lucas whispered.

"I like Lucas a lot better on this side," Cheryl said cheerfully.

Danielle turned back to Cheryl, who only gave a shrug and said, "I know you don't care. You have your soul mate. You're where you're supposed to be. And I suppose Lucas and I are where we are supposed to be—now. We could have stuck around longer had we not made such poor choices."

"Your cousin is right," Lucas said. "You do look radiant, by the way. I'm glad to see you are so happy."

Danielle turned to Lucas and frowned. "So you are okay with me and Walt?"

"Didn't Finn already tell you that?" Lucas asked.

Danielle abruptly turned from Lucas and looked straight ahead, facing the ocean. She shook her head and muttered, "Okay, this can't be a dream hop. It has to be a regular dream."

"Does it feel like a regular dream?" Cheryl asked.

Before either could respond, two new spirits appeared before Danielle—Rusty and Shannon Langdon. In Shannon's hand, she held a bouquet of white chrysanthemums. She offered the flowers to Danielle and said, "We brought them for you."

Reluctantly, Danielle took the flowers, not sure why she was dreaming about Shannon bringing her flowers.

"Rusty and I are so grateful for all Heather's help. We've moved on and are again with our parents and those on the other side who love us. But before we settle in, we wanted to bring you these. You need them."

"I need flowers?" Danielle frowned, telling herself this was a silly dream despite the fact it felt eerily like a dream hop.

"A white chrysanthemum represents truth," Shannon told her. "Remember that. And when someone brings you a message bearing white chrysanthemums, know it is the truth." The twins disappeared.

"Well, that was strange," Danielle muttered.

"Oh, Dani-Boo!" Cheryl laughed. "Of all the people to doubt someone like Finn Walsh, I would never have imagined you would be one. Especially considering you're a medium yourself."

"That's exactly why I know he's a fake," Danielle insisted.

"So am I lying? Is Lucas?"

"I don't even believe you're really here."

Cheryl grinned. "Then why are you arguing with me?"

Danielle stared at Cheryl yet didn't respond.

"Look at it like this, Dani-Boo. It's all about energy. There are different frequencies. You're wired to pick up spirits like Marie and Eva, who've decided to stick around. Whereas Finn is wired to pick up a different frequency. Those like me and Lucas, who have moved over to the other side. Finn can't see what you can, and you can't see what Finn can. Yet it doesn't make it any less real, no more than Lily not seeing what you do means it isn't real."

"Listen to her, Danielle," Lucas said.

"We love you, Dani-Boo. And remember, we are always there with you, watching over you. And by the way, you may want to cut down on those cinnamon rolls. Too much sugar."

The next moment Danielle woke up and found herself in her dark bedroom, Walt peacefully sleeping by her side. Eventually, she fell back to sleep.

WHEN DANIELLE WOKE up on Thursday morning, she found herself alone in her bedroom, sunshine streaming in the windows. Twenty minutes later, after dressing, fixing her hair, and applying a little makeup, she went downstairs and found Finn's and Madeline's suitcases stacked by the front door. She heard voices coming from the kitchen.

"Good morning, sleepyhead," Madeline greeted her when Danielle walked into the kitchen. Madeline sat with Walt and Finn at the table.

"I guess I overslept." Danielle glanced at the wall clock.

"I thought it best to let you sleep. You seemed to need it," Walt said.

"I was pretty tired."

Madeline smiled warmly at her former daughter-in-law. "Danielle needs a lot of extra sleep during this time."

"We really want to thank you for your hospitality, but I wish you would let me pay you for the extra days," Finn said.

Danielle shook her head. "Absolutely not." She walked to the table and sat down.

Walt stood up. "Let me get you some juice."

Danielle smiled up at Walt. "Thank you."

Walt walked to the counter and grabbed a glass from the overhead cabinet. "I was just trying to get Madeline and Finn to come back for Christmas. Of course, they should come as our guests."

Danielle looked in surprise at Walt and smiled when she realized she liked the idea.

"It's so sweet of Walt to invite us, but Finn has so many commitments," Madeline said.

Walt removed a carton of orange juice from the refrigerator and filled the glass. "If you find you have some free time and would like to come, you are more than welcome."

Finn reached over to Madeline, patted her hand, and looked to Walt. "We will definitely consider your generous invitation."

Madeline took Finn's hand in hers and smiled.

"I saw your suitcases out front. Are you leaving now?" Danielle accepted the glass of juice from Walt and then looked back at Madeline and Finn, waiting for their answer.

Finn set his coffee mug on the table and looked at Danielle. "Yes. Now that they've arrested that poor girl's killer."

"And to learn it was Charlie Cramer. He seemed like such a nice young man." Madeline shook her head at the idea.

"I have an event tomorrow night. I was hoping I wouldn't have to cancel. But this morning I was able to get us a flight. So it looks like the show will go on as planned," Finn said.

"It has been wonderful seeing you, Danielle. I'm so happy for you and Walt." Madeline reached over and kissed Danielle's cheek.

Walt sat back down at the table. He turned to Finn. "Do we get a final reading?"

"I was about to say something. They've been quite insistent," Finn said with a chuckle.

"They?" Danielle asked.

Finn nodded. "Rusty and Shannon are here. They have thanked me for trying to help, but say they understand why I couldn't. But they are together now, with their parents. Shannon is holding flowers. She keeps saying show these to Danielle."

Danielle's eyes widened. "Flowers?"

"Shannon wants me to tell you what kind they are. I believe they're chrysanthemums. White chrysanthemums."

WALT AND DANIELLE stood together on the sidewalk in front of Marlow House, waving goodbye to Finn and Madeline as they drove off in the blue sedan.

Walt looked at Danielle. "I dreamt about the twins and the

white chrysanthemums, too."

Danielle looked at Walt. "You didn't?"

Walt nodded. "My mother was also in the dream. She likes Finn."

"Oh my god, this can't be true!" Danielle closed her eyes and groaned.

Walt laughed. "Cheryl found it rather hilarious that you're having such a rough time processing all this."

"You dreamt about Cheryl, too?"

"She dropped in for a minute. Lucas was with her. She said they were on their way to meet you. They make a rather cute couple."

THE MEDIUMS of Beach Drive gathered in the living room at Marlow House on Friday evening. Also there were Ian, Lily, Connor, Police Chief MacDonald, Evan, and Brian, along with Marie and Eva. The chief's eldest son had gone to the movies with his friends. Melony and Adam had taken off for the weekend, which worked out for the friends, because they had things they needed to discuss without Melony and Adam present. As for Kelly and Joe, they had also left for the weekend.

Evan sat on the floor with Connor, playing with a wooden train set Walt had bought for the boys to keep at Marlow House, while Hunny and Sadie sat nearby watching, and Max napped under the coffee table. Not sleepy, Bella sat on the windowsill, looking out into the darkness, wondering what was out there.

Heather, who sat with Brian on the loveseat, looked to Ian and Lily. "Brian tells me this thing with Charlie has really hit Joe hard."

About to take a sip of his wine, Ian paused and looked at Heather. "That's the main reason they took off this weekend. Kelly said he needed to get away from Frederickport and work. He's still trying to process everything."

"I gave him some time off. Which wasn't easy considering we're shorthanded. But the way Joe was feeling, he was no good to anyone in his current condition," the chief said.

"So what exactly happened?" Lily asked. "From what I heard, none of it makes much sense."

Danielle looked at Lily. "Basically, the bike shop was about to go under. The possibility of losing it was more devastating for Charlie than it was for Rusty, because Charlie's mother had taken a loan out on her house to help them start the business. When she died, Charlie inherited her house, one that had a loan against it because of the bike shop. And Rusty admitted he wasn't good at business."

"Is that why Charlie killed Rusty, to cash in on the keyman insurance?" Lily asked.

Danielle shook her head. "I'm not sure if that was a motive or a perk. When they first opened, they got familiar with the local business community. Later, when Charlie was desperate to keep the bike shop open, he saw an opportunity. He had noticed how some of the local businesses were lax in their security. He had gotten to know their habits."

"And he started robbing them," Heather said. "And Rusty figured it out and confronted him. But I don't think it was for the keyman insurance. Rusty said Charlie just panicked when he realized he had been following him, and took pictures of Charlie breaking into one of the stores, and then threatened to turn him in to the police."

"I suspect Rusty wants to believe that," Chris said. "No one wants to imagine their best friend murdered them for the insurance money."

"Maybe we will never know all Charlie's motives, but he's undoubtably a murderer and a thief," Danielle said. "Perhaps Rusty's murder wasn't premeditated, but we know Shannon's was."

Heather then explained how she had trapped Charlie. When she finished her telling, she said, "Unlike what I told Charlie, Rusty never imagined Charlie would actually hurt him. When he stashed those photos under the floorboard in the bike shop, it was something he did at the last moment when he saw Charlie's car pull up to the shop. He's not even sure why he did it."

"It was probably his guardian angel warning him," Eva suggested.

"Rusty told us he often hid things from Shannon so she couldn't find them. He loved his sister, but she could be clingy," Danielle said.

"No kidding," Heather scoffed. "She totally fell apart after his death."

"Rusty told us about the hiding place in the bathroom at his parents' place. While Shannon wasn't aware of it, Charlie was. So when Heather told Charlie that's where she found the photos and fake letter, he believed her," Danielle explained.

"I suppose if things hadn't happened so fast over at Heather's, Charlie would have wondered why Rusty hid something from him in a hiding place he knew about, but his sister didn't," Walt said.

"Charlie must be one confused dude about now," Chris said. "He's probably still trying to figure out how Heather got his gun, or what she did with the bullets."

Brian looked over at Heather. "Yeah, well, I think Heather may have pushed him over the edge. She does that to men. Remember what happened to poor old Beau Stewart?"

Heather giggled. She also couldn't help but wonder what Kelly and Joe thought about Charlie being a serial killer. *Could they deem him a serial killer after killing two people and trying to kill her?* she wondered. She imagined Kelly and her mother were relieved Joe hadn't asked Charlie to be the best man. But she kept those thoughts to herself.

Lily looked at Danielle. "So is Finn really a medium?"

Danielle shrugged. "I guess so."

Heather let out a snort and looked at Lily. "Danielle is having a difficult time wrapping her brain around all this. But considering Walt, Danielle, and myself had practically the same dream Wednesday night involving the twins and white chrysanthemums, and then Finn gave his reading before he left, well, not sure what more proof we need."

"Yes, he is really a medium!" Danielle conceded.

"Why is this so hard for you?" Ian asked.

Danielle shrugged. "I suppose it's the universe's way of putting me in my place. Can't be too smug, can we? Thinking we know how all this works."

"I don't believe the universe is trying to put you in your place," Eva said. "It's just that we are not meant to understand how it all works, at least not on this plane."

Heather repeated Eva's words for the non-mediums and then asked, "What about when we move over to the other side?"

"I don't know." Eva looked at Danielle. "But I believe your cousin described it accurately. We are all energy, and when we leave behind our bodies, our energy remains. But the frequency we emit is not picked up by everyone. Which is why you can see me, but Lily and Finn can't. I also suspect Finn's reception is not as clear as yours."

Heather frowned at Eva. "What do you mean by that?"

"When Finn communicates with spirits, he often relies on imagery," Eva explained. "He interprets what he is seeing and hearing, as opposed to you simply listening to what I am saying."

"I did wonder why the spirits didn't just come out and tell him who they are," Danielle said.

"I believe you get a clearer image because the spirits you communicate with haven't moved to the other side," Eva said.

Again, Heather repeated Eva's words for the non-mediums.

"It's just a lot to take in." Danielle leaned back against Walt.

"What I want to know, while you three went dream hopping, did any of the visiting spirits happen to tell you what the baby's going to be?" Chris asked. "Are you having a boy or a girl?"

"No, they didn't say, and I didn't ask," Danielle said.

"I'm fine with waiting until our baby comes, like it's supposed to be," Walt said.

"That's how Ian and I felt. Well, after you got us to thinking about it." Lily looked to Danielle. "But I don't think Dani feels the same way. She has that ultrasound in a couple of weeks. You still want to know what you're having?"

"It will help when deciding how to decorate the baby's room," Danielle said.

"Oh pooh, you just hate waiting. I bet you used to peek at your Christmas gifts," Lily teased.

Chris's phone buzzed, indicating an incoming text. He read it while his friends continued to chat. After reading the message, he said, "Hey, that was from Brandon Purnell." Brandon Purnell was the man whose nonprofit organization had inherited the house next door to Marlow House.

All his friends stopped talking and looked to hear what Chris had to say.

"He was letting me know he contacted Adam tonight. All the repairs are done over at Pearl's, and he's having Adam list the house tomorrow. It's possible we could be getting a new neighbor before Christmas."

"Let the bidding war begin," Lily muttered.

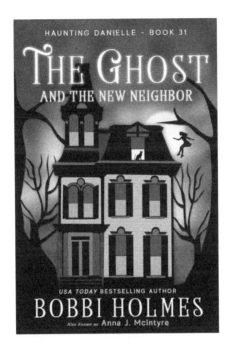

RETURN TO MARLOW HOUSE

THE GHOST AND THE NEW NEIGHBOR

HAUNTING DANIELLE, BOOK 31

Lots of activity on Beach Drive, with wedding plans and preparing for the stork's arrival. But it's the new neighbor moving into Pearl's house who has the neighborhood in a deadly uproar.

BOOKS BY ANNA J. MCINTYRE

COULSON FAMILY SAGA

COULSON'S WIFE

COULSON'S CRUCIBLE

COULSON'S LESSONS

COULSON'S SECRET

COULSON'S RECKONING

Now available in Audiobook Format

UNLOCKED 🔒 HEARTS

SUNDERED HEARTS

AFTER SUNDOWN

WHILE SNOWBOUND

SUGAR RUSH

NON-FICTION BY
BOBBI ANN JOHNSON HOLMES

HAVASU PALMS, A HOSTILE TAKEOVER

WHERE THE ROAD ENDS, RECIPES & REMEMBRANCES

MOTHERHOOD, A BOOK OF POETRY

THE STORY OF THE CHRISTMAS VILLAGE

CPSIA information can be obtained
at www.ICGtesting.com
Printed in the USA
LVHW101638090722
723112LV00004B/289